In the Shadow of the Cards

Frank Stanford

Published by Frank Stanford, 2022.

This is a work of fiction. Similarities to real people, places, or events are entirely coincidental.

IN THE SHADOW OF THE CARDS

First edition. November 9, 2022.

ISBN: 978-1738745708

Written by Frank Stanford.

Table of Contents

This book would not have happened without the encouragement of celebrated Canadian author Robert Wiersema and the members of his creative writing workshops in Victoria, BC. My thanks to you all for your sage advice.

My most profound thanks to my wife and first reader – my partner in all things, Janice.

And to Laura-Anne Passarello for her original cover illustration. It was a pleasure working with you.

Chapter one Teddy

The marble play area didn't have a name, so far as anyone in the school community was aware. And that was okay, in the minds of most eight-year-olds. Some of the adults might have found it frustrating, might have wanted to assign a word to it, but been unable to come up with the right one. They couldn't call it a marble "field" or "pitch;" those words were too grand to describe a tiny patch of hard-scrabble dirt. It certainly wasn't a "pit" or a "court;" there had been no improvements made to it. It was just the place where the boys gathered, off the end of the asphalt where the basketball and tetherball poles stood, before the grassed field that doubled as a soccer pitch and baseball diamond, depending on the season.

Marble season was never organized. No teacher coached or mentored the boys and there was minimal supervision. It was a spontaneous thing, lasting only from about the second week of school in September until the rains started in October, turning the playing surface to mud and rendering it useless.

Teddy missed playing his first marble season. Mom and Dad sent him to school with no idea that he might be expected to carry a bag, containing the spheroid gems that were both the tools and the trophies of the trade. But he was a curious little boy, and spent some of his recesses and lunch hours hanging around the fringes, watching and listening. He learned the names of the different sizes of marbles: Cat's-eyes; cobs; and giant cobs. He learned that crystals and crystal cobs were far more valuable than regular marbles.

He watched the game being played, absurdly simple, really. Somebody would drag his foot through the dirt to draw a line, and sit, three or four feet from it, placing a target on the ground between his outstretched legs. The target would usually be a small pyramid

1

of cat's-eyes, most often four, sometimes five, although the vendors who offered five would make a point of setting up a foot further back from the line. The shooters would flick their glass spheres from the line, trying to knock down the small pile. Whoever succeeded collected the prize.

He paid attention to who was vending and who was shooting from one day to the next, observing that, over time, the vendors seemed to do better. Most often there would be more than four or five marbles gathered in their crotches by the time somebody hit the target and they had to pay off.

Occasionally a vendor would be reluctant to pay off, claiming the shooter had "fudged" the line, or committed some other offence. There might be a shove or two, but the matters were almost always resolved without punches being thrown. An older boy would appoint himself arbiter and step in to settle the dispute. Teddy noticed some of the bigger boys were willing to provide that service whether they had actually witnessed the alleged transgression or not.

Teddy found it more interesting to watch the people than the game. He saw how intimidation was as much a part of it as an accurate thumb. Who tried to bully whom? Who got away with it, and who didn't? Rule one: *never touch a kid who's got an older brother around.*

It didn't occur to Teddy to wonder why he never saw any girls playing marbles. It might have been because they were taught not to let anybody look up their skirts.

* * * *

Teddy was a bright child, who paid attention in class and learned his lessons well. He started the year ahead of most of his contemporaries in reading and arithmetic, and by the end of the year the school recommended his parents consider enrolling him next September in third grade rather than second. "He'll have to work extra hard, but we think he can manage, and it will be good for him to challenge himself," said the report card.

Mr. and Mrs. Cronkite had what by their standards was a heated argument over it. Dad was smug, to think his first-born son was brighter than most, and couldn't see why anyone would think of it as anything other than an opportunity. Mom worried that her little boy would be lost among older children, "not academically," she agreed, "but how will he get along, having to start out making new friends all over again?"

"It won't be any worse for him than for any of the kids who are new in the neighbourhood," Dad argued. "People move all the time. And most of his friends will still be at the school. He'll see them on the playground."

"Maybe that's exactly what you don't want," insisted Mom. "He gets labelled a baby by his classmates because he hangs out with younger kids. He might never be accepted, and he won't understand why not."

* * * *

Teddy noticed some of the differences the instant he entered the grade three classroom - books on the shelves, where he was accustomed to seeing toys and models; printed words and photographs on the walls, rather than crepe-paper cut-outs. Teddy wasn't familiar with the word, but he would learn soon enough the biggest difference between grades one and three wasn't the way the room looked; it was the atmosphere, more businesslike. The teacher was older than Miss Johnson. In fact Mrs. Butters looked more like Teddy's Grandma than his Mom, and seemed a little grumpier than either.

She had a pencil in her hand as she began the rollcall.

"Teresa Adams?"

"Here."

"Charles Bond?"

No response.

Firmer: "Charles Bond?"

The children looked around at one another. "Does anyone know Charles?"

A boy raised his hand, slowly.

"Do you know why he's not here?" The boy shook his head.

"All right. Theodore Cronkite?"

"Here."

"Good. Do you like to be called Theodore or Ted?"

"Teddy."

A chorus of giggles rippled around the room.

"Quiet! Everyone." Mrs. Butters stared at Teddy, and he felt his cheeks getting warmer. He was relieved when she smiled slightly. "How about I call you Ted in class? Would that be all right?"

"Yeah."

"That's 'yes,' Ted, not 'yeah.'"

The teacher looked down at her list again. "Kellie Evans?"

"Present."

* * * *

When recess came Teddy rushed out to the marble zone, intending to set up his small pyramid of cat's-eyes and begin building on the assortment of glass treasures that Mom had bought for him last week at Hindle's five and dime. She didn't seem to understand his lack of interest in the paper, notebooks, pencils, crayons, and his very first pen, that comprised the grade three school supply list. He'd rushed to his room to rip open the package of marbles, and counted them repeatedly. He came to thirty-five a couple of times, more often thirty-six. What was sure was that two of them were the extra-valuable crystals! The store clerk had told him that he would be lucky to find any. One never knew prior to purchase what would be in the package, it was something called a "crapshoot." Mom had given the young man a dirty look when he uttered that word, and Teddy sensed that he probably shouldn't ask her why. He would just file it away in his memory as something really important.

Teddy eagerly pulled four cat's-eyes from his pocket, scuffed a line in the dirt, and sat down to wait for the game to begin. But none of the other boys showed up.

He was confused as he made his way back to class at the end of recess, both by the lack of players, and by the sneers from classmates. He could hear "Ted-dee, Ted-dee" as he walked past the tetherball game. He didn't know why the older boys would think his name was funny, but he knew the difference between a friendly laugh and an unfriendly one.

* * * *

By day three the marble game was thriving. Teddy wasn't sure who decided that's when it would start and why those boys hadn't been interested the day before, or the day before that.

He made his scuff mark in the dirt and sat down at the end of a line of boys to set up his pyramid, taking his cue from the others as to distance from the shooting line to target. He joined the chorus of calls, stating the obvious, to announce his readiness: "Four here! Four here!"

A couple of youngsters he recognized from his grade one class last year squatted down at the line, aimed carefully, and flicked their marbles at his target. There had been six or seven misses, a nice profit, when a bigger boy shouldered his way between them, placed his hand on the ground, clearly inside Teddy's line, and fired his shooter with his thumb. Even cheating, he missed once, but knocked down the pile on the second try.

Teddy wanted to protest the way the bigger kid had fudged the line, but he knew it would be pointless to try to take that up with a bully. Besides, he already had his profit, at the expense of the younger lads who'd played the game fairly.

He may have sensed something was wrong, but seven-year-old Teddy wasn't equipped to recognize a sentiment such as guilt, or to consider legalistic questions, like "who's the victim of the crime?" What he did know was that he didn't want to have to face down a bully, and he spent the next week watching again, lacking the confidence to participate. He noticed his acquaintances from the grade two class didn't make another appearance at all.

Teddy would count his marbles each night, although the number wouldn't vary. How could it, if they weren't in play? He rolled one of the crystals between his thumb and forefinger, admiring the way the tiny sparkles inside it reflected the light. How many regular cat's-eyes is it worth? Five? Ten? A hundred?

He tried to recall the few times he'd seen one actually in play at school. Obviously nobody would use one as a shooter. Would he be willing to put it up as a target? How many shooters would he have to collect to make it worthwhile?

He ate his breakfast quietly the day he decided to take his crystals to school.

"What's the matter, Teddy?" said Mom. "Are you feeling sick?"

"No."

"Is everything okay at school?"

"Yeah. Yes."

"Are you getting to know the other boys in your class? Are they nice?"

"Yeah," he lied.

Teddy was a bundle of nerves in class, stumbling when it was his turn to read aloud. Mrs. Butters cut him short. "Maybe we'll try again tomorrow, Ted. You should practice at home tonight."

There seemed to be more boys than ever playing marbles at recess, a rambunctious crowd. It might have meant a good opportunity for a vendor, but Teddy didn't see it that way. He swallowed, and thought about walking away, but his feet wouldn't turn. He studied the line of vendors sitting on the ground with their pyramids of four and five marbles. One boy was a foot further back than the others, calling out, "Six here! Six here!"

Teddy scraped a line in the dirt and sat down about the same distance from it as the boy hawking the six. He pulled a marble from his pocket reluctantly, and placed it on the ground between his legs. He could see some of the players looking at him.

"Crystal here!" he bawled. "Crystal here!"

Four boys materialized immediately at his line, jostling for position. Two of them still had their shooters in their hands when the second boy's marble grazed Teddy's crystal. The lad rushed forward gleefully to collect his prize, as Teddy stared in disbelief.

"Oh look," somebody sneered. "The whiddle boy is gonna cry!"

Teddy remained seated as he wiped his face and tried to fight back the tears. He thought about the second crystal, still in his pocket. The quartet of shooters stared at him. He reached into his corduroys and pulled out the marble.

"Come on!" somebody told him. "Put it down."

He set it on the ground a few inches further back than the first one had been.

"Uh-uh," said one of the boys. "You can't change the rules now."

Teddy reluctantly pushed the marble forward, dreading the outcome. The players lined up in front of him and began firing their shooters in turn: four misses, eight. "Shit!" snarled the boy who had won the first crystal, after his second miss. Twelve. Teddy stopped counting, enthralled by the growing mass of marbles between his legs. Two of the shooters gave up, but were replaced by another pair of boys. Others stood behind, watching. Teddy felt giddy as he gradually realized he had become the center of attention. For once he actually enjoyed some of the derisive remarks he overheard. "What the hell are you trying for, Wilson? You couldn't hit a barn."

The school bell rang, and he reached for his target. This was unbelievable! Winning all these marbles, and not even losing the crystal! The shooters got up, somewhat reluctantly, a couple of them eyeing Teddy's proceeds. One of the oldest boys, probably a sixth-grader, stood by while Teddy filled his pockets. It didn't occur to Teddy to thank him for being a guardian angel.

He felt like he was swimming in the clouds as he made his way back to class.

Chapter two Ante Up

Teddy finished sixth grade the summer Neil Armstrong and Buzz Aldrin walked on the moon. He didn't understand all the excitement; actually resented the way he was expected to be polite when his uncle would say something dumb, like, "So, I guess you wanna be an astronaut when you grow up, boy?" His father would smile knowingly.

As far as Teddy was concerned the whole moon thing was a monstrous bore, hours upon hours of "special" TV programming that served no purpose but to pre-empt his favourite shows. Things happened a lot faster on the starship Enterprise, and people didn't sit behind desks waving models and talking about them all day long. His ten – almost eleven - year old brain *knew*, but didn't quite *understand*, that one was fact and the other fiction. He was sure the planet Vulcan would be a much more interesting place to visit than Earth's moon.

He'd outgrown his obsession with marbles, only hung out at the games last fall to keep an eye on his younger brother. This year Bobby would enter grade three, and be big enough to take care of himself. And it wasn't as though he didn't have enough wealth to absorb a few losses. Teddy had passed down one of the largest collections in the entire school. *No. Grade sevens don't play marbles.* Some of them, toward the end of the year, anyway, actually seemed to take more interest in what the girls were doing, another reality that he witnessed but eluded his grasp.

Teddy's interests the last couple of years had leaned more toward outdoor sports. He was a better than average soccer player and took a dollar from Neil last year in a bet that neither boy's parents knew about: who would score more goals on the season? He'd tried to persuade some of the other boys to bet with him on the races at the year-end sports day, but one of the teachers got wind of it and shut him down. He was sent to see the Principal, where he was subjected to a lecture and barred from participating in any of the races. A stern letter went home to his parents the next day.

"So, that's what you've been doing with your allowance!" his father had said.

"It's not like I was gonna lose any of it," Ted mumbled.

"That's not the point," said Mom. "It's gambling, and it's not in the spirit of sports day. It's not in the spirit of any sports." She shook her head. "Wherever did you get such an idea?"

"Let's just drop it," said Dad. "I think Teddy's learned his lesson."

"Ted."

Dad looked at him, surprised. "I don't like to be called Teddy anymore."

He found himself less and less interested in family game time on Sunday nights, when Mom would invariably pull out Scrabble, or even worse Parcheesi, in an effort to keep Bobby involved. Ted could play a decent game of Scrabble, for a ten year old, but he was always disappointed that his parents refused to play card games.

"I wanna show you a trick," he would say. "Just take a card, any card." He'd spread his deck, face down on the kitchen table, but neither Mom nor Dad would play. The first time, they nearly took the deck away from him.

"Where did you get those?" Mom demanded.

"Hindle's. I bought it, with my allowance."

Mom and Dad looked at one another.

"I guess it's not hurting anything," Dad muttered.

The Yahtzee game he was given on his eleventh birthday was a big hit, more chance than Scrabble, and something Bobby could play too. It became the family standard through the latter half of the summer.

Ted would play solitaire games late into the night, becoming comfortable with the feel of fifty-two cards in his hands, shuffling smoothly, and learning to remember which cards had been turned. Sometimes he would pull out Yahtzee, playing against himself, maintaining a list of his five highest scores.

* * * *

Seventh grade was a triumph for Ted. He managed to keep his nose clean at school, never once had to deal with anybody picking on Bobby. There were no detentions, no letters home from "concerned" teachers. He won two races at the year-end sports day, plus a second and a third place. He was far too well-mannered not to smile when he was handed his ribbons, but a careful observer would have noticed the absence of joy on his face a minute later.

Ted should have had reason for boundless optimism. Not only his athletics, but his grades were among the highest in his class, and most importantly, a couple of the girls wondered what he would be doing for the summer!

"Maybe I'll see you at the beach," Carrie said. "We could hang out together."

It didn't occur to Ted to ask for a phone number.

His twelfth birthday, early in August, was a momentous occasion. After the oohing and ahhing over the new bicycle, and the cake and ice cream, and after the other kids had gone home, Dad took Ted aside.

"I'm going to cut off your allowance," he said. "But don't panic. I think you're old enough now to take some more responsibility, and part of that is going to be handling more money, not less." He offered a reassuring smile. "But it also means learning to earn it. I'll pay you three dollars for mowing the grass tomorrow. And there'll be other chores. That's better than a dollar a week, right?"

"I guess so."

"All right. First thing tomorrow I'll show you how to start the lawn mower. And you'll have to know how to keep gas and oil in it."

* * * *

He made a point of looking for Carrie in his home room on his first day at Junior High School. He recognized some of the faces, friends and foes. Some of the boys had played soccer against him in the elementary school league the past several years. He scowled at one particular boy, a kid he'd had a beef with on the field. Both boys had been red-carded that day after kicks and punches were thrown.

He didn't see Carrie in any of his morning classes, but noticed her strolling the halls at lunch hour, hand in hand with a boy Ted didn't know. *Dammit!* She didn't even let on she knew him when he walked by.

Ted wasn't particularly good with hand tools, and the shop classes the boys were encouraged to take were always an exercise in frustration. Mom and Dad would try to be encouraging when he would bring a project home from school, a patio planter or a new mailbox that he'd fashioned in his metalwork class. But he knew they were right when they didn't replace the one that was already attached to the front porch.

Ted's English, Math, and Science grades were good – nothing lower than a "B" – but his favourite class was Physical Education. He would invariably finish in the top three on cross-country runs, and he enjoyed the organized sports, baseball and soccer.

His recreational reading evolved away from boys' fiction (Hardy Boys weren't to be found in the Junior High library) to the essays of Isaac Asimov. Hailed as the greatest living teacher of science, and author of college texts as well as popular science fiction, Asimov was able to explain the interior of the atom and Euclidian geometry in ways that twelve and thirteen year olds found fascinating. At least, Ted did. If other kids didn't, that was their problem.

Most days he sat with Neil on the bus to and from school. Dad liked to rib the boys about it. "Back in our day we didn't have school busses. We'd walk – two miles each way – in the snow, uphill both ways."

The boys would grin at one another, although they much preferred bathroom humour. "Why do they make turds tapered?" "So that ass holes don't slam shut!"

* * * *

Ted's introduction to poker came on a Friday night, hanging out with friends in the rec room in Neil's basement. One of the boys had been shown the game by an older brother.

The cards were dealt, five to each player. "Don't let anybody see what you've got," the expert instructed. Ted held two threes, an ace, a king, and a four. "You get to change your cards once," he was told. "Then we see who's got the best hand."

"So what's a good hand?"

"Four aces or a royal flush. That's where you've got the ace-king-queen-jack-ten of the same suit."

Ted frowned at his cards and thought for a moment. He kept the ace, tossing the other four cards on the table, face up.

"Face down!" lectured the dealer. "Don't ever let anybody see your cards, even when you're throwing away."

He duly received his four replacement cards: a queen, a nine, a five and a three.

Neil won the hand with a pair of eights. The dealer had been trying to fill a straight.

"You could have won," he told Ted. "If you'd kept your threes. Never throw away a pair. You'd have had three of them."

The deal passed to Ted. He shuffled quickly and thoroughly, corner to corner, and reached for the top card to commence the deal.

"Uh-uh," said the teacher to his right. "You have to let me cut them."

Ted was smug as his fingers manipulated the cards, flicking them one at a time, to stop neatly in front of each boy. When it came Neil's turn to deal he laid the cards carefully into piles in front of himself and then passed the hands across the table to the various players. The self-styled expert frowned but didn't say anything.

Ted finally picked up a memorable hand the second time he dealt. His eyes widened and he smiled broadly when he saw three fives in his fingers. He didn't bother to think about the other cards as he tossed them away. He drew a pair of queens. Ted waited excitedly as the others showed their hands. "What have you got?"

"Full house!" he boasted, more satisfied with himself for knowing some of the jargon than for holding a winning hand.

"You win that one."

It was on the mentor's third deal – the eleventh overall – that the tone of the game shifted. "It's time to make it more interesting," the boy said, examining his cards. "I'll bet you a dollar that my hand's better than yours."

One of the other boys reached into a pocket tentatively and pulled out a bill. Neil shrugged and said, "I don't have any money."

"I don't want to bet with these cards," said Ted. He knew he was holding a handful of trash.

The dealer lay a straight on the table: four-five-six-seven-eight. "But you've got to pay me something for having the best hand," he claimed. "It's called an ante."

Ted reluctantly turned over a dollar. He was relieved when Neil announced he was getting bored and the game was called. Ted sensed he'd been cheated, but wasn't sure how.

Chapter three UBC

"All right," Neil shouted, loudly enough to be heard over the woofers in the back. "The white van! The one just on the other side of the light!" He slowed the car gradually as he approached the red light. "I'll take five!"

Ted waited for the other two guys to announce their bets, a seven and a one, before he settled on nine. All four held their dollar bills up as they waited for the selected licence plate to come into view. The last digit on it was a three, no winner.

"Okay," said one of the guys, scanning the oncoming traffic. "The green Honda. Who the fuck drives a green Honda?" He laughed derisively.

"Six!" shouted Ted. "My mother always said green cars are bad luck. Some kind of old superstition."

"Seven."

"Four."

"One."

The car came closer. "A four!" Larry shouted, gleefully, and grabbed the bills from his buddies' hands. "It's about time I won one!" Everybody waved and leered at the pretty blonde driving the Honda. Larry blew kisses out the open window but the girl didn't seem to notice.

Ted took a perverse pleasure in betting on licence plate numbers, something completely random, no thinking, no work involved. Winning or losing didn't matter. It was an amusing pastime, to ease the boredom on the drive to Vancouver, where he and his friends would commence their university careers next week.

Becoming the best poker player in high school had required concentration. Ted had learned the game fairly quickly, discovering it was less about the cards that were dealt than it was about reading the faces and the body language of all the players. It took longer to learn patience. There was no point emptying everybody else's pockets too quickly because they would simply refuse to play with him again. By his senior year in high school he had set a budget, to win as much money at cards as he earned working part-time at the super-market. No less and no more. *Keep the stakes low enough that the other guys'll play on a Friday night, and don't sweat it when somebody else wins once in a while.* Although there were some guys he particularly enjoyed beating. *Arrogant pricks!* He actually felt a twinge of regret occasionally, when Neil would be the biggest loser on the evening. Ted tried, with little success, to coach his best friend to be a smarter player.

There were times he tried to steer a sizeable pot Neil's way. He'd make some remark, like "I know you're bluffing," as he called Neil's raise in hopes of persuading other players to make a losing bet as well. Once, when Neil held an ace-high flush, Ted had feigned indecision, and finally called with nothing, not even a pair of jacks. Two other guys followed him in, and were completely pissed off when they fished his cards out of the pile and saw what he'd done. Ted decided that night to let Neil look out for himself for a while. *It's not like he can't afford it. His mom and dad are loaded anyway.*

The games balanced out in Ted's favour over the year, as he knew they would, keeping him in spending money so that his wages could go into the bank for tuition.

The licence plate game became boring and conversation died down in the car, just about the time they were passing Chilliwack on the way into Vancouver. Traffic became heavier and Neil concentrated on his driving. Ted smiled to himself as he thought about the three dollars he'd lost. *Better than paying for a bus ticket! That's probably what would have happened if I'd beaten up on Neil in those poker games. The downside to playing with friends.*

He looked forward to finding some new marks on campus, almost as much as he looked forward to meeting some of those hot college chicks he'd heard about. Joanie was a nice girl, but not the stuff of a life-long commitment. Of course, he hadn't told her that. He mumbled something unintelligible when she kissed him good-bye and told him she could barely wait for Christmas to see him again. "And I guess I'll be joining you at university next year."

* * * *

Ted was comfortable in his surroundings, knew how to find the cafeteria and the library as well as his classes, the first time he noticed a card game going on in the lobby of the student union building. Five people around a table right below the sign that proclaimed "no gambling allowed." He edged closer, watched the cards being dealt, the entire deck, into four hands. *They're not playing poker! And who's the fifth wheel?*

He studied the group more carefully. There were actually four guys at the table; the young woman was seated to the side and slightly behind one of them. He sidled up to her and whispered, "What's the game?"

"Bridge."

He'd heard it mentioned occasionally but never been exposed to it. "How come you're not playing?"

"It needs exactly four players – you can't play it with five."

"Oh. Do you play it for money?"

"You can," the girl said, "but usually not."

One of the players looked their way and scowled. The girl put a finger to her lips. "Pull up a chair if you want to watch, but stop talking. Kibitzers aren't allowed to say anything."

Say anything? Shit! A poker player would never let anybody sit behind him at all!

He heard somebody announce "four hearts," and the other three players said "pass" in turn. One of the guys threw a card face up on the middle of the table and the player to his left spread his cards, face up, in front of him. Ted watched as thirteen tricks were played. He could see how hearts were trump, when a small one captured a club honour during the play, but he didn't understand why the tricks only went into two piles, not four.

"It's a partnership game," the girl explained, smiling at him. "You play with the person across from you."

"Down one," somebody proclaimed. Two of the guys jotted numbers on scoresheets.

Ted watched a few more hands, until he was satisfied he'd picked up the basic mechanics of the game. He waited until the play of a hand was finished before he got up and spoke to the girl again.

"I'm going to get a coffee. Would you like one?"

"Why not? Actually, I'll go with you." The fellow she'd been watching frowned as she got out of her seat. "Back in just a minute," she sang, pinching the guy's ear.

"That's Frank. My boyfriend," she explained, as they walked to the concession.

"Oh. Sorry, I..."

"Don't worry about it." She chuckled. "It's not like we're going to be out of sight."

"So, do you play bridge too?"

"Oh yeah, I play. But not like they do. Those guys are *good*. That's why I kibitz sometimes. You can learn a lot that way."

"What's to learn?" asked Ted, as he paid for the coffees. "It doesn't look that hard."

She gave him a pained look. "It's the most complicated game there is. You have to know what all the bids mean, and there's the play of the hand, and defence..." He looked at her doubtfully. "You don't seem convinced."

"What about...?"

"What about chess? Everybody says that. You know, they've got computers that play chess, and pretty soon they're going to beat the best human players. But they can't teach bridge to a computer."

Or poker, I bet.

"There might be more moves you can make on a chess board, but it doesn't require the partnership understandings that bridge does. Getting two heads to think as one is part of the challenge. If you're really interested you should get a book on it, play some, and then you'll understand what's going on when you watch these guys."

Ted thought about it, thought about how he'd never actually read a book on poker. *That's not how you learn a card game. But then, poker's not a card game.*

"I'd better get back. Nice talking to you."

"Yeah, you too." He put out a hand. "I'm Ted, by the way."

"Lily."

Ted noticed Frank gave him a long sideways stare as he headed for the exit.

* * * *

He found a copy of **Goren's Contract Bridge Complete** the next time he was at the library.

Holy shit! Five hundred pages! It wasn't something he could sit down and read on a single weekend. He'd have to find one at the bookstore. He paid for it out of savings. His first university poker game hadn't gone well. The guys who invited him to play weren't the putzes he expected them to be.

Chapter four Disco Madness

The rain pelted his face as Ted stepped off the bus in the pricey Kerrisdale district. The sky had been threatening and sprinkling on and off all day and the clouds chose the most inopportune moment to open up. At least it wasn't a cold rain, but the old line about April showers had no romantic appeal for him in the few minutes it took to walk to the appointed address.

Ted knew the promise of a pool party, like something out of Hollywood movie, would be off, but he had decided he wasn't going to miss the festivities no matter what. He didn't have many excuses to get off campus.

As he expected, he found everybody had retreated indoors by the time he arrived, at least fifty people crammed into the ground floor party room, plus those lining the stairwell and who knew how many upstairs. There was no sign of the hostess, Lily, or of birthday boy Frank, but Ted figured they'd be together, somewhere in the mass of bodies.

I hope she has her mom and dad's permission for this!

Ted squeezed his way into the main room and stood against a wall, across the room from the speakers pounding out a continuous disco thump. Most of the people seemed to be swaying more or less in time with the music, but he couldn't tell who was dancing with whom, or if anybody was actually paired off at all. He enjoyed the pulsating beat as much as the next guy, but the disco lyrics failed to interest him. "Boogie Shoes" would never resonate like the words of Mick Jagger. Ted was on a losing streak, at the card table as well as with girls.

He waved and nodded in the direction of a couple of acquaintances from his European History class, but there was no point shouting "hello." He wouldn't be heard across the room. He shrugged and reached into his jacket pocket for the mickey of rye he'd scored after three tries at different liquor stores. Ted wasn't a heavy drinker, just as well since he was still underage. He tried to persuade himself that he liked his whiskey straight, when he did drink, fortunate in this setting because it would have taken him twenty minutes to push through the crowd to the kitchen sink for a little water, much less any other mix.

He had the bottle to his lips when a petite young woman, twisting to the music, backed into him. A whiff of her perfume was almost enough to drown out the odour of marijuana that permeated the air. He was astonished when she didn't recoil forward, away from him. Instead, she bent slightly forward and wiggled her rear against his hips. He was conscious of the fact his equipment was rising to the occasion, but he had little idea what to do about it.

Do I push back? Or does that just get me slapped in the face?

He wondered if the girl even knew who she was flirting with. He tried to remember whether she'd looked his way before stepping in front of him, but he hadn't noticed. He replaced the cap on his flask and slipped it back into his pocket, and placed his hands tentatively on the girl's shoulders. He massaged gently when she didn't flinch, lifting her hair off her neck, and focused for a moment on the white bra straps. She turned abruptly and pressed herself against him.

"Come on. Dance with me," she purred. He caught only a fleeting glimpse of her boobs, she had turned so quickly, but they felt magnificent against his chest. She put her hands behind his neck and lay her face against his. He put his arms around her back. *Am I supposed to grab her ass? Do I dare?* He swiveled his hips gently at first, then with more enthusiasm. The girl moved with him.

Jesus Christ! This is unbelievable! He wondered how much the girl had had to drink, or smoke. She wasn't falling down, or even the least bit sloppy. In fact her movements were precise as well as provocative. He allowed his hands to drop to her rear. It didn't seem to cause a problem.

What the hell do I say to her? "This is nice," he managed.

"Shut up and dance."

Ted allowed his pelvis to move forward and back as well as side to side. Her cheek rubbed on his.

How long do we do this for? Does she expect to keep it up all night?

"Try this," she said. The girl peeled herself off of him and performed a body ripple. Ted tried to imitate it, bending forward and back from the waist.

"No. Start by bending your knees, and lower your butt straight down. Then you pull yourself up and forward, through the thighs, then the hips, the belly, and then your shoulders." She demonstrated again.

God, she makes that look sexy.

The girl broke the body contact and stepped to the side, swaying her hips. "Come on. Bump!" Ted thrust his hip to the side in time with the beat. He closed his eyes and embraced her when she stepped in front of him again. He shut out the room, the world around him, conscious of nothing but the scent and the warm body of the beautiful young woman in his arms, moving in unison with him.

Until she was yanked away. He heard the girl gasp and opened his eyes barely in time to see the fist driving toward his face. The second punch was to the solar plexus, and Ted doubled over. A knee to the chest completed the job. Ted slumped to the floor, gasping for breath and bleeding from the mouth.

Hands materialized under his arms and pulled him to his feet. A third hand reached into the back of his pants and gave him what seemed an overly enthusiastic wedgie. The sea of bodies parted, clearing a path for him as he staggered toward the exit, with the weight of a hundred eyeballs on his back. The dancing queen was laughing as hard as anybody. Somebody pulled the door open and he slipped out, stopping in the driveway to regain his breath and look for a dark spot in the garden where he could unbuckle his pants and adjust the underwear.

What the fuck was that!? Psycho bitch set me up!

He managed to pull himself upright and did his best to appear dignified as he weaved up the street toward the bus stop.

Fuck, I hate disco!

He slipped his jacket off of one shoulder and used a shirt sleeve to mop most of the blood from his face. He checked with his tongue; all of his teeth seemed still to be in place.

* * * *

"What the fuck happened to you?" Neil said, when Ted arrived back at the dorm.

"I don't fuckin' know."

"Whaddaya mean, 'you don't know?' Somebody punched you in the face and you don't know?" Neil looked at him more closely. "Are you stoned?"

"No."

Ted went to the bathroom to study his fat lip in the mirror.

"What the fuck happened?"

"Somebody punched me in the face, all right? I don't know who it was."

"What? At the party?"

Ted nodded.

"I told you you shouldn't try to hang out with third and fourth years. What the fuck did you go for, anyway?"

"I like Lily. And I thought Frank was okay too – but some of the people they hang out with..."

"What? Did you say something to somebody's girlfriend?"

"There was a girl, yeah. But I didn't do anything. She was all over me."

Disbelief was written on Neil's face.

"Seriously! I thought she was coming on to me. But it was all some fucking set-up. I should have known." Ted was quiet for a moment. "I thought the hazing was all over last fall."

Chapter five Joanie

"So, who are you gonna call first when we get home? Joanie or your old boss?"

"Bill, I guess. Have to get as much work as I can this summer. Might as well get started early." Ted knew the answer, but good manners required he ask anyway. "What about you?"

"I'll be working for Dad again. "

The ride home was less rambunctious than the drive to school had been eight months earlier, just Neil and Ted in the car. Ted reflected on the highs and lows of his first year away from home. *Grades, good. Women? A disaster.* Bridge had become more than a casual pastime, although he knew he wasn't a strong enough player yet to look for money games. He'd tried to resist the lure of poker, but there were too many nights when it seemed the only way to break up the monotony of studying. And if it cost a few bucks to play, well, *A guy's allowed to spend his money on something, right? At least I didn't turn into a pot head like so many of them.*

Neil had been a good roommate, but he was a year older, not having skipped a grade in primary school. They hadn't talked about sharing accommodations again. *Maybe it's been enough of a good thing.*

Mom had tried to persuade Ted to take a year off before heading to university. "You're only just seventeen, after all," she'd said. *She's always treated me like a baby.* She tried to keep it a secret, but Ted knew she'd spoken to Neil about "keeping an eye on Teddy. Make sure he's okay down there, will you?"

* * * *

He reached Joanie the third time he called. She hadn't returned his first two messages.

"Hey."

"Oh, hi." There was a distant tone in her voice.

"How've you been?"

"Fine." Awkward pause. "How about you?"

"Fine. Just got back in town a couple of days ago."

"Yeah, I figured. Did you have a good time at school?"

"Yeah, it was good."

"You didn't burn the place down?"

He forced a chuckle at her ridiculous joke. "No. Nothing like that." Awkward pause.

"So, I thought we could get together today. Maybe catch up over lunch?" His gut knew what the answer was going to be.

"I don't know, Ted. I'm not sure it's a good idea." Longer awkward pause. "I've been seeing somebody else."

"Oh." He tried not to sound devastated. "Somebody I know?"

"I don't think so. His family just moved here this year."

"Oh."

"We're going to go to the prom together."

"Oh. Well, have a good time." *What else am I supposed to say?*

"Thanks. Maybe I'll see you around, eh?"

"Yeah. Probably."

* * * *

Ted spent the afternoon in his room, on the pretense of trying to sleep in advance of an overnight shift, unloading trucks at the supermarket. *At least Bill wanted me back.* He recalled the conversation as he stared at the ceiling. "We've been waiting for you to come home, Ted. When can you start?"

"Maybe tomorrow? Mom wants to have a big welcome home dinner tonight."

That was the first time he called Joanie's house. Mom had insisted that she be invited.

How am I going to tell her that we're done? She always liked Joanie.

He rolled over and stared at the clock for a time. The roar of a lawn mower shattered the silence, as Bobby set about cutting the grass below his window. *Whatever. It's not like I was actually going to get any sleep anyway.*

He gazed around the room. *This is still home.* The dorm room had been okay, but it always felt temporary, no matter how many Stones or Elton John posters he and Neil tacked to the walls, how many knick-knacks they placed on the limited shelf space.

He stood up and opened the closet, found the old Yahtzee game still in its place on the top shelf. He hadn't touched it in, what, three? four? years, but pulling it down felt like the most natural thing in the world. The list of high scores was still in the box, in his child's handwriting.

His first roll of the dice produced two deuces, a three, a five, and a six. *Fuck. Keep the deuces? Or try to fill the straight?* He knew the odds were against him, but he picked up one of the two's and tossed it again. A five. *I can bail out into fives, or try for the straight again.* The decision was far more important than anything Joanie could possibly be doing that afternoon. He picked up a five and shook the die vigorously in his fist. A four! *All right!* It was better than sex.

* * * *

Summertime in Penticton was an experience not to be taken for granted, judging by the way tourists would descend on it from the middle of June until Labour Day. Long time locals had learned to endure the way their city would bulge with thousands of visitors, soaking up the sunshine on the warm beaches of Okanagan and Skaha Lakes.

Freelance teenage boys, Ted among them, prowled the beaches in search of a presumed smorgasbord of bikinis, but more often found their styles cramped by hordes of families – little kids splashing in the water under the watchful eyes of concerned mothers, while overweight dads sunned themselves in Speedos that they really oughtn't have been wearing.

Grocers adjusted their stocks to accommodate the demand for the quick and easy microwavable meals that budget conscious motel residents would live on, eschewing healthy diets for two weeks of casual ambrosia.

Ted noticed the change in deliveries ahead of the start of the season.

"Got to give the market what it wants," he was told. "The customer is always right."

For some reason the lesson left an indelible impression.

* * * *

It was late July when he bumped into Joanie in the grocery aisles.

"Hey."

"Hi Ted. How've you been doing?"

"Oh, fine. Help you find something?"

"No. No, thanks. I know where everything is." But she didn't reach for anything on the shelf. "You've got a birthday coming up pretty soon."

"Yeah."

"Going to have a party?" She smiled at him.

"Not really. Just family. We'll probably barbecue some steaks." She lingered, seemed to want to chat. *What the hell?* "Do you want to come?"

"Yeah. I'd like that."

* * * *

The store gave him a cake, large enough to feed an army, decorated elaborately around the words, "Happy 18th Ted."

His mom and dad greeted Joanie warmly. She hugged Ted and gave him a peck on the cheek, *not the mouth,* he noticed.

"You sure you don't want another piece of cake?" insisted Mom, after dinner.

"No, thank you, Mrs. Cronkite. I'm stuffed. That was fantastic." Joanie got up and began gathering plates. "Let me help you tidy up."

"Don't be ridiculous. You two visit." She gave Dad a pointed look. "We'll take care of it."

"You want to go for a walk?" she asked Ted, after his parents disappeared inside.

"Sure."

She didn't offer him a hand as they strolled together toward the water. "I missed you when you were away," she said. "Wondered for a long time what you were doing."

"I'm sorry," Ted mumbled. "It was busier than I realized."

"What's it like?"

"It's big. Not like high school. Takes forever to walk from one class to another. The library's always busy – line-ups everywhere."

"What about those crazy parties I hear about?"

"Yeah, I guess they have those too. I only went to one." He didn't tell her how badly it had ended. "So, you're going in September? I presume you were accepted?"

"Oh, yeah. It's not like you have to have straight A's to get in."

"What about your boyfriend?"

She stopped walking. "That's off. We broke up a month ago. Prom night, actually. He thought I was going to put out."

Shit! "And you wouldn't?"

She shook her head.

"Aww, Joanie. I'm sorry." He reached for her, squeezed her tightly when she accepted the embrace. She kissed him, closed mouth, but on the lips.

Chapter six A Christmas Carol

Frank received his Business degree at the spring Convocation and went to work for a downtown advertising agency. Lily was a year behind, and without Frank around Ted found her available for bridge at the university club from time to time. He knew enough not to try to make any more of the relationship than that.

The first time he was invited to join some of the players in the student pub after a game, Ted was ID'd at the door and denied entry.

"You guys go on ahead," said Lily. "I'll catch up with you." She and Ted sat on a bench in the October sunshine.

"So, how old are you, anyway? When are you nineteen?"

"Not 'till next August."

"You're kidding! I guess you'll have a big party then?" She became serious. "So, that means you were still seventeen at that party at my house."

"Yeah." He pulled a piece of long grass and twisted it in his fingers.

"I heard what happened – I hope they weren't too hard on you."

Ted snapped the grass. *Yeah, but I bet you didn't do anything about it.* "No lasting damage," he muttered.

"Listen. You're a nice kid. And you're obviously smart, to be here that young. But you're not the smartest guy here. Some of the guys thought you needed to be taken down a peg or two. That's all it was."

Ted struggled to remain expressionless.

Lily brushed a lock of hair away from her eyes. "You're second year now. You know your way around. But don't let it go to your head." She smiled. "We can play bridge once in a while, but you should really be hanging out with people your own age. Have you got a girlfriend?"

"Sort of. My high school girlfriend's here now – we still hang out sometimes."

"Well, there you go. Show her the ropes. Be there for her. You know, women can be just as nasty to the new kids as guys are." She patted his arm as she got to her feet. "I'll see you around, okay?"

* * * *

Santa Claus came early to the Cronkite household in 1976, the night Ted arrived home for the holidays. Mom and Dad had decided to be the first on the block, for once, to acquire the latest technology – a brand new VCR.

"A what?" said Ted.

"Video cassette recorder."

Oddly, it was Bobby who knew what it was. "Cindy's family got one a few months ago – when they first came out."

"Oh, yeah? How come you never mentioned it?"

Bobby shrugged. "Here. I can show you how to set it up. The cable goes from the wall into 'input'. And then from 'output' to the TV. You can record programs whenever you want, and watch them later. You should be able to record one program while you're watching another, so you don't have to miss anything." He pointed to the control pad. "And look. You can fast forward the tape so you don't have to watch the commercials!"

He arrived home the next day with an oblong plastic box in his bag. "Here. Cindy loaned this to us. They recorded it last week."

The hand-printed label read "Christmas Carol," the version with Alistair Sim as Scrooge.

Ted was intrigued.

"You can record on one machine and play it on another?"

"Should be able to."

"And they just *loaned* it to you?"

"Well, yeah. I don't think they want to give it away."

"No, that's not what I..."

The conversation was interrupted when Mom came into the living room with a pitcher of eggnog and a plate of fruit cake.

Nobody seemed to notice how Ted was lost in thought through the movie.

Chapter seven The Camaro

It was Neil who first heard the rumours about a gambling club in Vancouver's east end – maybe legal, maybe pushing the envelope. That was part of the appeal.

"We should check it out," he told Ted. "I hear they play for some serious stakes. Not the penny-ante social games."

"Are you sure?" Ted laughed. "Wait a minute. You're serious, aren't you?" He'd been doing better in recent months, picking up a few bucks here and there from fellow students. But Neil was right. *If you're going to play, you might as well make it worthwhile.*

The address was a rundown building in a seedy neighbourhood. There was no off-street parking, and no flashing neon sign over the non-descript entrance.

"How'd you find out about this place?" asked Ted.

"Just a guy in one of my classes. Says his dad comes here sometimes."

The room was lit by bare overhead light bulbs, no decorative features. The carpet was worn and the wallpaper was peeling in places. It seemed the only thing in the place that was well maintained was the green felt on the pool and card tables. Half of them were unoccupied. A nudie calendar hung on the wall behind a desk, where a middle-aged man sat, reading a racing form.

He glanced up as the boys entered. "Yeah?"

"We heard we might find a poker game here."

The man scowled. "Can you kids afford it? We don't want any jokers in here."

Neil and Ted each showed a wad of cash.

"Okay," the man groused. He took their money and handed them each three hundred dollars in chips. "The house doesn't take any cut of winnings. You pay two dollars every thirty minutes for a seat. The players set the table stakes." He pointed to a rack of mugs hanging on a wall. "A buck for coffee. No booze allowed." Snacks were in a vending machine.

The boys looked at one another, and handed over another eight dollars apiece.

"Okay. No refunds!"

"Friendly guy," Ted whispered, as they stood uncertainly in the middle of the room.

One of the players at a table of three looked directly at them and pointed to the two empty chairs. Ted shrugged and approached the table. "Ten dollar ante," said the man. Ted looked at Neil and nodded.

The game started slowly enough. Ted won an early hand with a straight, but only one other player had called, not the guy who'd invited them to play. "Fuckin' shithouse luck!" snarled the guy who'd bet against him. He flung his chair back and stomped out.

Too bad, thought Ted. He'd made the guy as a patsy. The first man who'd spoken was obviously going to be the toughest challenge. He had the largest stack of chips in front of him and played like a shark. Ted detected no obvious tells. When the proprietor wandered over to the table the guy flipped him a ten dollar chip. "For an hour. Keep the change."

Two more men joined the table, one of them staring harder at Ted than at anybody else.

That's right, you idiot. I'm the guy you should be worried about.

Ted was up a fairly pedestrian two hundred dollars, and Neil, unaccustomedly, almost double that, before things turned ugly. Neil had won a large pot when the shark made what seemed an ill-advised call, but Ted sensed it was more a matter of research on his part. *Find out if this kid thinks he can bluff in here.* Something about the guy made it clear he had deep pockets.

Ted folded two pairs a few deals later when the shark made a modest second raise. *He's trying to slow play us.* He knew better than to say anything, and pleaded silently for Neil to stay out of the water. Neil leaned back in his chair, studying his cards. *Neil, please. Don't!*

"Are you in or out?"

Neil set his cards face down on the table. "I'm in – and raise you five hundred." He pushed an entire stack of chips forward.

There was no doubt in Ted's mind the shark was going to call. The guy looked at his stacks of chips, and reached into his pocket for a wad of bills. "Five hundred – and another thousand."

I've got to say something! "You can't expect him to bet more than he's got." The shark glowered and blew cigarette smoke in Ted's direction.

"It's okay, Ted." Neil reached into his pocket and dropped his car keys on the table.

"What the fuck is that?"

"1967 Camaro. It's worth a lot more than a thousand dollars."

The shark stared at him. "Okay." He counted another ten hundreds into the pot. "Let's not quibble. Is that enough?"

Neil looked as though he'd just won the Irish Sweepstakes. He faced his cards and reached for the pot. "Full house. Jacks over aces."

"Hold it! Kings over threes."

Fuck! Neil… Ted saw his friend slump in his chair, as though he'd been stabbed through the heart. The guy pocketed the cash and dangled the car keys from his fingers. "You know these are no good to me until you sign transfer papers." Neil stared wordlessly. Two thugs who'd been drinking coffee quietly in a corner wandered over and stood behind his chair.

"Everything okay, Gerry?"

"I think so. This gentleman was just explaining to me how he's going to deliver me an automobile."

The smile disappeared from Gerry's face. "Let me see your wallet!"

"My wallet?" Neil croaked.

"I need to know who you are and how to find you." He helped himself to Neil's driver's licence. "You get this back after we meet at motor vehicles. Nine o'clock Monday. Be there."

Ted stole a glance at the two henchmen standing over Neil. Nobody was smiling.

* * * *

Neither of the boys noticed the heavy winter rain when they walked out onto the crumbling sidewalk.

"I think we go this way for a bus," Ted suggested, trying to steer Neil away from the Camaro, parked just up the street. He didn't succeed. "Are you okay?"

Neil looked at him as though he was from Mars. "No, I'm not fucking okay. What do you think?" He ran a hand along the roof of the car, before he spun and kicked the passenger door. Ted looked back at the club, hoping nobody was watching out a window.

"I know. I just meant..." *I don't know what the fuck I meant.* "I know you loved your car." *Probably spent more time under the hood than driving it.* "But we can't take it."

"I know that! Fuck 'em! I didn't tell anybody what condition it was in."

Ted put a hand on his friend's shoulder and urged him away from the vehicle.

"Let's just go, before anything else happens, okay? If somebody saw you..."

"I don't fuckin' care!" Neil boasted, but he turned with Ted and walked up the street. "That fuckin' guy must have cheated," he declared. "He had to have. How the fuck do you have two hands that good on one deal?"

"I don't know," admitted Ted. "I didn't see anything."

"No. You wouldn't. He's a fucking pro. A professional cheater!"

It could be. But it's not like there's anybody you can complain to. "He's certainly a professional poker player."

Neil kicked a garbage can. "You knew that, didn't you? How the fuck did you know?"

"When you won that big pot early on. He was testing you."

"Fuck! I guess you're right. I should've fucking known!"

Do I tell him what he shouldn't have done? No. Nobody wants to hear that. This isn't the time for a lesson.

Ted paid the bus fares.

"You want me to go with you on Monday?"

"I don't know that I'm going to."

"Jesus, Neil. You have to. These aren't guys that you can fuck with."

"Maybe I can buy it back from him."

"Have you got two grand?"

"No. I'd have to ask Mom and Dad." There was a crack in his forced stoicism. "How am I going to tell them?"

There's that. And there's the matter of another repair bill after you put the boot to it.

Neil hung back when Ted opened the front door at the rez. "Aren't you coming in?"

"Nah. I want to be alone for a while. I'm going to have a cigarette."

"You sure?"

Neil nodded. "Don't wait up for me."

At least it's stopped raining. "Okay."

Ted tossed and turned, unable to sleep for what seemed like hours. He looked at the bunk across the room when he woke up just after ten o'clock Sunday morning. The top cover was spread neatly, with no lump beneath it. It didn't appear to have been slept in. *What the fuck?* He decided to check some usual haunts before sounding unnecessary alarm bells.

* * * *

He couldn't possibly have missed the buzz in the cafeteria.

"Who was it? Anybody know?"

"No. They haven't said yet."

"A student?"

"Apparently. Probably flunked an exam or something."

"Or maybe his girlfriend dumped him."

Ted leaned on the counter for support as his knees buckled beneath him. He turned to somebody at one of the tables. "What happened?"

Neil didn't hang himself in a private shower stall someplace. No, he made a statement. He did it in a tree on the university endowment lands, in clear view of traffic on the Tenth Avenue arterial into the campus. The spectacle was blamed for a chain reaction crash, where at least five vehicles rear-ended each other.

* * * *

Ted was weeping into his pillow when a couple of cops banged on the door shortly after noon.

"Ted Cronkite?"

"Yes."

"We're here about your roommate. I take it you've heard what's happened?"

His red eyes confirmed the answer. He wiped his face with a sleeve.

"Mind if we have a look around?"

"Sure." He stepped aside and waved an arm grandly, inviting the officers in.

"You look pretty shaken up. You fellows were close?" One of them asked the questions while the other pulled back the spread on Neil's bed. *No sheets!*

"Yeah. Friends for almost ten years."

"Any idea why he would have taken his own life? Anything been bothering him?"

"Yeah," Ted affirmed dully. "I know exactly what it was about."

The cop's eyebrows went up in surprise. "He talked to you about it?"

"No. No, I had no idea he was going to do this." He related the story about the poker game, and the timeline as best he could, recalling the way Neil hadn't gone to bed immediately.

The second cop picked up a piece of paper from the desk. The note was short – "I'm sorry Dad."

"Does that look like Neil's handwriting?"

"I think so, yes."

"And you haven't touched this? You didn't notice it here?

Ted shook his head.

"Any idea why he'd address it just to his father? Are his parents together?"

"Yeah, they are. It's probably because his dad got him the car. He runs a dealership up in Penticton." *Jesus Christ!* He looked up from the floor, wide-eyed. "Do they know yet?"

"Actually, no. We haven't been able to reach them yet. I guess they went to church or something. Give us a few hours before you call them, okay?"

Ted nodded. *Fuck! I hadn't even thought about that. Am I supposed to?*

The cop seemed to look at him sympathetically. "I'm sorry for your loss, Mr. Cronkite. Are you going to be all right? I hope you'll talk to a counsellor."

* * * *

He curled up on his bunk in the fetal position.

He had no sense of time, other than the lack of daylight streaming in the window, when he heard another tap on the door.

"Joanie!" She was crying.

"Oh my God, Teddy." She folded into his arms. She was the only beautiful thing in the world.

Chapter eight George Who?

Joanie's face darkened and her body stiffened visibly as Ted related the events of Saturday night.

"A card game! That's what this was about? A fucking card game!?"

Ted felt his own face redden. "Joanie – not so loud." People at nearby tables were looking at them.

"I don't fucking care! A fucking card game?"

"It was Neil's idea – he wanted to go."

"Yeah, sure. To humour you, maybe." Joanie's voice caught as she tried to fight back tears. "How could you let this happen?"

"I didn't exactly 'let it happen.' I..."

He reached for her hand, but she yanked her arm away. "You let him go there. You let him make a bet he couldn't afford. And you left him alone afterwards."

The last part he did feel badly about. *Was it my fault?* He gazed into her flaming eyes, thinking about the night they had just spent together. *Not what I had in mind for the first time with a girl in the dorm.* Nothing had happened – they spent the night in one another/'s arms, fully clothed, on the single mattress. *Actually, I felt closer to her than I would have if we'd fucked each other's brains out.*

"Joanie..."

"Don't talk to me!" Her eyes teared up again as she stared into space.

"He was my friend, too, you know."

"I know you think that!" She scowled. "Do you even know what a friend is, Ted? You're supposed to take care of each other. But you're too wrapped up in your fucking card game!" She slammed her fork down and pointed a finger at him as she stood up. "Everybody's just a mark to you, aren't they? How much can you take them for? What are the odds on the next deal?" She turned her back and stormed out.

Ted tried to focus on his breakfast, but there was no way he could eat, with everyone in the cafeteria staring at him, no matter that he hadn't touched a thing yesterday. He took the toast with him, but left the omelet.

* * * *

He didn't see Joanie again until the funeral, where she sat immediately behind Neil's family.

He couldn't bring himself to approach the McKenzies. *No doubt she's told them it's all my fault.* He dropped a condolence card into the mailbox at their house, but didn't knock on the door. He was sure he wouldn't be welcome at the reception.

'A fucking card game! Everybody's just a mark to you, aren't they?' Joanie's tirade echoed in his head. *Fuck, Neil. Why were you so stupid? And why this?* He kicked a garbage can on the street corner, and the image of Neil doing the same thing on a rainy night in a sleazy downtown alleyway replayed in his head. *It was just a car! Just a fucking thing – and things can be replaced.*

He remembered Neil's easy laugh, how they'd punch each other in the arm on the school bus when they were kids. He recalled trying to tell his friend about the number "one" – the seemingly simple concept magically rendered mysterious in one of Asimov's essays. (If you break a piece of chalk are you left with a broken chalk, or do you now have two of them?) Neil had made some dumb remark about how "everybody knows the difference between number one and number two."

Joanie didn't even know who we were back then! She's got no right! No fucking right to be so pissed off at me.

* * * *

Most people would have no reason to know, much less care, about the cultural significance of one George Atkinson.

But Ted did.

Bastard!

He clipped the article from a popular motion picture magazine. Buried among the gossip items about the latest sexcapades and divorces of the Hollywood stars was a sarcastic piece, predicting the first video rental store, on Wilshire Boulevard, would close as quickly as a bad Broadway play.

Fucking idiots! Can't they see this guy's going to make millions?

Ted was in the middle of his third year at UBC, and the pressure was on to make some decisions about his future.

"You're nineteen now," Dad had said, back in the summer. "It's about time you start planning what happens after college."

Ted frowned as he cracked another beer.

"You know, you might want to specialize in business. Maybe be the manager at the supermarket someday. Or do you think you might want to go to law school? Your grades are probably good enough."

"I don't know, Dad. I don't see myself working for somebody else."

"What? You want to open your own grocery or something?"

"Or something. Maybe."

* * * *

Ted was on auto pilot through the autumn of that year. Earning a BA was just too easy. *But Dad's right. Then what?* He couldn't shake the feeling there was an opportunity waiting to be seized.

And then that story, that somebody else had seen it too. Somebody who had the financial wherewithal, or at least the credit, to do something about it. *Fuck! I was born ten years too late.*

It seemed everywhere he went he would overhear that absurd **SaturdayNight** utterance – "ex-kyooze mee!" *Everybody thinks he's Steve Martin!* Odd thing was the number of people who didn't actually watch the show **live**, despite its name. Video recording had caught on fast and was taking the world by storm.

* * * *

He was surprised to find personal mail awaiting him when he arrived in Penticton for Christmas break – an invitation for Ted and guest to attend the wedding of Lily Jacobs and Frank Hamilton, St. Stephen's United Church, 7025 Granville Street, reception to follow at the Shaughnessy Golf and Country Club, Southwest Marine Drive.

"That's nice," said Mom, as Ted handed her the invitation to read. "I guess that's a pretty exclusive club."

"Yes." He studied the card again, as though there would be some nugget, some important clue that he'd missed, to a question he couldn't think to ask.

"They're friends of yours? Of course they are. Or do you just know one of them?"

"I know them both. I guess I know Lily better. She taught me to play bridge. I haven't seen her since she graduated last spring. And Frank was the year before that."

"You're going to go, aren't you?"

"I guess so."

"Well, you have to send your RSVP – let them know whether you'll be bringing a guest. Will you?" Mom asked, pointedly.

"I don't know."

"What about Joanie?"

His mother's face fell when Ted shook his head.

She paused before she tried to brighten the mood. "Well, I guess I should take you shopping for a gift. Men are hopeless at picking out wedding gifts."

"A gift?"

"See? That's what I mean."

* * * *

Ted posted a letter to his parents in March.

Mom – Dad

I've got some news, and I'm writing instead of phoning because I don't want to get yelled at. Please understand this is a done deal. There's no point telling me not to go ahead.

I've quit school, and taken a job down here in Vancouver – Coquitlam, actually, but that's just a line on a map. Make a note of the address. I'm living in a basement suite, at Frank and Lily's house. You remember they're the couple who just got married on Valentine's Day. (By the way, Mom, they really liked the crystal bowl you picked out for them.)

*Please don't blow your stack, Dad. I told you a long time ago I was going to go into business, and I've been thinking about pretty much nothing else. I'm going to rent movies! You know, video cassettes. It's like **everybody** is buying VCR's now - watching movies at home is going to be huge. I've never been so sure about anything in my life. There are already shops opening up – first one was in Hollywood, naturally enough – and I've got to get in before it's too late.*

I'm not going to ask you to loan me any money, but I have to start getting my stake together. I can't afford to waste any more time on a degree that isn't going to make any difference.

I have taken a full time job – pretty good pay, and it can be more than full time if I want it to (which I do) so it might not be long before a bank will at least give me the time of day.

I won't be coming home for the summers anymore – hope to see you all at Christmas.

Love you both, and wish me luck!

* * * *

Dad, of course, did blow his stack. "'Waste his time' finishing a degree! What sort of bloody nonsense is that!?"

Mom re-read the letter in stunned silence while her husband vented.

"Of all the bloody irresponsible, ungrateful stunts to pull! We break our backs to give him an opportunity and he just up and throws it away!" He paced the living room. "'Not going to ask us to loan him any money.' How nice! How much have we already invested in UBC?"

Mom glanced at the TV and the gray box sitting on top of it.

"He might be on to something, you know. People thought waterbeds were going to be a passing fad - micro-wave ovens..."

Dad stopped pacing and glared at his wife. "Yeah, and I suppose you still think pet rocks were a good idea too!"

Chapter nine Alice

Ted was awake with the sun Saturday morning – Easter weekend, 1980. He sensed the warm body in the bed beside him, but still, a reality check seemed compulsory. He reached out to touch her.

Alice. That was her name. Alice.

She didn't move, curled up peacefully on her side, facing away from him, her breathing slow and steady. Not like last night. *A real minx. I wonder if Lily and Frank heard? Probably.* No doubt Lily's face would give it away. *She never could hide a smirk.*

He thought about the events that brought them together last night – a few drinks over a social bridge game, and Lily's insistence that Alice stay the night rather than driving. She'd protested, until Ted suggested she bunk in his suite, downstairs. A sixth sense told him it might be one of those occasions when boldness could be rewarded.

Alice shrugged. "Why not?" She followed him into his kitchen, and stood closer to him than necessary as he poured a glass of water.

"Would you like one?"

"Sure."

She'd barely wetted her lips before she stepped into his space and turned her face upward. Her kiss was warm and thorough. "Touch me!" she commanded. "Put your hands where you like."

Her reactions to his probing fingertips served only to amplify the curiosity. Her breathing quickened and her grip on his shoulders tightened. Of those things he was certain – it couldn't have been his imagination. Less sure was the gentle moan that seemed to escape her throat, and the word "harder" that he thought he heard.

Preliminaries diverted to the living room couch prior to the main event in the bedroom.

* * * *

Ted kissed the young woman's shoulder, gently, not so as to awaken her, and slipped out from beneath the covers as quietly as possible. He was out of the shower and in the kitchen in time to hear the seven o'clock news on the radio. Still no sound from the bedroom.

He started the coffee, quietly, but the cupboard door banged – a deliberate accident? - when he pulled out a frying pan for scrambled eggs. Four slices of cracked wheat bread went into the toaster. Strawberry jam, not jelly. Whisk the eggs in a bowl first, with a quarter cup of milk to fluff them up. *Don't measure. Eyeballing's good enough.* A little salt and pepper when they're done.

Alice was stirring when he carried a tray into the bedroom. He set breakfast on the dresser and handed her a coffee.

"Wow." She smiled her thanks. She sat up, holding the sheet over her chest with one hand as she lifted the mug to her lips with the other.

"Good morning! Sleep well?"

"Eventually."

She set the coffee on the bedside table and tilted her face up as Ted handed her a plate. "Wow again. Breakfast in bed!" Ted leaned down to plant a kiss on her mouth.

"I hope it's all right."

"Looks wonderful."

She struggled with her modesty, holding the sheet and the plate with her left hand, picking at the food with her right.

"You're shaved and everything. How long have you been up?"

"A little over half an hour, I guess." Ted sat on the edge of the bed, doing a balancing act with his own plate. His coffee was just out of reach on the dresser.

Alice smiled. "You know, this would've been easier at the table."

"I know. Breakfast in bed is supposed to be romantic." Ted grinned. "I'm not sure I get it." They both laughed. The sheet slipped down. Ted pretended not to stare.

Alice looked at him thoughtfully. "Listen – I want you to know I don't – you know – do that, on the first date. This was the first time."

For just a second Ted thought he detected a pleading look on her face. "I know," he told her. He couldn't possibly know but it seemed to be what she wanted to hear. She smiled slightly.

"Anyway, I'm glad you made an exception this time. You were..." *Maybe I better not say any more.*

"So am I."

Ted took a bite of his toast. "You know, maybe you haven't broken your rule. Was that even a first date? I mean, we played bridge with my landlords. It's not like it was a real date."

"That's true! Lily set it up. It's not like you called me."

"That's right. I don't even know your phone number."

Ted waited until they'd both stopped laughing. "So, what do you think? Would you like to go out? Maybe tonight?" *Or is that too pushy?*

"Saturday night? Let me check my calendar." She set her plate on the bed and pretended to thumb through a non-existent note book. "Saturday – Saturday – I guess I could be free."

"A movie? Or would you rather go out to dinner?"

"Hmm. Tough choice."

Ted got up. "Why don't you think about it for a minute while I get you another coffee?"

"That would be nice. But take your time. I'll get dressed and join you."

Ted carried the mugs to the kitchen. Alice appeared a few minutes later, dressed, and carrying the breakfast tray. "Couldn't find my bra," she mumbled. "Did you do something with it?"

Ted laughed and pointed to the couch.

"Oh yeah – I remember." She pulled her shirt off and picked up the undergarment, with her back to him. "Some help, please?"

Ted resisted the temptation to reach in front for a bonus squeeze before connecting the hasp in back, but he ran his fingertips slowly down her bare arms. She seemed to shiver slightly before she turned to look at him with puppy-dog eyes.

"You know," he said, "you're easy to be around in the morning. Some girls are really up tight the morning after."

"Some girls?'" She feigned shock. "Just how many girls are you talking about?"

Ted blushed. "Not that many, really. I mean – one - or two, maybe..." He let his voice trail off.

Alice gave him a playful peck on the cheek. "Only one or two? It seemed to me like you'd had a lot of practice!"

Ted blushed again. "I've got to get moving," he announced. "Have to work today." He scrambled in a drawer for pen and paper. "Leave me your address and phone number for later."

Alice wrote her information on the page, along with a couple of little hearts and flowers. "Come straight to my place after work? What time'll that be?"

* * * *

Ted pulled up in front of Alice's apartment building in his six year old Ambassador. He hadn't intended that his first car would be an AMC product, until Neil's suicide. After that he could barely look at a Camaro without bile rising in his throat, and he quickly enough came to realize that all the GM vehicles featured similar sleek, curved lines. The Rambler looked more like a box on wheels, and he decided if he had to accept the necessity of owning the most ubiquitous of all symbols of North American lifestyle, it would be the car with which to punish himself. The fact 1974 was the last year the model was built was a bonus for Ted alone to understand.

Alice buzzed him into the building and met him at the door of her second floor suite. She was dressed in a smart but comfortable-looking pant suit. Her hair was pulled back in a ponytail, and she displayed a little more jewelry than she had the night before. There was a brooch on her lapel and a silver charm bracelet adorned her right wrist. Ted's eyes spent more time on her hips.

"Wow!" he said. "You look fabulous!"

She smiled coyly and ushered him in. There was an awkward moment when Ted stopped in the entrance. *Am I supposed to kiss her?* He tilted his head forward but pulled it back when she didn't respond, only to notice she lifted her face toward him a second later.

"Okay. How do we...?"

They settled on a gentle bear hug and rubbed cheeks for a moment. Her perfume was intoxicating.

"Would you like a drink before we go?"

"Maybe just a beer if you've got one?"

He watched her reach into the cupboard for a glass, accentuating her bust line for just a few seconds. Ted shook his head. "So, would you like to go for dinner first? Or maybe we could catch an early movie and grab a pizza after?"

"That sounds good," she said, agreeably. "What sort of movies do you like?"

"I'm not big on the slasher stuff."

"Me neither. There's gotta be something without the blood and guts."

April was not prime season for the blockbuster new releases. They settled on American Gigolo. *I can live with two-fifty apiece, but it's the concession that kills you!*

* * * *

"Anything to drink while you're waiting?"

Ted studied the waiter carefully. *Looks younger than I do! I wonder if he's even allowed to bring us a beer?*

Alice glanced up from the cocktail menu. "I think I'll have a Harvey Wallbanger."

Ted shrugged. "Sure. Might as well make it two."

"So," she said, as they waited for the drinks to arrive. "How do you know Lily and Frank? I kind of got a sense it's more than just a landlord-tenant thing."

Sharp girl. Smart as well as good looking. "Yeah, I met them at university. Four years ago now, I guess. Played a little bridge with Lily at the UBC club. 'Course Frank was one of the stars there. I think he was a Life Master less than a year after he graduated."

"Life Master?"

"Yeah, it's an American Contract Bridge League designation. They keep track of all your master points, and run the big tournaments."

"They have tournaments?"

"Yeah, it's quite an elaborate organization. Publish a magazine and everything." He looked at her q uizzically. "How did you learn to play?"

"My parents," she said. "But they never went to tournaments. They'd just get together with friends in the living room, and sometimes they'd need a fourth – like last night."

"Well, maybe we can try a club game sometime, just for the hell of it." Ted tried to smile encouragingly. He changed the subject when she didn't answer. "What about you? You work with Lily?"

"Sort of. I'm in the office. I do the in-house paperwork for all the sales people."

"They don't do that themselves?"

"No. They're pretty much done after the subject-to clauses come off the interim agreements. I have to make sure the real estate board gets notified when a property's off the market, and calculate the commission splits."

"Am I allowed to ask how Lily's doing?"

"You're allowed to ask." Alice frowned slightly. "She's not one of the top sales people in the office. But she's young, and she does all right."

The drinks arrived.

"Some people in the office must be starving. They never bring in any deals. I think a lot of people get a rude awakening when they find out real estate isn't the easy money they think it is." She paused as they watched the waiter carry a pizza to a nearby table. "The way the market's been booming the past few years, a lot of new people have gone into it. But I guess it's like anything else – the top guys get rich and the rest get left behind."

"What about you? You think you could sell?"

Alice shrugged. "I don't know. It's a big gamble. Lot of work to get licenced, and even if you're good it's going to take some time to build up a client list. And I don't mind the job I've got." She took a sip of her drink. "I like having my weekends free."

Ted nodded thoughtfully.

"What about you? What do you do?"

"Me? Oh, I sell rabbit food." He laughed at the perplexed expression on her face. "I'm a produce manager at Safeway. For the moment."

"For the moment? You're pretty young to be a manager."

"Started in groceries when I was in high school." He swirled his drink. "But I'm going to go into business for myself."

"Doing what?"

"Movie rentals."

Alice leaned forward with an expression of interest. "I've heard about that. Mom and Dad have a VCR – I haven't got one yet."

"I'm guessing you will pretty soon."

"Maybe."

The pizza came – Hawaiian with extra cheese. Ted touched it first.

"Little too hot yet – let's give it a minute."

Alice returned to the subject. "I've heard people argue about different kinds of tapes – what do they call them? Alpha and Beta?"

"See? You are interested." Ted smiled. "VHS or Beta. And it's looking now as though VHS has won." She looked at him with an uncertain expression. "Actually, it might be a good thing I didn't get in as early as I wanted to. I might have got it wrong. I think anybody who invested in Beta has wasted his money."

"So how much investment are you talking about? It always costs money to set up a business."

"Actually, it's not that bad. I don't need a bunch of expensive equipment like refrigerators and freezers. It's basically just shelves and a cash register – plus the stock, of course." He hesitated. *Does she really want to hear all this?* Her face seemed to say yes. "I've been thinking a lot about locations. Seems to me I don't need to be in a high rent building. I think neighbourhood strip malls are the place to be." He slid his knife under a piece of pizza and lifted it to his plate.

"They say the only things that matter in real estate are location, location, and location," said Alice.

Ted's knife clattered to the floor. "Dammit! I hate the way they make these knives with all the weight in the handles, so they won't stay on your plate!"

She grinned at him and twirled a brush of hair in her fingers as she watched him lean down to pick up the knife.

"So, what else bugs you? Is that really your biggest pet peeve?"

Ted paused to consider. "I don't know. I don't have a lot of them."

"Well, that sounds like a pretty easy life." She twirled her hair again.

"What are yours?"

She put on an exaggerated pout. "I hate the way they always use more glue than they need to hold down the first sheet of toilet paper on the roll."

Ted chuckled. "Yeah! You're right! And I hate that you can't get anything out of the ketchup bottle, and when it finally does come it gets all over!"

"I hate that you can only use Krazy Glue once, 'cause the cap gets glued on solid."

"And I hate that they won't give you your deposit back on pop cans if you've squashed them!"

"I hate that when you turn a box to look at the instructions you always find the French side first!"

"I hate that the commercials on TV are always louder than the programs. And I really hate that they think they can lie to us about it!"

Alice laughed out loud. "Who *are* these bastards that want to make our lives miserable?" She reached across the table and took his hand, as their laughter subsided. Other diners were staring at them.

"So, do you have any places in mind? When do you think you'll be ready to open up?"

Her interest appeared sincere.

"Lily's kind of keeping an eye out for me. Problem is, I don't think it makes sense to open up in one location. I want to wait 'till I can make a bigger splash."

"Pourquoi?"

Ah, she knows more French than she was letting on. Ted picked up a slice of pizza. "I'd rather eat pizza by hand anyway."

Alice chuckled again. "Yeah." She pushed her cutlery aside.

"The way I figure it, the best locations might be right next door to a laundromat. What do people do while they're waiting for their laundry? Pick out movies!" He took a bite of pizza. "Easy parking, and close to home. I think it's going to be important to have a bunch of little locations instead of one big one." Alice nodded.

God, it's nice to talk to somebody who understands.

"Are you going to be able to afford to do that?" she asked.

"I don't think I can afford not to. These places are springing up all over the country. I don't know that any one of them is making anybody rich. But if each location nets fifteen or twenty grand a year and you have six or seven of them..."

Alice's eyes widened.

"And it is going to grow. It's gonna grow faster than any other business you can think of."

* * * *

They lingered over the good night kiss at Alice's door.

"I had a good time. That was a really nice first date."

So she's not going to invite me in. Fair enough. "So you think you might like to do it again? Maybe next weekend?"

"Maybe. Call me, okay?"

Ted couldn't stop thinking about her on the drive home. Smart, sexy, funny. *Bit of a women's libber. Got to remember not to talk about 'salesman' or 'chairman' when she's around.*

She was a bigger fan of the Doors and Led Zeppelin than the Rolling Stones, but that was okay. *At least she doesn't think Abba is God's gift to music.*

* * * *

Ted was in the upstairs kitchen in time to help peel potatoes and cut vegetables for Easter dinner. Lily was basting the turkey. She greeted him with a song.

"Ted and Alice sitting in a tree – K-I-S..." Ted didn't take the bait. "Man, you are smitten with her, aren't you?" She snapped her fingers. "Earth to Ted."

"Oh. Oh, yeah, sorry."

"'Oh yeah' you're here? Or 'oh yeah' it is love at first sight?"

Ted pondered. "I don't know. She is an interesting girl."

"You are going to see her again, then?"

"I think so."

"You didn't invite her for dinner tonight? You could have, you know."

"She's at her parents' place for Easter. I think I'll see her again next weekend." He bent down to retrieve a piece of potato skin that had fallen to the floor.

"Good. Good for you." She turned to face him. "Don't blow this. Alice is a great girl."

Chapter ten Pete

He phoned Alice Wednesday night to suggest drinks on Friday. "Maybe you'd like to go skating or bowling first?"

"God, I haven't done either of those in years. How about bowling?"

"Sure. Is seven o'clock a good time?"

* * * *

Ted picked up a half sack of beer on his way to Pete's house to see if the regular Friday night poker game might get underway early enough to squeeze in a few hands before his date with Alice. It had been a stressful day, and he hadn't taken a lunch break. His sandwich and bag of cheezies would make for a quick supper at the card table. At least there would be some company, better than grabbing a hamburger alone.

Pete Lambert lived on a street of older houses, most of them in need of repair, all of them with dandelion-infested front yards. The sidewalk was crumbling, as were most of the driveways. Ted could see Lambert's place had had a new roof installed since he'd been there last, no doubt the biggest news on the block in at least a month.

Lambert was a bearded, burly man, somewhere in his mid thirties.. He walked with a limp, frequently wincing in pain. Ted knew he lived on a veterans' disability pension, a result of an injury acquired on peacekeeping duty in Cyprus. Common knowledge was that he spent most nights on a cot in his basement, unable or unmotivated to climb the stairs to the bedroom – not that there was any compelling reason to make the effort. His wife was home as infrequently as possible. Everybody knew she was biding her time with Pete, waiting for the day one of her lovers would invite her to move in.

Ted found Pete and another man tinkering with the elaborate model railroad at one end of the basement. *Probably the only thing that keeps him alive.* He offered both of them a beer and sat down to eat his sandwich.

"'Bout time you dropped in," said Pete. "Was starting to wonder if you'd fallen off the face of the Earth."

"No. Just been busy," said Ted. "Can't stay long tonight, either."

"What? You're going to ditch us for some broad or something?"

"Actually, yes."

"Ohhh…" Pete looked at the other fellow and laughed. "The kid's got a hot date. Probably thinks we're going to pay for it for him!"

The other man laughed nasally.

"Why don't you get the cards out, kid? We'll start when Joe gets here."

Six-thirty came and went on the clock while Ted was counting his losses. "Just a couple more hands," he told the guys. "You've got to give me a chance to get even."

Two became four, became six, then ten, as frustration mounted. Ted lost track of time completely. He knew it was poor strategy when he bet heavily on a marginal hand in an attempt to recover his money in one shot, and lost.

Fuck! He stretched, and stared up at the small window, noticing the blackness outside. He jumped when he heard what sounded like an explosion, echoing through the neighbourhood.

"What the fuck was that?!"

"A rifle," said Pete. "Big one. Not a twenty-two."

"Jesus," said Joe. "Should we call the cops?"

"I suppose so," said Pete. "I'll phone. You guys go check it out."

"Are you sure that's what it was?" said Ted. "Couldn't have been a car backfiring or something?"

Everybody looked at him as though he was daft. "No, it couldn't have been a fucking car backfiring. I think I know the difference."

The three men made their way upstairs and peeked out the front window, in time to catch a glimpse of a car backing out of a driveway across the street, with its headlights out. The tires screeched as it roared off into the darkness.

Ted squinted at the house. "Looks like the front door's open."

"Ya think?" sneered Joe. Light poured out onto the porch.

Pete lumbered up the stairs. "Cops are coming. You guys see anything?"

"Looks like it was across the street." Pete peered out the window. "Somebody took off without closing the door."

"I'm gonna get out of here," said the man with the nasal voice. "I wasn't here, all right?"

"All right," said Pete, looking pointedly at Ted.

Neighbours started pouring out of houses. There were more than a dozen people milling around the middle of the street by the time police arrived. Everybody was eager to confirm hearing exactly one shot – the one they would later learn left Mrs. Hadfield dead in her bathroom – but nobody had a good look at the person who fled the scene. The police initiated a manhunt for Mr. Hadfield.

With nothing useful to add, Ted was on his way home within thirty minutes of the murder.

It was past eleven o'clock when he slunk in the door, feeling deflated and slightly shaken. He found his way to the bedroom without switching on a light. He tried not to think about the hundreds of dollars he'd lost, a pittance against other events of the evening. But it still stung. *And Alice! How pissed off is she going to be?*

He couldn't deal with it before morning.

* * * *

"Alice? Ted. I'm sorry about last night."

"What the hell happened to you? I thought you were in an accident or something."

"Had to work late," he lied. "They found some bad produce on one of the trucks and I had to stay to supervise the unloading."

"Well, you could have called, you know." He didn't detect any disbelief in her voice.

"I know. I'm sorry." Awkward pause. "Are you mad?" He beat down the urge to admit his actual whereabouts and tell her the news about last night.

"Yes, I'm mad." She hesitated again. "Look, Ted, I understand you've got to work. And it's not like I would have had time to make any other plans at the last minute anyway, but you should have called."

"I know. Can we do it tonight instead?"

"That's not going to work. I've got other plans."

"Oh." Awkward pause.

"I'm going out with an old girlfriend." Relief. "Listen, Ted, I know we haven't talked about being exclusive or anything, but just so you know, I'm not seeing any other guys at the moment. But I do have a life. And I was really worried about you last night."

* * * *

Ted lacked the chutzpah to call her during the following week. He was thinking about heading to the bridge club to look for a game on Friday night, when his phone rang at suppertime.

"Ted – Alice."

"Hi!"

"I haven't heard from you. Have things been okay at work, and everything?"

"Oh, yeah. Fine."

"I need to see you this weekend."

He sat up straighter, mood brightening immediately. "Tomorrow night? You want to go out for dinner?"

"No. Tomorrow, if you're not working."

"I'm off. What's going on?"

"I don't want to talk about it on the phone. Can I see you tomorrow morning?"

"Sure."

"I'll come over early, maybe eight-thirty or nine."

"That'll work. I'll make breakfast." He glanced at the fridge, trying to remember how many eggs he had on hand.

"You don't have to do that."

He placed third in the Friday night club game, with a pick-up partner. Frank and Lily were first, despite a heated argument after an early deal, when Lily forgot a bidding convention.

* * * *

Alice and Ted sat on the swings in the playground of a nearby elementary school.

"So, what's up?" *Please don't say you want to break it off.*

"I'm worried, Ted. I'm late. A week."

"Late? Ohhh..." *Shit.* "Is that a big deal? I mean, a week – might not mean anything."

"I'm pretty regular."

He stared at the ground between his feet. "But you're not sure yet. You haven't been tested yet?"

"No. I see a doctor on Tuesday."

"Am I supposed to go with you?"

She chuckled drily. "No. I don't think that's necessary." She hesitated. "But what if I am?"

Ted looked at her without speaking.

"Just for the record, if I am, it's yours."

"Well, if you are, I'll be there for you. Whatever you want to do."

* * * *

Ted went directly to her apartment after work Tuesday, with a grocery bag containing the makings for spaghetti sauce.

Alice's hair was disheveled and her face was drawn.

"It's positive." Ted didn't phrase it as a question. She nodded.

He set the grocery bag on the floor and reached for her. She evaded his embrace.

"Not now, Ted." She bent to pick up the grocery bag, but her shaking hand knocked it over – onions and peppers rolled onto the floor. "Dammit!"

"It's okay," said Ted. "I'll get it." He collected the vegetables and carried them to the kitchen counter.

Alice sat at the table with her face in her hands, as Ted busied himself cutting vegetables. "Have you thought about what you want to do?"

"I don't know."

"Have you told anybody else?"

"Are you serious?" She gave him a withering look. "Mom and Dad don't even know I've got a boyfriend, much less this."

Boyfriend! "Yeah, I'm sorry. I guess that was a dumb thing to say." He went to her and rubbed her shoulders. She looked up with tears in her eyes.

"Ted, what am I going to do?"

"What are *we* going to do. I'm not going to leave you alone in this."

She choked, once, twice, and then burst out crying openly.

"It's okay." He squeezed her in his arms and buried his face in her hair. "It'll be all right." *Won't it?*

* * * *

"This is good," said Alice, twisting a mouthful of spaghetti onto her fork. "You're a good cook."

Ted grinned. "Maybe that's one more reason we could get married."

"Oh, Ted, don't be ridiculous. We haven't even known each other for a month." She stopped the fork in mid-air and studied his face. "Wait a minute. You're serious, aren't you?"

"I know it hasn't been long, but I feel like I know you well."

"We can't know each other that well." She paused to consider. "And we can't be in love."

Ted shrugged. "I already told you how much I like having you around in the morning." He smirked. "And we know how good the nights can be." *Okay. Maybe that was the wrong thing to say.* "You know what I mean."

"I don't know, Ted. I can't decide something like this so fast." Her lip quivered. "I just don't know."

Chapter eleven Moving Mountains

Ted lay in bed, half awake, on a Sunday morning, contemplating his winnings at last night's poker game, when the air shook with a thunder such as he'd not heard before. It wasn't painfully loud, but it was more than sound, a force of nature that he literally felt deep in his being. He didn't know how to describe the sensation after the fact – certainly he heard many different people attempt to.

The phone rang a few seconds later.

"Ted!" He recognized Alice's voice. "Did you feel that?"

"Yeah. What was it?"

"An earthquake?"

"I don't think so." He looked around his living room. "A window shook a little bit, but nothing fell."

"Yeah – here too."

"Were you scared?" He tried to hold the phone on his shoulder while pulling on his pants.

"I don't think I was scared. I don't know what I was. It wasn't like anything..." She paused. "I reached out for you, and you weren't there."

"I know. I'm sorry."

"Ted, I wanted you to be there. I want you to marry me."

"I'll come over right now."

He was in the car in time to hear the tail end of the nine o'clock news on the radio. Mount St. Helens had blown its top, more than two hundred miles away, in Washington. The time was 8:32 a.m., May 18. It took almost twenty minutes for the shock wave to reach Vancouver.

She wants to marry me! That was the earthquake.

She'd made it clear enough she didn't want to be a single mom, but still she'd been reluctant to commit. "There are other options," she'd said. "We need more reason than a baby to get married. I'd think you'd want that too – I don't want you to feel pressured."

He'd tried to show her how happy she made him. A one month courtship was lightning fast by anybody's standards, but they'd crammed a lot into it. Good times, and sharing dreams for the future. And the sex, *well, that gets an A-plus.*

Alice met him at the door with a smile as wide as the great outdoors.

"You heard what it was?"

"Yeah, it was on the news."

"Mount St. Helens. We should have figured. It's not like it's a big surprise."

"So, you were serious, about..."

"Yes! Yes, I am!"

Ted got down on one knee and took her hand. "I don't have a ring for you yet." He kissed her hand. "Alice Johnson, will you marry me?"

"Yes! Arise, Sir Ted. Yes, I will!"

Ted sensed another tenant stepping out of his suite into the hall as he took her into his arms and kissed her. *Go ahead and stare, Mac.*

* * * *

"So, I guess the next thing to decide is when?"

"Well, we could rush off and do it before I'm showing, and hope nobody notices. Or we take some time and have a more traditional wedding." A serious expression came over her face. "Either way, you're going to have to meet my family. It's not going to be pleasant for you, when they find out you got me knocked up."

"I guess there's no point trying to sneak it past them. That might piss everybody off even more." A light went on in Ted's head. "And I've got to tell my family too."

"Here's what we do." There was an earnestness in Alice's voice. "Don't tell them, ever, that this happened the night we met. Tell them we've been dating for a while. Since January, anyway."

"What about Lily and Frank? They'll know, and they might blab."

"We'll have to have a talk with them. Can you do that? Will they listen to you?"

Ted nodded slowly. "I think so." He thought for a moment. "Lily'll be sympathetic, and I don't think Frank'll care one way or the other. Only risk is that he'll blow it without even thinking about it."

"Well, we just have to get through to him how important it is not to."

Ted got up to help himself to a glass of water. "So, do we go to see your folks today?"

Alice shook her head. "We can't. We have to go shopping first. I can't show up without showing off a ring – they'd know right away this was a snap decision."

The tri-lite in Ted's head switched up to level two. He smiled. "Good thing you're the one figuring these things out. I never would have thought of that!"

"I've been thinking about nothing but this stuff."

"Yeah, I guess you have." He squeezed her hand. "Am I allowed to tell my parents yet?"

"Christ, no! What would you tell them?" Alice's voice rose in exasperation. "That we haven't decided whether we're eloping or not?" She forced herself to speak calmly. "We talk to my mom and dad. We tell them you proposed, I accepted. We let them help us decide what the date should be. They won't want us to elope, so it'll probably be sometime in August. June is too soon. By then I'll be showing, but they'll have had a chance to get used to you. We'll tell them we were going to get married anyway."

Ted took a long draught of water and ran his fingers through his hair. "Were we?"

"Jeez, Ted. Don't ask me that right now."

He set his glass on the table and wrung his hands together. "I do love you, you know. Call it fate, call it whatever you like. I think it's the luckiest hand I've ever been dealt."

She smiled and squeezed his hand. "There is one more thing, but I guess we don't have to think about it right now."

He looked at her curiously.

"Where are we going to live?"

The tri-lite snapped up to intensity three.

"There isn't really room for you to move into this apartment, and there certainly isn't room for a baby."

"There's room at my place. I don't know if you noticed I don't have the whole basement. Part of it's not finished yet. We could offer to pay for that, or maybe Frank and Lily would rather do it and raise the rent."

"Can you afford that? I mean, I'm working now, but I'll have to be off when the baby comes."

"I've got the cash I've been setting aside to set up the business." Ted frowned. "It'll set me back a few months, but c'est la vie, right?"

"Okay. Just one more thing, then." She smiled at him. "You want to spend the night tonight?"

* * * *

They lay side by side in Alice's bed a few hours later, fingertips idly tracing patterns on one another's skin, ultra-sensitive in lovers' afterglow.

"Ted?" No hint of sleepiness in Alice's voice.

"Yeah?"

"Do you think I need a boob job?"

"What!?" He lurched upright.

Alice giggled. "You heard me. Do you like my boobs?"

"Of course I do. I think they're perfect." He reached out to squeeze one.

"Do you like my ass?"

He twisted his arm to give it a gentle slap. "What the hell kind of questions are these?"

"Which do you like better?" He stared at her, open-mouthed. "Come on. Tits or ass?"

I don't know what I'm being set up for, but there can't possibly be a right answer. "Neither. I mean, both. What the hell are you getting...?"

"I'm serious." She tried not to laugh. "It's a psychological test. It's a measure of how grown up you are."

"How grown up *I* am?"

"Yeah."

"Horse shit."

"I read somewhere that one way to tell the difference between boys and men is whether they stare at your tits or your ass."

"I don't know what kind of horse shit you're reading."

Alice sputtered with laughter.

"But," Ted rubbed his chin, doing his best to look professorial. "If it's to have any scientific validity at all, Dr. Johnson, you have to observe the subject, like a rat in a cage. You can't come out and ask him." He extended an arm to tickle her tummy. "He might lie to you, you know."

Alice turned and leaned on one elbow. "Would you, Ted? Would you ever lie to me?"

"Why would I?" He latched on to one of her ankles and tickled the sole of her foot. "What does your magazine say about this?"

Alice screeched with laughter as she tried to kick her leg free.

Chapter twelve Bunny

Three months' salary? Is that really a thing, or is it just marketing by greedy jewelers?

Ted wished he had the option of asking for his mother's advice. *I mean, I don't mind whatever it costs to make Alice happy. But I really hate the smell of bullshit!*

The stuffed-shirt jeweler seemed to make a point of ignoring the doubt on Ted's face, focusing his attention on Alice's glow. "I think everyone's happier when ladies come in to try on their own engagement rings," he bubbled. "This one's just made for your hand."

Ted recognized the upselling tactic, but said nothing.

The shirt finally had no choice but to acknowledge him once they moved from the display case to the till. "It's never going to go down in value," he promised, staring at the wallet in Ted's hand.

Ted failed to stifle his sarcasm. "Exactly when do you suppose we're going to try to sell it?"

"Well, uh..."

Yeah, you dumb fuck.

He paid cash.

* * * *

Ted made a point of finding a drive-through car wash on the way to the Johnsons' house. His shoes were freshly polished, and he wore a sports jacket and tie. His one black suit seemed unnecessarily formal for a dinner engagement, the importance of first impressions notwithstanding.

"Wow!" he said, pulling up in front of the house. "Somebody's a pretty serious gardener!"

Rows of neatly spaced bedding plants lined both sides of the driveway, a trio of rhododendrons were in full bloom, and a Hallelujah chorus of colours burst from the ornate urns on the front steps. But Ted couldn't take his eyes off the lawn. It looked like a putting green, or what a non-golfer might expect a putting green to look like, with nary a weed in evidence.

"Yeah," laughed Alice. "Mom likes to tend the flowers herself, but they do get some help from a landscaper. You should see the back yard!"

The cheery picture was consistent with her mauve sundress, spotted with embroidered daisies. Her hair was up, and a string of faux pearls hung around her neck. She carried a sweater as they entered the house, in case the air was chilly when it came time to leave, but more importantly, to conceal her hand until the ideal moment.

Her father met them at the door.

"Hi, Bunny!"

"Hi, Daddy!" She threw her arms around him.

"Long time no see." He took a step back and looked pointedly at Ted.

"Daddy, this is Ted. Ted Cronkite.""

"Ted." Dad put out his hand.

"Sir."

"Cronkite. Like the news guy on television?"

"Yes."

"Any relation?"

Jeez. Like I haven't heard that one before. "No. No, I don't think so."

"Well, come on in. Can I get you two a drink before dinner?"

"Maybe just a beer if you've got one?"

"Sure. And wine for you, Bunny? White or red this time?"

"Not right now. Maybe with dinner."

Alice's mother appeared, wiping her hands on a dish towel. "So this is Ted?"

"Nice to meet you, Mrs. Johnson."

"You want a glass for your beer?" asked Dad, as he turned toward the kitchen.

"Yes, please."

"Come on in," said Mrs. Johnson. "Sit. Dinner'll be about half an hour."

Alice sat with Ted on the love seat. Her mother took a spot on the couch, and studied Ted curiously.

"So, we've got to hear all about it. How did you two meet?"

"Turns out Ted's landlady is one of the sales people in our office," Alice explained. "They had me over for a bridge game, and we kind of hit it off." The story had been rehearsed, as close to the truth as possible, fudging only the date and the extra-curriculars.

"Yes," said Mrs. Johnson, looking at Ted. "Alice told us you're a pretty good card player."

"Not like Frank and Lily," said Ted. "But I do go to the duplicate club sometimes."

"Well, we'll find out after dinner, eh?"

Alice's father reappeared, with drinks for his wife and Ted. "You sure you don't want something, Bunny? How about a coke?"

"Sure." He went back to the fridge for the soft drink and another beer.

"So, is your family here, Ted? Did you grow up in Coquitlam?"

"No, I'm from Penticton, actually."

"Penticton!" repeated Dad, as he re-entered the room. "We've been there a few times, when the kids were young. You remember, Bunny?"

Ted glanced around for a coaster to set his drink on.

"Here." Mr. Johnson recognized what he was doing, and handed him one.

Guess I get a brownie point for that.

"So, what do you do, Ted? Are you in real estate too?"

"No, I run the produce section at a Safeway."

"You run it?" The future father-in-law's eyebrows went up slightly.

"Yes, Sir. It's a pretty good job, but it's only temporary."

The eyebrows went up further.

"Yeah, I've got plans to start up a business of my own."

Alice interrupted. "He can tell you all about that later. We've got some other news first."

With both her parents' attention on her, Alice draped the sweater over the back of the seat and held out her left hand. "We're going to get married!"

The silence lasted just a few seconds, as Ted studied their faces for reaction.

Doesn't look too bad. Actually, they don't look completely surprised.

Alice giggled and stood up, with her arm extended. Her mother jumped up and stepped over to examine the ring.

"Wow! That's quite a rock!"

"It's beautiful, isn't it?" Alice tilted her hand this way and that, both women admiring the sparkle.

"Look at this, Bob," said Mrs. Johnson. "It's lovely."

He got up, perhaps a little grudgingly, and took his daughter's hand. "It is a very nice ring. Congratulations, Bunny." He stared at Ted. "This is rather sudden, isn't it?"

Ted allowed Alice to do the talking. "Maybe a little. But we love each other. I've never met anybody like Ted."

She kissed him lightly and he put an arm around her. Everybody remained standing.

"So, how soon do you think you're going to get married? Have you set a date?"

"That's one of the things we wanted to talk to you about." Alice's voice bubbled with enthusiasm. "We figure this summer sometime. Weddings should be in the summer, right?"

"Your sister had a six month engagement."

"I don't have to do everything the way Connie did, do I?"

"Well," said Bob, turning to Ted. "Congratulations, young man. I guess we'll be getting to know each other better, eh?"

Ted smiled. "I'm looking forward to it, Sir." There was no suggestion that he drop the formal honourific.

* * * *

The bridge game after dinner was only slightly painful, rotating partners after each rubber. Ted bit his tongue at one point, playing with Alice's mother. She opened a no trump and then inexplicably passed his three spade bid. Ted chalked it up to the fact the ladies were both less focused on the game than on the vital issues of flowers and the colours of bridesmaids' dresses.

Alice was right. A lot easier to get her mom on side with this thing by asking her to help plan it.

Dad – Sir – was more interested in how large the guest list was going to be, and whether the kids had any particular plans for their honeymoon yet?

"I don't think it'll be very exotic," said Ted. "I am trying to build up my capital to open some stores."

"Selling what?"

"Video rentals." Mrs. Johnson's interest seemed nothing more than polite, but Ted was sure he detected more than that in Mr. Johnson's reaction.

"You think there's money in that?"

"If I can go big enough. It's definitely a growing business, and I want to own a piece of it. I'm thinking a bunch of locations, not just one."

"So, you've been doing your research? You know how much space you need, and I guess there's licencing, and staff..."

"Oh, yeah," said Ted, as he dealt the cards for the next hand. "I've been thinking about it for a long time. I'm pretty sure I've got a good idea what's involved. I think it's still early enough – there isn't a store on every corner yet."

Mr. Johnson sat back in his chair, and tilted his glass slightly toward Ted. "Good luck to you!"

* * * *

Alice beamed with delight in the car. "Well, that went better than I expected. They seemed to like you. What do you think?"

"Yeah, they seem okay." He fidgeted, unaccustomed to riding in the passenger seat of his own car. "You don't think they suspect anything? Your dad asked a couple of times why you weren't having a drink."

"It's simple enough – my turn to drive. I think it makes it seem like we've been going out longer than we have."

"Yeah. Maybe."

"So, what do you think about the honeymoon? I hadn't even thought about it until Dad brought it up."

The car lurched slightly as Alice touched the brake pedal – more sensitive than the one she was accustomed to.

"Dammit," she mumbled, gliding to a stop at a traffic light.

"I haven't either," said Ted.

She turned to look at him. "Haven't what?"

"Thought about a honeymoon." He reflected on his depleted bank account. The diamond, combined with Frank and Lily's acceptance of his offer to improve their house, added up to a number well into five figures. And there'd be other wedding expenses. Even with the Johnsons' promise to rent the hall and pay for the dinner, tradition apparently called for Ted to fund the liquor, and there'd be suits to rent, and probably unforeseen other expenses. *Glad I'm only going to do this once!* "Have you got any ideas?"

"Just about anything but Niagara Falls. That would be too cliché."

"Niagara Falls! Can't we do something closer to home? Maybe go to Lake Louise or something?"

Alice glanced over at him. "Connie and Dean went to Paris and the French Riviera. I don't need anything that fancy, but Mom and Dad would be disappointed if we don't at least get out of BC. "

Better not tell her Lake Louise is in Alberta. No need for this to turn into a fight.

"What about somewhere in the States?" she suggested. "San Francisco's supposed to be a romantic place to go. We could even drive. The coast highway is apparently nice."

"That could be okay," Ted agreed. The light bulb in his head flashed on again. "If we're going to drive, maybe we don't just do one place. Spend a couple of nights in San Francisco and then pop over to Las Vegas before we come home?" He tried to suggest it casually, belying the depth of his interest.

Alice seemed to buy into the idea. "Maybe. And then we could stop in Yellowstone on our way back to Canada. Would be cool to see Old Faithful!"

Ted nodded noncommittally. *Not like some geyser is high on my list, but it is a landmark, and we'll have to pick some route north.* "We can look at a map when we get home, see if it works."

"When we get home? Mr. Cronkite, what are you suggesting?"

"Well, I do have a map of North America at my place, if you want to see it."

"Nothing turns a girl on more!"

This could actually work out, Ted thought. *A touring holiday actually sounds like fun.*

Alice laughed as she turned the car toward Ted's house. "It's a good thing I've got an overnight bag there. Saves us a stop."

Chapter thirteen Trophy

Ted's fears about his family's reaction to the news were allayed quickly. His mother, in particular, was delighted, although she chided him for not staying in closer touch.

"How come we never knew you had a girlfriend, much less a fiancée?"

"I'm sorry, Mom. I'm just so busy all the time – it seems every time I'm about to pick up the phone something comes up."

"Well, at least we get to meet her before the wedding?"

"I don't know, Mom. It's coming up pretty soon, and there's a lot of planning."

"I know that," she said. "But you can spare at least one weekend. We're only five or six hours away."

Ted looked across the breakfast table and shrugged. "We've got to go to Penticton," he mouthed. Alice nodded understandingly.

"We've just missed the holiday," he observed. "And there isn't another one until July. What about this weekend?"

"That won't work. Your dad's away at a convention. But I want you to make it as early as you can."

"Okay. I'll talk to Alice and see if there's a Friday that we can both knock off early."

"All right," said Mom. "Let us know as soon as you can." Ted watched Alice gather up the breakfast dishes. "Now tell me, when you come, do you need me to make up a couch for you? Alice – that's her name? – is obviously going to be in your room."

Ted grinned broadly. "I was wondering how I would ask you about that."

He held out the telephone receiver toward Alice so that she could hear his mother as well.

"Well, it is 1980 after all. I don't necessarily approve, but I'm not an idiot!"

Alice put her hand to her mouth, trying to stifle a giggle.

"I think I'm going to like your family," she told Ted, after he hung up the phone.

* * * *

They were upstairs for coffee five minutes later.

"Holy shit! You guys won the open pairs?"

Lily beamed with obvious delight as she held the trophy aloft. Frank appeared more smug than happy. The Vancouver Regional only happened once every two years, and winning one of its flagship events was a big deal.

"Were you that good, or were you lucky?" Ted kidded.

"Little of both," said Frank. "You know how it goes. You make no mistakes, and cash in when the opponents do." He reached for a pencil. "But there was one board where we earned our own top – you want me to write it out?"

"No," said Ted. "I'll remember it."

"Okay. Second seat, nobody vul. You hold two small, two small, ace-queen-nine-seven, and five to the nine spot." Ted knew that bridge players always describe their cards in the same order when boasting about a hand: spades, hearts, diamonds and clubs. "RHO opens a club."

"Pass," Ted offered immediately. Alice nodded.

"Okay," said Frank. "LHO bids a diamond, and partner doubles." He looked at Alice. "That's takeout for the majors," he elaborated, for her benefit. "RHO passes."

"Yuck," said Ted. "I'm a little light for one no trump, but I don't think I have any choice. Certainly can't bid two clubs."

"That much is right," said Frank. "But you do have a choice."

Ted scrunched his face. "I'm not bidding a spade or a heart on a crappy doubleton. What did you do?"

"Pass!"

"You passed a one-level double?"

Frank nodded. "With my fingers crossed. Partner leads a club, and dummy hits with queen-third, jack-third, doubleton jack, and ace-king-queen-fifth of clubs."

"He probably should have bid one no," suggested Ted.

"She." Frank chortled. "Probably expected me to bid, and decided she liked her cards better for defence. Not an unreasonable call, actually. Anyway, declarer wins the first trick in dummy, and then comes off the board with a trump."

By this time Alice was looking confused but Ted kept up. "You grab your ace right away and return a club."

"Obviously. Praying that partner started with the stiff."

"She did?"

Frank nodded. "She ruffed with the *ten!* I'm looking at my spots, thinking 'holy shit!' I've got two more trump tricks coming. Lily cashed the ace-king of both majors – down two, for all the matchpoints!"

"It's a good thing partner had as much as she did," observed Ted.

"She had to have! It's one of the things that the average player has to learn – some of them have to learn it the hard way. Make disciplined takeout doubles. You can't do it on shape alone – double shows values!"

Ted nodded his understanding. "So," he said, "it might not be as big a deal as winning open pairs, but we've got some news too."

"What's that?' said Lily. "You already told us you're getting married – when you asked about finishing the basement."

"Yeah, well, we've set a date," said Alice. "September 6th. It's a Saturday. We talked to my folks about it yesterday."

"How'd they take the news?"

"Well, we haven't exactly told them the whole story yet."

Frank and Lily looked at one another and rolled their eyes.

"They don't know yet that I'm pregnant, and they don't know how sudden this all is. If anybody asks you – ever – you introduced us in January, not April. Okay?"

"Why would anybody ask?" said Frank.

"Well," said Ted, "We're presuming you'll meet both families. You're invited to the wedding, and I'm hoping you'll be a groomsman!"

Frank stood up and put his hand out to Ted. "I'd be honoured, sir!"

"And if you need any help, with food or anything, don't hesitate to ask," offered Lily.

"Thank you. But I think we should be okay. Mom and Dad are arranging catering."

"All right, then!" Lily clapped her hands together. "I've got to get going – off to work today. Do you want a lift, Alice? Or is your car here?"

"You're not playing bridge again?"

"No. But Frank is." Lily smiled at her husband. "He's off work all week."

"Yeah. One of the duffers is paying me fifty bucks to play." He snickered. "If I'd known I was going to have championship credentials I'd have charged a hundred!"

Ted was intrigued. "You get paid just to play? Whether you place or not?"

"Yup. 'Course, I have to be ready to give her some pointers. I guess the money is more about the lesson than the results."

Frank poured another couple of coffees after the women left.

"Are you sure you're doing the right thing, Ted?"

"What do you mean?"

"I think you know what I mean. You've only known Alice for a few weeks. Are you in love with her?"

Ted leaned back on the chair and stretched his legs out while he considered the question. "I'm not sure I know what love is," he admitted. "Does anybody?" He forced a chuckle, but stopped when Frank didn't smile. "I'm certainly comfortable around her. She makes me feel whole. And it's not like there've been a lot of women swarming around."

"I know. That's part of what worries me. You haven't played the field much. Do you really know what you're doing?" Frank drummed his fingers on the table. "I mean – a wife and a baby – that's a lot of life changes all at once. Did you talk about maybe another solution?"

"Needing a solution implies there's a problem. Besides, it's Alice's call." Ted took another gulp of coffee before he spoke again. "I guess I'm all in."

* * * *

It was July by the time Alice and Ted paid their obligatory visit to Penticton. Traffic was heavy, in the middle of the summer vacation season.

"So, I gather you don't see your family often?" Alice said. "Do you not get along with them?"

"Oh, yeah. They're fine. I should stay in closer touch. Don't really know why I don't." He frowned. "I guess you just take things for granted after a while."

"Is your brother going to be there?"

"Yeah. He's home all summer." Ted made a shoulder check and switched into the fast lane.

"And his name is Bobby, right?"

Ted nodded.

"Bobby or Bob? Most guys like to drop the 'y' when they think they're grown up."

Ted frowned and touched the brake as a van pulled into the lane in front of them. "He hasn't said anything about it. Well, last I talked to him, anyway." He didn't tell her how much he disliked being called 'Teddy' in his pre-teen years.

"What does your dad do?"

"He works for the city. A bureaucrat." He glanced at Alice. "I mean, he's not a bad guy, but I don't think he understands that I couldn't stand that life. He's not exactly sold on my business plan."

"Mmm."

"I'm not sure he's ever taken a chance on anything in his life. He's probably the least exciting guy I know. Never took us fishing or hunting, or..."

"That's too bad. You never had a chance to be really close with him?"

Ted shrugged. "Like I say, he's not a bad guy. We'd throw a baseball around from time to time - he just wasn't in to teaching us the macho stuff, so I spent more time reading when I was growing up."

* * * *

Darren and Barbara Cronkite liked Alice instantly. By the time dinner was over the conversation had turned from "Where are you from?" and "How did you meet?" to "What do you do?"

"I handle the admin for a real estate office," she explained. "Somebody has to check the sales peoples' spelling, so they don't give anybody an excuse to collapse a deal."

Darren chuckled. "Yeah. Realtors."

"What about you? Ted said you work for the city?"

"Municipal planning department."

Alice looked at him attentively. "Really! That's fascinating work."

"Fascinating? Most people don't think so." Darren took a sip of his drink. "You can't get anybody to come out to a public hearing when you're updating the Community Plan, but as soon as somebody wants to put up an apartment building on their street people start having conniptions!"

"Is anybody building apartments in Penticton? Down in Coquitlam it's all condos – nobody seems to think there's any money in rentals."

He pointed a finger at her. "You're right. More and more cities are coming to realize that is a problem. We were just talking about it at a convention..."

Ted sat back and gazed proudly at his fiancée, holding her own in an increasingly technical discussion about building heights, setbacks, and the cost of underground parking. But his eyes glazed over when the conversation turned to the pros and cons of the federal government's MURB tax incentive program.

Mom smiled at him. "Why don't you come and help me with the dishes, Ted? Let these two talk."

"Sure."

Bobby stayed in the living room with Alice and his father.

"You know the drill," said Mom. "Plates and cutlery to the dishwasher, pots and pans to the sink." She opened the fridge to stow leftovers. "You're a lucky boy, to be marrying such a lovely girl." She hesitated. "Are you sure it's what you want to do?"

"Yeah. Why would you ask that?"

"I just wonder if you're being pushed into it."

Ted stopped what he was doing and stared at her.

"Yes. She's showing. How far along is she?"

"Little over three months now."

"You know a lot of marriages don't work out these days. And a baby right away can put extra strain on any relationship." Ted didn't speak.

"I don't doubt that you think you're in love with her. I just hope you realize it takes work to make any marriage last. You're going to go from no responsibilities at all to having to take care of two people, all within a few months."

"I know."

"And, you're still thinking about starting up a business? How's that coming?"

Ted shifted uncomfortably. "Money is going to be a little bit tight for a while. We have to use most of my savings. I could lose a year – maybe more."

Mom nodded thoughtfully. "Well, I don't want to sound negative." She threw her arms out for a hug. "My baby's getting married!"

Ted grinned. "How come I'm your baby? Bobby's the youngest."

"Bleah! The first one's always special. Second one you let play with knives in the street." Mom laughed. "You'll find out soon enough."

Chapter fourteen Honeymoon

The Johnson-Cronkite wedding was a comparatively small affair – compared, at least, to that of Alice's sister. Certainly all the relatives were invited and most came, as did friends of the bride and groom. The pews that were empty might have been filled with friends and acquaintances of the respective families, particularly the Johnson side. There was an unspoken reluctance to put Alice's obvious condition on display for anyone other than closest friends.

The bridal party numbered three on each side, which suited Ted perfectly. Nobody could have replaced Neil in that group, although Bobby was elevated to the status of best man.

Ted's first boss, Bill, was asked, and did a creditable job as MC at the reception.

Alice was radiant in her maternity wedding gown. The Pastor, with the young couple's blessing, acknowledged the issue that was no doubt on everybody's mind, expressing his approval of the fact the child would be born into a loving home.

Ted spoke his vow clearly and confidently, remembering the simple statement in the Johnsons' church was not what he was accustomed to hearing in the movies and television programs. "I will," rather than "I do."

He lingered over the first kiss, whispering in her ear. "I really do love you. You know that, right?"

She squeezed his hand, hard.

"Just in case people think it's only about – you know..."

Alice kissed him again, more deeply than the first time.

Ted shuffled his feet and let the bride lead her own turns and spins to the music she'd selected for the first dance, Jane Olivor's version of "L'Important C'est La Rose." Handkerchiefs came out all over the room.

* * * *

Alice's car was selected for the road trip, being a little newer and presumed more reliable, but mostly because it burned less gasoline. Ted was at the wheel when they crossed the border and belted through Washington on the Interstate. They switched drivers after a pit stop in Portland, and Alice steered west to the ocean to follow the scenic route south. There was a stop for photographs at Haystack Rock, with the sunset in the background, and a night in a motel in one of quaint villages that dotted the coast, within earshot of the pounding surf.

Ted set one of the suitcases on a table and heaved the larger onto the bed.

"You want to go for dinner right away? Or maybe take a walk on the beach first?"

Alice smiled playfully. "Actually, I'm not hungry yet. At least, not for the kind of food you're talking about." She fingered a strap of her blouse, pushing it off her shoulder. "Oopsie!"

Ted stared in fascination as she dropped the coyness, lifting the garment over her head and tossing it aside. "I think they're getting bigger already. What do you think?"

"Uh, well, um. I..."

"Well, here's how you tell!" She pulled one of his hands to her chest. "There! Whaddaya think?"

"I, um...I dunno. I guess so."

She looked at him as though he was daft, squeezing the girls between her elbows.

Ted's face reddened. "Can...? Should we...? I mean..."

"Of course we can." She pulled his head to her chest. "If you're worried you forgot to bring condoms, don't you think it's a little late?"

His blush deepened.

"Although..." Alice turned away from him with an exaggerated pout. "Maybe you're right. Maybe we shouldn't do anything until after the baby comes. Or..." she pushed him backward onto the bed. "Would you be happier if you let me do the riding for a while?"

The suitcase thumped heavily onto the floor.

* * * *

Two days later they rolled through Sausalito and onto the Golden Gate Bridge. Ted had to admit the city skyline was impressive, but his thoughts were more about the budget – two nights in the expensive downtown hotel would allow time to walk Haight-Ashbury, ride the cable cars, and tour Alcatraz. On the third day they would check out of the hotel, have a late lunch at Fisherman's Wharf, and drive over the Bay Bridge to Oakland in plenty of time for the first game of an A's – Royals series. It wasn't a hard sell; Alice had surprised Ted with her interest in and knowledge of pro sports.

He was jittery in the car following the ball game, thinking about the four hundred dollars he'd managed to squirrel into his pocket without his bride's knowledge. The plan was to grab a cheap motel somewhere in the middle of California, but Ted drove well into the night with Alice dozing peacefully beside him. *Only three and a half hours to Reno – we'll get there before sun-up.* Las Vegas had come off the itinerary the first time they studied the map – too far south - but it turned out Nevada's second city lay directly in the path of the eastbound Interstate.

God, she's beautiful. He glanced over as the interior of the car was bathed in the dim light from an overhead lamp standard. *She's got that glow, even in the dark.* His fingers ceased their nervous tapping on the steering wheel as he thought about her. *What kind of fate brought us together?* He replayed the day he stumbled onto that bridge game at the university, and how Lily had made it seem interesting enough to learn it. *Never would have met Alice otherwise. Did I ever say 'thank you' to Lily?*

Alice interrupted his reverie just about the time the city's lights came into view on the horizon.

"Where are we?"

"Just about in Reno. How long have you been awake?"

"Only a minute." She yawned and stretched. "I thought we were going to stop and grab a room?"

"Yeah, I know. It was pretty late by the time we got out of Oakland, and I kind of felt like driving anyway, so..."

"What time is it?"

"Little before three." He glanced over at her. "How do you feel? I don't think it makes any sense to try to get a room now for tonight. Why don't we stop for breakfast someplace and then see what time check-in is?"

"I could use a bathroom."

"Right now? Do we have to find a gas station? Or can you hold on until we get to a restaurant?"

"I guess I can wait." She unbuckled the seat belt and twisted in her seat. "That's a little better. Bad enough to have one thing pressing on my bladder – don't need two." She reached for the dial on the radio.

Ted grinned. "So how is little Teddy?"

"Quiet. But hungry. He wants an anchovy pizza."

"For breakfast?!"

"He doesn't know what time it is." She slapped Ted's arm lightly. "And what makes you think it's a 'he,' anyway?"

"It's obvious. A girl would want pickles and ice cream."

Alice guffawed. "Don't make me laugh! I think I peed myself!"

She reached into her purse for the directions to their hotel. They'd chosen the El Dorado because it claimed to have the largest and most modern showroom in the state. "Might as well go straight to the hotel," she said. "Even if we can't check in yet we'll be able to get some food – and it's not like there's much else to do at this time of day."

They left the luggage in the trunk after Ted parked the car, but Alice rummaged in her suitcase for a clean pair of underwear and slipped it into her purse.

Ted's body tingled as he gazed into the casino, while waiting for Alice outside the ladies' restroom. The crowd seemed to be thinning out – more people boarding the elevators than stepping off them. His practiced eye had no trouble separating the winners from the losers. One couple in particular drew his attention – a balding man with his arm wrapped around a much younger-looking woman, wearing too much make-up, a flimsy spaghetti-strap blouse, and an absurdly short skirt – short enough that Ted could see the tops of her fishnet stockings. It didn't dawn on him what was going on until the pair stepped into the elevator, and the man dropped his hand to his escort's rear, apparently oblivious to Ted's scrutiny.

He didn't notice the security guard until the man stepped in front of him.

"Can I help you with something, sir?"

"Oh. Oh, no, thank you." Ted blushed slightly. "Just waiting for my wife." He nodded toward the restrooms.

The guard didn't seem convinced. "Are you a guest here?"

"Yes. Well, we will be. We haven't checked in yet."

Fortunately, Alice appeared in time to interrupt the cross examination. She looked freshened-up.

"Ready to go for breakfast?" she asked, innocently.

"Yup." Ted turned to the uniformed man again. "Can we get a pizza at this time of day?"

The man pointed without smiling. "Enjoy your stay." Ted felt the eyes on his back as he and Alice walked in the indicated direction.

"You sure you want a pizza?" he said.

"No," admitted Alice. "Actually, I changed my mind. I need some sugar. Let's get some pancakes and lots of syrup."

Ted laughed. He was getting used to the abrupt shifts in Alice's cravings. This time it was for the better. He couldn't stomach the idea of sharing anchovies with her.

They dawdled for almost an hour over breakfast, but it was still just past four when they stepped out of the restaurant, and early check-in wouldn't be until nine.

"Now what?"

Ted shrugged. "Guess we can check out the casino." He knew enough not to go near a poker table when he was half asleep, and he wasn't about to suggest Alice play anyway. *Ridiculous to play against your own money!* They found stools at a couple of slot machines.

"I thought these things had an arm to pull on the side," Alice groused. "Might have helped to keep me awake." They burned a few minutes trying to figure out how to load money into the machines, in the coin-free environment. Even at a quarter a spin, a twenty dollar credit was reduced to seventeen or eighteen within minutes. Win nothing, win nothing, win nothing, win nothing, win nothing, win seventy-five cents. Ted resisted the urge to increase his bets in frustration, and frowned when he watched Alice punch the one dollar button before pressing 'spin.' The machine issued a series of clangs and whistles and some sort of a "whah-hoo" that sounded more like a synthesizer suffering influenza than anything else.

"Look!" cheered Alice. "Eleven dollars!"

"That's great, babe. Way to go!" He didn't think about the arithmetic – it formed itself organically in his head. *That buys eleven more wasted spins – at fifteen seconds apiece that's enough to sit here for another three minutes.* "Do you think you should dial it back now? You don't really expect to win two in a row?"

Alice shrugged. "Maybe you're right. What if we cash out and see if they've got some five cent machines?"

They wandered among the rows of machines. Alice was looking for a place to sit again, but Ted was distracted by the cheering at a craps table.

Alice stopped and looked at him. "You wanna try craps?"

He thought for a moment, but wisely shook his head. "No. I have no idea how to play it, and I'm way too tired to learn."

Alice studied her watch for the twentieth time. "Let's go outside and get some air."

The orange glow in the eastern sky might have been pretty, but for the flashing neon distractions. "Should have driven out to the desert to watch the sun come up," Ted mumbled. Alice nodded.

He took her hand as they meandered to the edge of the parking lot, and then angled toward their own car. *Nowhere else to go!* Ted unlocked the passenger door. "Think we might be able to nap for a bit?" Alice shrugged.

They settled into the car, tilting the seats back to try to get comfortable. "I think we should have got a motel," said Alice.

"Yeah," he admitted. "You're probably right."

* * * *

The sun was up when Ted snapped awake from a nightmare – Gerry – *That was that fucker's name?* – dangling Alice's car keys from his fingers and laughing at him.

Alice was wide awake. "Who's Neil?" she asked him.

Shit. "Neil?"

"You kept saying his name. Sounded like you were having a nightmare."

"I dunno. I don't remember what I was dreaming about." He closed his eyes again and felt the chill leave his body as Alice put a hand on his arm. "I did have a friend named Neil – best friend, actually. He died a couple of years ago."

"Oh, no! That must be what you were dreaming about." She looked at him sympathetically. "How come you haven't mentioned him until now? What happened to him?"

"I try not to think about it." He hesitated. "He committed suicide."

The shock on Alice's face was clear. Ted shook his head; she must have picked up the cue and didn't pry any further.

He leaned over to kiss her. "God, you're a pretty sight to wake up to in the morning. What time is it, anyway?"

"Almost seven-thirty. We might as well head in." She glanced into the back seat. "Or would you rather we take our time?"

Ted came up for air, cursing the console between the bucket seats. And the fact cars and people were already moving about the parking lot.

"Little bit too much activity," he mumbled. "I think we have to wait. Dammit."

Alice put on an artificial pout before she kissed him again. "I suppose you're right." She withdrew her hand from his pants.

Ted stepped out of the car, stretched, and shifted his weight uncomfortably. He gazed around, trying to focus on the surroundings while he waited for the adrenaline surge to settle down. *There really isn't anything here but the casinos. Why else would anybody come here?*

They left the brand new luggage – an easy wedding gift – at the front desk. "Still over an hour to kill," Alice observed.

"Back to the armless bandits?" suggested Ted.

"Whatever. Let's see who can lose twenty bucks faster."

Ted was a little more awake, less inclined to be negative about the experience. "Maybe. Or maybe we're due to get lucky."

Alice had six dollars left in her bank when Ted was cleaned out for the second time. *Fifty-four dollars down the drain. That would've paid for a motel.*

He flopped on the bed when they finally got to their room. He was asleep before Alice stepped out of the shower and joined him.

* * * *

The newlyweds were awake in time to visit the pool before dinner and the evening comedy show. Alice brought some brochures from the front desk to read poolside.

"They do have some museums here. We don't have to spend the whole time gambling, you know. They say Reno has more history than Vegas does."

"Mmm."

"What if we get out and look around tomorrow?"

"Maybe."

There was no denying the comics were funny. The profanity-laced routines of the first two set up the third, a woman, to be particularly hilarious with her carefully cultured language. Alice howled in delight at the stories about pregnancy and child birth.

Ted kissed her good night at the elevator. "I'm going to go play some blackjack. You'll be all right?"

"Yeah, I'm going to go straight to bed. Try to get back into a normal routine." She let go of his hand. "No more than a hundred dollars, right? You lose that much, you quit."

"Absolutely."

Ted marched past the slot machines, determined to ignore the cacophony of clangs and whistles and excited shouts of the occasional winner.

He stood for a moment behind a chair at a five-to-two hundred table, watching the play. Most of the players were betting five or ten dollars each hand; one fellow's minimum bet was twenty-five. The most striking thing was the way the cards were dealt, *all face up!* Except one of the dealer's, of course. *That's not how we did it in school! Actually,* he thought, *it must be an advantage to see all the others players' cards.*

He pulled the chair back and sat down, tossing a couple of fifties on the table, and smiled slightly as the dealer made a show of counting his five-dollar chips, first into four piles, then two. None of the other players seemed impatient. The fellow to his left took the opportunity to light a cigarette, one of those harsh-smelling American brands. It competed with the scent of perfume from the woman to his right. Ted glanced behind him – an old poker habit – before he pushed two of his chips forward.

He eyed the cards carefully. Nobody had a twenty. In fact, of the eleven cards showing there was only one face. The woman to his right had an easy choice, to hit nine. She held at sixteen. Ted studied his thirteen, an eight and a five. *Not an auspicious start!* Eight cards could help, five would see him go bust. But his odds were no better than fifty-fifty, since an ace, two, or three would leave him at no better than sixteen anyway. He looked at the dealer's six, and waved her off. *Better to make sure I stay in and hope for the best. Let the dealer go bust and we all win.*

His face fell when the dealer flipped her down card, another six. *Come on!* A queen! *All right! This game is too easy.*

He took half his winnings off the table, leaving a fifteen dollar bet. There was a flurry of tens, *not unexpected.* Ted and one of the other men at the table showed twenty. The house's card was an ace.

"Insurance?" The woman to Ted's right shook her head. The dealer looked at Ted.

"What's insurance?"

"You buy it to protect your bet in case I have a blackjack."

Ted shook his head.

The dealer flipped her down card, a seven. *Eighteen! Win again!*

He fidgeted nervously. *Increase the bet again? Or am I due to lose one?* He looked at the other players. There seemed to be a camaraderie among them, a sense of teamwork in the air.

"Bets down!"

He left twenty five dollars on the table. *What the hell? It's all the house's money.*

He stared unhappily at his fifteen. The dealer showed a seven. *Shit! If there's a ten under there I lose.* Everybody stood pat. The dealer flipped her down card, a deuce. *Fuck!* She reached for the shoe and pulled ... a five! *Double fuck! I'd have had twenty.* But the house still had to hit fourteen, and went bust with a king. There were fist pumps and high fives among the players. *That's something that never happens at a poker table!* Ted knew, and he could tell everybody else did too, that had he taken the five the dealer would have ended with nineteen, and he would have been the only winner.

The dealer smiled at her group. "Well done, everybody."

It was two-thirty in the morning when Ted made his way upstairs. Alice was sleeping peacefully. He reached into his pocket and pulled out the eight crisp new hundred dollar bills the cashier had handed him when he turned in his chips. He beat down the temptation to wake his wife. *Just leave it here for her to see in the morning.* He thought about the four hundred that he'd brought with him on the sly. *More than a grand? She'll shit herself!* He fanned the eight hundred onto the table beside the t-v, switched the set off, and climbed into bed.

Alice rolled over to face him.

"Did you have a good time?" she mumbled.

"Yeah."

He put an arm around her back and snuggled close.

Alice was suitably impressed in the morning. "You won *eight hundred dollars* last night?"

"Well, no, not exactly."

She appeared confused.

"A hundred bucks of it was ours. I only won seven."

She laughed and threw her arms around him. "You've gotta go back and see if you can do it again tonight!"

Ted nodded.

"So, what do you want for breakfast?" Alice picked up the in-house telephone directory. "I think this means we can afford to order room service!"

"Actually, if it's okay with you, I'd rather be around people this morning." He searched for the words to explain to her the almost sexual thrill of the teamwork at the table last night, how everybody seemed to be of like mind, to nail the dealer. "I never thought of cards as a team sport – except for bridge, of course. It was weird – you know – it wasn't really even so much about how much money..."

* * * *

Ted's success was not duplicated on the second night of blackjack, not necessarily any fault of the players. The house had a seemingly endless stream of good luck – eighteens and nineteens, one after another. Ted burned his hundred dollar budget within minutes, and dipped into his secret stash. He managed to walk away from the table with a little over a hundred dollars still in his pocket. Fortunately the bulk of last night's winnings were in Alice's purse.

He found her seated at a slot machine.

"How are you doing?"

"Bleah. Lost about thirty-five dollars. How 'bout you?" She looked at him hopefully.

Ted shook his head.

"It's all gone? The whole hundred?"

And then some. But I guess I don't have to tell her that.

They checked out immediately after breakfast on day three, consciously ignoring the lure of an encore visit to the casino. Ted pulled into a remote gas station just before the Utah border.

"Can you handle the gas? I've got to go to the can."

A slot machine leered at him from the wall above the urinal. "You've got to be fucking kidding me!" *They're fuckin' everywhere!*

He toyed with the idea of directing his stream upward. *Aw, fuck it! Probably couldn't reach anyway.*

Chapter fifteen Sgt. Strickland

The daily ritual of diapers, feeding, and trying to establish regular naptimes was interrupted by the telephone on a Tuesday. Alice tried to grab it quickly enough that it wouldn't wake the baby.

"I'm looking for Ted Cronkite, please," said the stranger's voice.

"He's at work right now. Can I take a message?"

"Detective Sergeant Strickland, Coquitlam RCMP."

"Hang on a second – I have to find a piece of paper." Alice could hear the baby crying. *Shit.* She made a detour to turn down the heat under a pot on the stove. She was still trying to get used to the lay-out of Ted's basement suite – *our suite.* In her apartment the telephone had been on the kitchen counter, within reach of everything important.

"Okay. You said Sergeant Strickland?"

"Yes, with the General Investigation Section." He gave Alice a phone number.

"What's going on? Is my husband in some sort of trouble?"

"No, no. Nothing to worry about. He's a witness in a matter we're investigating."

"What? A traffic accident or something?"

The cop hesitated. "No. It's more serious than that. Listen, Mrs. Cronkite, I assume? It's quite important that we speak to him. Do you know when he'll be home?"

* * * *

"What's this?" said Ted, when Alice handed him the note. "The cops want to talk to me?"

"Something or other investigation section. He said he's a detective."

Ted looked confused.

"What do you think it's about?"

"I've got no idea."

Alice rocked the baby in her arms.

"Can you take him to the other room, so he doesn't cry when I'm on the phone?"

"No." Her eyes narrowed slightly. "I want to hear what's going on."

Ted shrugged and dialed the telephone.

Alice heard him ask for Strickland. He looked at her and shrugged again as he waited.

"Yes! Sergeant Strickland. Ted Cronkite."

"Oh, yeah, that. Yes, I was there. I talked to you guys that night."

The baby spit out his soother and fussed in his mother's arms.

"Well, I don't know any more than what I already told you."

"All right. I was at Pete's house, right across the street. Yes, Pete Lambert. We were in his basement when we heard the shot. I didn't know what it was right away – Pete said it was a rifle. I figured he would know, because he was an army guy."

Alice's mouth fell open at the words "rifle" and "shot."

"Yeah, it was Pete who called you guys – the rest of us ran upstairs to see if we could tell what was going on."

"I don't know. Sixty seconds probably?"

What the hell?

"No. We didn't go outside right away. We looked out the front window."

Alice was relieved to hear that detail.

"No, I didn't see anybody come out of the house. The guy was already in the car, and took off like a bat out of hell."

The baby fussed. Alice struggled to wrap him tighter in the receiving blanket.

"No, I didn't see him at all."

Ted's face seemed to go blank. "I guess that's true. I don't actually know that it was a guy."

Visions of courtroom dramas on t-v flashed in Alice's head. *They're going to need better witnesses than Ted.*

"I think it might have been a Camaro. I don't know a lot about cars, but I knew a guy who had a Camaro..." He waved at the sink and mouthed a word to Alice. "Water?"

She poured a glass and brought it to him.

"Yeah. He backed out fast. I heard him lay rubber when he took off. I remember noticing the headlights weren't on."

"Yeah, I'm sure about that."

Ted held the receiver away from his ear, looked at Alice, and shrugged.

"No, we – I - didn't hear anything before the shot."

"No, I got to Pete's place way before it happened. Probably four or five hours."

She tried to whisper a message to him. "Ask him if they've caught anybody!"

Ted put his hand up. "I mean, you guys already know all this. Do you really need me to...?"

"So, you think you've caught the guy?"

Alice struggled to hear what the cop was saying down the line.

"Yeah. Yeah, I understand."

"So, if you do need me to testify, when would it be? When's the trial?"

Good question!

"A year! Holy shit!"

"Well, I guess so. We're not planning to go anywhere."

* * * *

Alice waited until the baby settled down before she accepted a glass of wine and began her cross-examination.

"So, what the hell happened? Somebody got shot? How come you never mentioned it?"

Ted shrugged evasively.

"Come on. This doesn't sound like something that happens every day. I mean, if you've got to go to court..."

"There's a chance I won't."

"So, what happened?"

"Apparently a domestic dispute. Cops seem to think a guy shot his wife."

"Holy shit! Is she dead?"

"Yeah."

"And you were there?"

"You heard me on the phone. I just happened to be in the neighbourhood."

"Where was it?"

"Out toward Poco."

"So, why didn't you ever mention this? I'd have thought..."

Ted shrugged again, and reached the for the TV remote. "Just never came up."

Alice pushed the little box away from him. "Whaddaya mean, 'never came up?' It's the sort of thing you bring up. You didn't think I'd be interested?" She took a drink of her wine. "I mean, how many murders do we have?" She tried to recall the last time she heard something on the news. "When did this happen? Was it before we met?"

"No."

"How come you don't want to tell me about it?" *Why is this like pulling hens' teeth?*

"I don't know." Ted sounded defensive. "I really don't know much about it, that's all."

Alice took another sip of wine before she tried another tack. "So, who's Pete?"

"Just a guy I know."

She threw her hands up in the air. "'Just a guy you know?' But you know him well enough to hang out with him for the entire evening?"

Ted squirmed uncomfortably.

"Come on, Ted. No secrets." She tried to smile encouragingly. "Who else was there? Was it a party? Were there women there? Is that why you won't tell me?"

"No."

"You knew me when it happened, but you didn't tell me about it. There has to be a reason." She thought back to their whirlwind courtship. "Wait a minute!" The pieces fell into place. "That night you stood me up! Was supposed to be our second date."

Ted nodded sheepishly.

"You told me you were at work." She tried to say it casually, not overly accusing.

Ted nodded again.

"Why? You were partying and just forgot about me?"

"Yeah. I'm sorry." He went to the kitchen for a refill.

If he thinks that's my cue to drop it he's got another think coming.

Ted sat down again, with the wine bottle in his hand. "How's yours?"

She waved him off. "Who's Pete? Somebody you work with? I don't remember a Pete at the wedding."

"He's kind of down on weddings. He and his wife are kind of on the rocks, and he's not happy about it."

"So you were there to console him? You're kind of new at this to be much of a marriage counsellor."

Ted didn't laugh.

"So, why didn't you call me? I might have been mad that you blew me off, but at least I would have known what was going on."

Ted shrugged again.

"You guys were drinking. Were you drunk? That's why you forgot?"

He shook his head.

"Then what?!" Her voice rose in exasperation. "Ted, this shouldn't be such a big deal! I don't want to fight with you about it, but you're obviously hiding something!"

"We were playing poker."

She leaned back on the couch and stared at him for almost a minute.

"What? What are you looking at?"

"You played poker. And you forgot about a date with a girl you knew for barely a week. I mean, I'm obviously not happy, but I don't know why you're invoking the Official Secrets Act."

Ted spoke quietly. "I didn't forget about you."

Alice jerked her head in surprise.

He shrugged again. "I was losing. And I kept thinking my luck had to change. Just a couple more hands and I'd get it back. And it just got worse and worse, and I couldn't face talking to you about it after."

She sighed heavily. "And that was more important than our date."

She moved from the couch to the armrest of his chair, pulled his head to her breast, and rocked quietly for a moment.

"How much money did you lose?"

"I had to use some of my savings to pay the rent."

Shit! "And how often do you do that?" She released his head and looked into his eyes.

"Not very." He forced a childish grin. "I do win sometimes."

She chose her words carefully. "Okay, Ted. Here's the deal. You hang out with these guys once a month. You take a hundred bucks. It's your allowance. There's enough room in our budget for it." *He doesn't exactly seem delighted.*

"You're okay with it?"

"Ted, some husbands spend five times that much playing golf. You're allowed to have some sort of an outlet." She pulled his ear. "But you've got know you can be honest with me about it. I'd better not hear about any women hanging out at these things!"

Chapter sixteen Cronkite

"So, what are you planning to call them?" Frank wondered.

Ted was finally ready to pull the trigger on a trio of leases Lily had found, and Frank attended the meeting – half business, half social – as a courtesy. He took a sip of his drink and reached for a petit four.

Ted shrugged. "I've always just thought Ted's Videos, I suppose."

"Why don't you use your last name?" suggested Frank.

Ted set his drink on the table and pushed his fingers through his hair.

"I – I dunno. A lot of small businesses don't."

"I think it might set you apart from the crowd. You've got one of the most recognizable names there is. Why not use it?" Frank paused for emphasis. "It's not like Walter can complain. It is actually your own name, after all."

"Cronkite's Videos," Alice mused aloud. "Sounds all right."

"Not Cronkite's," said Frank. "Cronkite. No 's.' Don't muddy the water."

Ted mulled the idea as he watched Alice heave herself out of her chair and toddle toward the nursery, where two-year-old Robert was crying again. He smiled as his mind went to memories of the day they'd painted the room, how it turned into a playfight, stabbing one another with their brushes, making a hell of a mess. *Not sure we've ever laughed so hard!* And then it had turned into a different kind of play – the kind that might well have conceived the second child that day.

Lily had said the house was perfect for a young, growing family, and it looked as though she was right. It was a standard west coast two-level, in a quiet neighbourhood, close to schools. True, the kitchen was a little dated, but it opened onto a south-facing back patio and mature garden that wouldn't require a lot of work immediately. Likewise, the unfinished full basement could wait. Planning the renovations would bring as much joy as watching the kids romp in the playroom that would eventually be built for them. Alice was happy enough, for the time being, to devote all the savings to realizing Ted's business dream.

There was enough money in the bank to cover rent for the first six months, as well as licencing and purchase of enough tapes to get started. But there was no line of credit. Banks felt safer loaning mortgage money against residential property than a start-up business venture.

"You are sure about this, right?" Alice had said. "You're talking about quitting a perfectly good job."

"Never been so sure of anything in my life!" Ted forced himself to ignore the self-doubt. He rolled over and buried his face in her chest. "Except you, of course."

Frank and Lily were staring at him when his mind snapped back to the present.

"You dog!" said Frank, with a chuckle. "We saw the way you were looking at her."

Ted grinned sheepishly. "I guess you're the advertising expert."

"That's good," said Lily. "You get your signs made right away and get them up, with some sort of 'opening soon' messaging. You can have occupancy of two of them at the end of the month. The other one's still waiting for the receiver to clear everything out."

"He will do that, right? Last thing I need is to end up with a whole shitload of shoes." Everybody laughed. *Actually, might not hurt to open two – see how it goes. Third one can wait a couple of months.*

* * * *

Cronkite Video opened August fifth, 1983 – a Friday, Ted's twenty fifth birthday – with two hundred titles at each store. He made sure to have three copies of each of the previous year's top rentals on hand, the first year those statistics were available. Six of each of what looked like the hottest current releases.

Three or four dozen curious onlookers watched as Ted ceremoniously cut a ribbon in front of his flagship location, hamming it up for the camera as Alice took the pictures. Her father snapped photos of Ted and Alice standing below the sign. Half the crowd pushed into the store. Ted wasn't entirely sure whether the round of applause was for his opening or for the kiss he shared with Alice.

It was an hour before he was able to catch his breath and call his assistant manager at the satellite location.

"Jesus Christ!" Jenny told him. "We're already out of 'Wrath of Khan' and 'Officer and a Gentleman!'"

"Holy shit!" said Ted. "How's 'Star Wars' doing?"

"Not so much. Guess everybody's already seen that one on the big screen. What about you?"

"Pretty much the same. How many people have been in?"

"Nineteen so far. Half of them rented two"

"And you and Tim are getting along? He's doing his share of the work?"

"Oh yeah. Listen, gotta go. More customers."

He hung up the phone and glanced at Alice at the till. *What a trooper! Eight months pregnant and still on her feet.*

He sidled up beside her and copped a squeeze of her backside. "You ready to let me take over again?"

"Absolutely!"

"You think maybe you should slide out to the liquor store? Pick up a bottle of champagne? This is looking like we should celebrate a little."

"We?"

"I don't think the baby'll mind if you have a glass or two." He paused. "Maybe your Mom and Dad'll keep Robbie overnight, give you a break. You can drop me here in the morning and then go pick him up."

Alice proved a perfectly capable bookkeeper, working at home after the second child's arrival. Ted's draws in the first year were less than the six figures he had forecast for himself, but they were enough. Almost.

* * * *

An urgent message from one of the stores awaited him when he came in late on a Friday night, months later.

"Where've you been?" demanded Alice. She was in a housecoat. "Linda's in a panic."

Fuck The one time we go to the track instead of hanging out at Pete's house. Ted was in a filthy mood. He didn't know the first thing about horse racing, and it showed in his betting results. Picking one winner out of nine was no way to accumulate wealth.

He took it out on his wife. "What do you want me to do about it?"

"Call her, for Christ's sake!"

"Now?" He made a production of examining his watch.

Alice glowered at him.

"I'll go see her in the morning."

Alice adjusted the shoulders of her housecoat. "So, how much did you lose tonight?" Ted wouldn't look her in the eye.

"Where were you? I must've called Pete's number five times."

He threw his coat down and went to the sink for a glass of water.

"Ted?"

"We went to the race track. All right!?" He reached into his pocket and handed her a small wad of bills.

"Twenty-two dollars? That's what you've got left?" He tried to rub the back of her neck; she twisted away from him and fell into an armchair.

"I won't go out for lunch next week, all right? I'll brown bag it."

"Ted, that's three times this month." She carried on, muttering something unintelligible.

"What? What did you say?"

"You can make them yourself!" Alice slapped the arms of the chair and stood up. "I'm going back to bed." She rolled away from him when he crawled under the covers beside her.

* * * *

Linda was busy with customers when Ted entered the store a little after noon. He spent several minutes placing returns on the shelf before they were able to speak privately.

"No James today?"

"No, he went home sick yesterday afternoon."

"Yeah, I got your message about that. So, what was the problem? It was too busy to handle yourself?"

"No, it's not that." Linda stared at her feet and shifted uncomfortably. "The police came. Well, some sort of police. I don't think they were actually RCMP."

"Who the hell were they, then?"

"I don't know exactly." She took a step back from him and reached under the counter for a sheaf of papers.

"Sorry," Ted mumbled. "I didn't mean to yell."

"They locked up the back room. Said we couldn't rent any X-rated stuff, because I'm only seventeen."

Ted glanced at the door to the adults-only room. *A fucking padlock! Shit!*

He took the papers from Linda. A citation with a two hundred dollar fine, and some sort of an order that he provide details of satisfactory staffing before he would be allowed to reopen.

"I'm sorry, Mr. Cronkite."

"It's not your fault." *Fuck.* "Did you actually rent any of that stuff last night? Was there some sort of complaint?" *Why would there be? People who watch "Naughty Nurses" wouldn't generally want to tell the cops about it.*

"No," she said. "They told me it was just a spot check. Apparently I was supposed to lock it up and not let anybody in there as soon as James went home. I tried to tell them there was an adult scheduled to be here, but they wouldn't listen to me."

Ted sat down to study the paperwork. *Going to have to send this to the lawyer,* he decided. *He'll probably say there's no point fighting the fine. But closing down is going to be expensive.* The profit margin on porn was huge, in comparison to mainstream movies.

Have to get a memo out to everybody at all the stores. Tell them how to make sure this doesn't happen again.

"Are you okay?" he asked. "Did you open on time this morning?"

"Oh, yeah. I came in early 'cause I knew James wouldn't be here."

Ted smiled. "You're a trooper! Why don't you knock off early today?" He looked at the box of returns. "Just take care of these. I'll finish up, and pay you for the whole day."

"Thanks, Mr. Cronkite, but..."

"No buts."

Chapter seventeen Block Party

Ted felt the bulge in his pants as he drove, part of it the wad of bills in his left side pocket. A stack of twenties the likes of which he'd never seen before. *Mickey Mouse charity casino. They'd have given me hundreds in Reno.* He chortled to himself. *They did say they'd never seen anybody win that big here before.* What a run! He'd been unable to do anything wrong at the blackjack table. Nineteens and twenties all night long, and the odd time he decided to stand on a crappy thirteen he'd watched the dealer go bust. *What a night!*

The light was on in the carport but he found the door locked when he tried to turn the handle. He glanced at his watch before he entered the house. *Wonder if anybody's still awake?* He took off his coat and shoes at the door and crept into the kitchen. There was no light pouring into the hall from any of the bedrooms. He pulled a carton of apple juice and some leftover macaroni and cheese from the refrigerator, and paused for a moment in front of the micro-wave. *Heat it up? Yeah.* He thought cold pasta was overrated, but he winced and waited several seconds when his plate clattered on the glass bottom of the appliance. The noise didn't seem to wake the household.

Ted was still giddy when he sat down and counted fifteen bills onto the kitchen table, couldn't wait 'till morning to make his first phone call.

Lily sounded groggy when she picked up on the fifth ring.

"Lily! It's Ted!" He made an effort to keep his voice low.

"Ted! What's wrong?"

"Nothing's wrong. I..."

"For Christ's sake, Ted, it's after midnight. We're asleep over here."

"Oh, well. Listen, this'll just take a minute. Is Frank home this weekend?"

"Yes. He's not going to New Orleans until Tuesday."

"Good! I want you guys to come to a little soiree tomorrow. We're going to do a barbecue for the neighbourhood. Block party kind of a thing."

"Okay - Ted, have you been drinking?""

"Not at all. Just feeling good. So you can make it?"

"I guess so."

"Good. See you about four. Just come right to the back yard. Don't bother ringing the doorbell."

"It'll probably be closer to five. Frank and I are playing at the club tomorrow afternoon."

"Okay. Whatever." Ted couldn't resist blurting it out. "God, you sound sexy when you're asleep."

There was a pause on the other end. "Good night, Ted."

* * * *

He tidied up after himself in the kitchen and crawled into bed without waking Alice, drifting off with a hand on her backside. She let him sleep until eight before calling him for breakfast. Ted hugged the kids, stopped for a moment to share a laugh with them at the slapstick Saturday morning cartoon, and took a detour to the liquor cabinet on his way to the table. He poured a shot into his wife's coffee as well as his own.

Alice raised her eyebrows. "You seem to be a in a good mood. I guess you did all right last night?" Her eyes went to the money, stacked neatly on the table. He guessed, correctly, that she'd already counted it.

"All right!? Yeah, I guess you could say I did all right." He took a swallow of coffee.

"Listen, I want to have a barbecue tonight. Invite the neighbours. I think we should do it once every summer."

"Do you think we can afford it right now?" She picked up the cash. "I mean, this is..."

"Not all of it," he boasted.

"So...?" She obviously wanted more information, but Ted decided to play coy.

"You put that away. I've got enough to do the shopping. Maybe you can go knock on doors while I'm out. Invite everybody, whether we know them or not. Tell them it's a block party."

Ted edged and mowed the lawn and moved a couple of the kitchen chairs outside before he left the house. He bought a case of premium wine, at over a hundred dollars a bottle. He had to sign a paper acknowledging he was not in possession of a licence, but wouldn't be charging for drinks. "Private party," he assured the skeptical clerk.

"Fuckin' doorknob," he muttered to himself as he climbed back into the car. But he did kick himself over the cost of the food. *Should have looked at grocery flyers, see who's got steaks on this week.* He shrugged and decided on Superstore, where he picked up an assortment of rib-eyes, t-bones and New Yorks, a dozen of each. And, he remembered to buy a bag of briquettes. *Have to pull out the old barbecue. Won't be able to get all these on the gas.*

He was still in a good mood when he arrived home, so much so that he didn't curse when he found he had to scrub the rust off the grill that hadn't been used in years. *We should use this more often. A lot to be said for tradition.* He dug a cooler out of the basement for the wine, sat down on the patio with a half-sack of beer, and began to wonder what happened to Alice.

"Where've you been?" he asked, when she showed up just after three.

"I took the kids to Mom and Dad's."

"Mmm. Not a bad idea," he said. "Are they going to keep them overnight?"

"They offered," said Alice. "I'll phone and let them know once we see how late things go. At least I don't have to run over with a diaper bag if they do."

Ted nodded and grinned. "Yeah. Thank God we're past all that part." Alice frowned slightly as he lit a cigarette. "So how many are coming? I bought three dozen steaks."

"Good God! That's way too many!"

"I had to be sure we had enough. You can always freeze some of them."

"I guess so," Alice muttered. "There'll probably be about sixteen. A lot of people weren't home, some have plans tonight. It is short notice." She popped the cap off a beer. "Even Lily and Frank aren't around. It'll seem strange to have a party with a bunch of strangers and not our best friends."

"They're coming," said Ted, with an excess of pride. "I phoned them last night."

* * * *

The guests started arriving at ten after four, Tom and Erica from next door. They weren't close friends, but knew their neighbours well enough to be comfortable showing up first. Ted opened a cooler and pulled out a bottle of champagne. He peeled away the foil top, and tilted the bottle toward the house next door before pushing on the cork. "See if I can break a window with this," he joked. The cork flew halfway to the property line.

Alice stared at the label. "What the hell is this?" she demanded.

"Dom Perignon. We're celebrating tonight."

"We're celebrating!?" Alice gritted her teeth, as Tom and Erica looked at one another, shuffling uncomfortably.

Ted poured three drinks, and reached for the fourth cup. "None for me," said Alice. "I'd better go get the corn started. Come inside and help for me for a minute."

Uh-oh. Ted followed her into the kitchen.

"Just exactly how much money did you win last night?" she hissed.

"A little over twenty-one hundred dollars."

"And you thought it was a good idea to spend it on champagne?"

"Do we have to talk about this now? I can't leave company alone outside." Ted was pretty sure his wife wouldn't make a scene within earshot of visitors. She flounced about the kitchen as he stepped outside again, and forced a smile. Tom and Erica didn't ask any questions, they were already chatting with the couple from across the street. Ted poured two more drinks, less exuberantly than the first three.

* * * *

"Let me pour you a drink now, Alice. At least try to look like you're having a good time."

Ted didn't hear her muttered response, turning his attention instead to the two couples who had appeared from around the side of the house.

"Hey, Frank! Lily! About time you got here! How are you?"

"Great!" said Lily. "Listen, I don't suppose you've met Roger and Carol Meyers yet? I just sold them the place on the corner."

Roger shook hands; Carol extended a large bowl of potato salad, with a questioning look. Ted waved vaguely at one of the tables. "Just set it over there, I guess. My wife's coordinating all that – where'd she get to, anyway? Alice!" he bellowed.

"I think she went in the house," said Lily. "I should go see if she needs a hand."

"Have a drink first. Hey, Frank, how about you pour? Top mine up too. I've got to keep an eye on these steaks." Ted tried to do another head count of the people milling around the back yard, but lost track and turned his attention back to the grills. *Hopefully eighteen'll be enough. Maybe better throw a couple more on just to be sure.*

Frank opened a cooler on the patio near the back door. "Dom Perignon? What's the occasion?"

"Had a big night at the casino!" Ted dropped his voice to a conspiratorial whisper. "Big night! What better to do with it than share it with your friends, right?" He squirted some barbecue sauce onto the meat.

Alice stepped outside, with a stack of plates and napkins. "Hey, babe! Somebody you've gotta meet! My wife, Alice, this is Roger, and – sorry - I didn't get your name..."

"Carol." She smiled politely and shook hands with Alice.

Frank glanced around for glasses but everybody seemed to have patio beer cups in their hands. "Never had champagne out of one of these before."

"Whatever works, right?" Ted grinned broadly. "Gotta love that sound!" he proclaimed, as Frank popped the cork off another bottle.

Lily disappeared into the house with Alice and reappeared a moment later carrying a tray of corn-on-the-cob.

"Who wants their meat rare?" Ted bellowed. A few of the guests, who'd been watching the bocce game, began moving toward the patio.

"Somebody might as well go first," offered Harry, as he stepped forward and pointed to a rib-eye. "How about that one?"

"Good choice!" said Ted. "Cooked the old fashioned way. We don't use the briquettes often enough. The gas is just too easy."

Harry poured himself another generous cup of wine and sat down with his wife at a table. Other couples tried to balance plates on their laps, or sat on the lawn, eschewing chairs altogether. Alice winced when she noticed at least one cup go over, spilling its contents on the grass.

* * * *

Ted sat back on the lounge chair with a self-satisfied smile. "Well, that was a great party, eh?"

"Hmph."

"What's your problem? You've been grumpy all night." He tried to focus on his wife, through an alcohol fog. "Steak for breakfast tomorrow – doesn't get any better." He waved at the left-over meat piled on one side of the grill.

Alice moved about the back yard, collecting bottles; several empty, some half full. "Jesus, they could have left us one still corked. This is all going to go to waste!"

"Come on, Alice. Everybody had a good time. That's the important thing." He made no move to help with the clean-up. "What's the matter with you?"

She turned and glared at him. "I'll tell you what the matter is. This party – was ridiculous. Twelve hundred dollars in wine and three or four hundred for steaks for a bunch of people you hardly even know. Just so you can feel like a big shot for a day!"

"It's important to get on with the neighbours. They'll remember this – the best party of the season."

"Oh, come on Ted. Most of those people don't know the difference between Dom Perignon and Canada Duck, and the ones who do are laughing at you over the way you served it." She shook her head. "If you wanted to have a get-together to meet the neighbours, they'd have been just as happy with beer and burgers. The ones who are actually your friends weren't celebrating with you, they were embarrassed for you. Frank and Lily know we can't afford this."

"It was free money, for Christ's sake! I told everybody I won it!"

"Ted, can't you see this gambling thing is a problem? You go to the casino, four out of five times you lose. And when you do finally win once you don't pay yourself back, you blow it on something ridiculous." She poured herself a cup of champagne. "Might as well try to drink this before it goes flat."

Ted swatted at a wasp as he reached for another cigarette. "Whaddaya want from me?"

"I want you - I need you - to grow up. Be smarter. Put your own family first."

"Like how?"

She gave him a withering look. "Gee. Lemme think. Get the brakes done on the car. Buy some new tires. Put something away for the kids' coats and shoes so I don't have to worry about whether we can afford them in September. We can't even talk about the fact the kitchen needs painting, or, God forbid, make a payment on the line of credit."

"I gave you three hundred dollars."

"Yeah, hopefully that'll keep us in groceries the rest of the summer. We barely made the mortgage payment this month." She sat beside him and lowered her voice. "Ted, you have to promise me you won't go to the casino again. I've told you before - I can't live like this."

He stared blankly.

"I'm serious, Ted."

Was it her tone? Or was the sudden chill in the evening air real?

Once more, he thought. *Just once more. I win big one more time and she'll be happy again.*

Chapter eighteen Laundromat

Alice heard the side door bang and the excited laughter of the kids clumping into the utility room. It was one of those rare west coast snow days, the one day each winter Vancouver would be blanketed deeply enough that schools would close and the radio would advise everybody to "stay off the roads, unless absolutely necessary." Ted used a garden rake to push snow from the driveway before venturing out on the new all season tires. He hadn't thought it necessary to invest in a snow shovel. Alice decided to let Robbie stay home from school and enjoy it, even before the District confirmed it would shut down for the day.

"Stop right there," she called, as she switched off the vacuum cleaner and headed for the laundry room. "Don't come into the house!"

She found the kids pulling off their boots. "Did you see our snowman? Did you, Mommy?"

"Yes, I watched you out the window."

"Do you think it'll still be there when Daddy comes home?"

"I don't know, Emily. Sometimes the snow turns to rain pretty quickly." She smiled at her four-year-old. "Take all your wet clothes off right here. We don't want to drip all over the house. We'll throw them straight into the washer." She lifted the lid on the top-loading machine. "Then maybe we can have some hot chocolate with lunch."

Boots were left by the back door, wet coveralls were hung to dry, and socks, pants, shirts, and even underwear went into the washing machine on top of the accumulated load. Alice measured a half cup of detergent and turned the dial. Nothing!

Jesus! Are the pipes frozen or something? She shook the machine. There was no sound of a pump struggling to pull water. *Dammit.* She checked the power cord. *Of all the days.*

"What's wrong, Mommy?"

"Nothing, Robbie. Just go to your room and get dressed, okay? You can't spend the day wrapped in a towel."

She abandoned the laundry and turned her attention to getting Emily into some dry clothes. Robbie had switched on the TV by the time she was ready to call the kids for lunch.

* * * *

"So, was it busy at the store today, Ted?" She ladled some green beans onto the plates beside the meatloaf.

"Actually, not too bad," he said. "I guess everybody's planning to stay in tonight, so we had a fair number of customers." He chuckled. "Whoever would have thought renting videos would be an essential service?"

Yeah, right. You didn't think maybe it might have been essential to stay home for once and help the kids build a snow fort?

Alice cleared her throat. "There is something we have to talk about."

Ted speared another piece of meatloaf and looked at her.

"The washing machine quit today."

"Quit?"

"Actually, just wouldn't run. I don't know what's wrong it, but I think it's time to get a new one. We've already had a repairman out once."

Ted nodded as he chewed. "You're probably right. It is more than six years old."

"A lot more. Remember it was at least five years old when we moved in here. And so is the dryer. That's my problem. I don't know whether we should just buy a new washer, or replace the set."

"Why would we do that? This meatloaf is good, by the way."

She smiled thinly at the compliment. "I did two of them this time. You get your onions and some of the spices that the kids won't eat."

Ted nodded, and she returned to the subject. "Because they're more than ten years old. If we have to replace them both separately it'll cost more than buying the set together. But I have no way of knowing whether the dryer's going to last another week or another ten years."

Ted shrugged. "What are the odds? How long is a dryer supposed to last?"

"I don't know. I suppose there's more that can go wrong with the washer, but I don't want to guess wrong, and I sure as hell don't want to get shit from you if I do!" *I knew I shouldn't bring this up before the kids go to bed!* She winced as she watched the four-year-old stuff a handful of food into her mouth.

"Emily, use your fork!" It came out more sharply than she intended.

Robbie stuck his tongue out. "Yeah, Emily. Use your fork."

"That's enough," said Ted. "No fighting at the table." He jumped up for a dishrag to mop up the milk his daughter spilled.

* * * *

Alice parked the car between two mountains of melting snow, and stepped out into three inches of water and slush.

"Dammit!" She was already in a bad mood, left to her own devices to decide how many appliances to buy. She debated herself for the hundredth time while she pulled the stroller from the trunk. *Not that Emily can't walk of her own, but one of us should try to keep our clothes dry!* The child squawked and struggled as Alice loaded her into the stroller and pushed toward the mall entrance. *Probably be the last time I use this thing. Maybe have a garage sale in the spring.*

The post-Christmas sales lent credence to her suspicion. All the stores seemed to trumpet the same special offers, geared toward encouraging her to spend more money, not less. Buy the washer at the regular price, and the dryer would be a half price add-on.

She was in and out of three stores before she made her decision, and was shocked when the rug was yanked out from under her at the till.

"I'm sorry. Ma'am. Your credit card's been declined."

"What? That must be a mistake! Stop that, Emily."

The child was fussing and kicking her from the stroller. Alice bent to pick up the dropped sippy cup.

"Can you try it again?"

The clerk shrugged. "I can try, but..."

* * * *

"You didn't know about the credit card?"

Lily poured two glasses of wine, an unusual weekday indulgence. Alice had left Emily with her mother, on the excuse of needing a mental health break from the children, but it was her husband that weighed on her mind.

"I've never been so embarrassed in my life! Some stranger telling me that my account's been frozen! I couldn't even have bought lunch, much less appliances!"

"Shit!" Lily gazed at her sympathetically. "So, did you get it straightened out? Did you go to the bank and pay it?"

"That's the worse of it ! Everything's maxed – overdraft protection, line of credit." Alice shook her head, and tried unsuccessfully to hide the fact she was wiping tears from her eyes. "I don't know what to do. Ted's gambling is out of control. Between that and having to buy another car - I mean, I love him, but I can't carry on like this."

"He's playing that much?"

Alice struggled to maintain her composure. "It was supposed to be once a month, to hang out with friends. But ever since that God damned casino opened it doesn't seem to matter whether there's a poker game or not."

She stared into her friend's eyes. "You don't look surprised."

Lily sighed and shrugged.

Alice could hear the ticking of the grandfather clock, the only sound as she composed herself. She looked around the living room, at the lush sofa and chairs, solid wood tables, and tasteful art on the walls. "This is a nice condo. But aren't you a little young to be downsizing?"

"Frank's on the road more than twenty-six weeks a year, since he turned pro, and I couldn't do the upkeep at the house on my own. This way I can go with him to some of the tournaments when I want, without worrying about security and making sure somebody's cutting the grass."

Couldn't have that life if you had kids, Alice thought. "He's really into this bridge thing, I guess?" She managed to make the question sound sincere, despite her own distractions. "He's not going to get tired of it and have to look for a real job again?"

"It is a real job." Lily frowned for a moment, then smiled. "I know - a lot of people don't get it. But some people want to play with an expert, and they're willing to pay for the privilege." She stopped to listen to an incoming message, being recorded by her telephone answering machine. Alice took a mouthful of wine and looked at her expectantly.

"Not important," said Lily. "I can call him back later."

"You were telling me about Frank?"

"Yeah. He's got clients in Toronto and Montreal, Los Angeles, Houston. Not so much New York yet. But he's making more of a name for himself."

"Is it worth it? I mean, does he actually make enough money to cover all the travel?"

Lily nodded. "I wouldn't pay it. But I guess some people have more money than they know what to do with. So yeah, they pay his expenses plus his fees. Some of the top pros make a really good buck."

"And you manage on your own? I don't mean the housekeeping, I mean how do you avoid going stir-crazy?"

"I work long hours – when I need to. When I feel like it. You know the drill in real estate. Lot of weekends." Lily drained her wine glass. "If I don't feel like cooking, I go out. If I want to treat myself to a spa, I do." She looked at Alice's empty glass. "More wine?"

"I'd better not. Can't have liquor on my breath when I pick up Robbie from school." Alice tried to smile, but sensed the effort produced something more grotesque than merry. "Listen, I really hate to ask you this, but..."

"Anything I can do," said Lily.

"Do you think you might have a couple of dollars in coins? I've got to get to a laundromat – things have been kind of backing up since our washing machine packed it in."

Lily didn't answer for a moment. She got out of her chair and walked to the kitchen. Alice heard a metallic rattling. Lily reappeared with a coffee can in her hand.

"Here." She tipped at least five dollars in coins from the tin. "And this." She pushed a wad of twenties toward Alice.

"Oh, no! Thank you, but no, I couldn't." *Take it, dammit!*

"Alice, you need some walking around money. But this comes with a condition."

Alice twisted uncomfortably.

"You cannot tell Ted about it!"

That goes without saying.

"Thank you. I'll pay you back. I promise. Thank you."

"When you can."

Lily hugged her good-bye at the door.

"You're a good friend."

She didn't count just how good a friend until she was seated in the car. *Three hundred dollars! At least Robbie gets a cake for his birthday next week.*

Her plans for a low-key affair, with a few of the boy's friends over to the house, were trumped when Ted announced at the last minute he would take everybody horseback riding. Weather permitting, of course.

Chapter nineteen Daffodils

Alice demurred the first time Lily phoned to tell her about a support group she'd found, for families struggling with a loved one's addiction.

"Most of it's about booze and drugs," said Lily. "But gambling addiction is real, and you need help!"

"What are a bunch of strangers going to do for me? They're not going to understand."

"You might be surprised."

Alice hesitated and fumbled for an excuse. "How do you know so much about these things, anyway?"

"I have a cousin who's an addictions counsellor."

"For Christ's sake, Lily! You told your cousin!?"

"Of course not. At least, not in so many words. No names."

It was a week before Alice cooled off enough to speak to Lily again, and agreed to attend a meeting.

"Remember, these aren't addicts. These are people just like you, having to live with the fallout from somebody else's problem."

The meeting was in a United Church basement – not Alice's denomination, a fact which provided her a comforting degree of anonymity, although it did bring back memories of her childhood Sunday school classes: large, open, with miniature chairs stacked neatly in the corner and a small kitchen to one side. A tray of sandwiches sat on a table just outside the kitchen, and a man was carrying what she assumed was a coffee urn. He set it on the table, plugged it in to a wall outlet, and turned to greet the newcomers.

"Welcome," he said. "The coffee'll be a few minutes." He glanced at his watch.

Alice nodded and mumbled a "Thank you."

The man smiled. "My name's Bruce. I'm the facilitator. But we're pretty informal here. The less I talk, the better, right?"

Lily chuckled and offered her hand.

"Why don't you ladies grab a seat? We'll get going in about ten minutes." He nodded to the center of the room, where another couple were unfolding chairs and arranging them in a circle. Alice pulled a chair off the dolly and unfolded it herself.

Speakers on the first night included a couple grieving the loss of a daughter, whose descent into prostitution had gone hand in hand with a growing heroin dependency. It obviously wasn't their first time in the group; people seemed to recognize the story. But the update was shocking.

"We'll never know which one led to the other," said the tearful father. "But we know it was the drugs that took her life." The room filled with gasps and "Oh no's!"

Alice's thoughts were of little Emily.

One woman removed a pair of sunglasses as she spoke. "My name is Jennifer – and this is what my husband does to me when he drinks!"

"For Christ's sake," muttered Alice. "Somebody tell her to just leave him."

"That's not what the group is for," whispered Lily. "She has to decide for herself. Our listening to her will help her do that."

Bruce nodded when Jennifer was done, and spoke somberly. "Why don't we take a break for a few minutes?"

Alice helped herself to a Styrofoam cup of coffee and stood off to one side, reluctant to partake of the food. Bruce came to her. "Don't be shy. Why don't you have a sandwich?"

"Thank you, but I'm okay."

"Does either of you wish to share tonight?"

Alice looked at her feet, allowing Lily to do the talking.

"I'm just here with my friend. I hope that's okay. She was reluctant to come."

"Of course it's okay. Alice, do you want to tell us your story?"

Alice felt her face redden. She shook her head without looking up from her shoes.

"Jesus Christ," she whispered to Lily after Bruce stepped away. "I can't talk to these people. My problems are nothing, compared to..."

"They're not, Alice. They're real. And these people aren't here to judge you. Here. Have a doughnut."

The facilitator intercepted them again on the way to the door. "Thank you for coming, both of you. I hope you'll join us again."

* * * *

By the third week some of the faces and stories had become familiar. Alice decided she was ready to speak. She stood behind her chair, leaning on it for support, but the words wouldn't come.

"It's all right," Bruce told her. "You can sit if you'd rather."

Alice shook her head. "I'm ready now," she squeaked, barely audibly. She hesitated for another several seconds.

"My name is Alice," she began.

"Hello, Alice!"

"And my husband gambles." She looked into the two dozen faces in the audience – many of them staring blankly, a handful appearing attentive. *Guess it'll be interesting for them to hear something different!* She decided to focus on those who wanted to hear what she had to say. It would help to quell her nerves.

"I guess I've known it almost since the day we were married – coming up on eight years now. I guess I was naïve, or stupid – I didn't realize for the longest time it was a problem. I mean, I thought if a guy takes a hundred dollars to a poker game with his friends once a month that's okay, right?" She cleared her throat. "I mean, that's what guys do, right? And Ted could afford to have some fun. It's not like he didn't have a good job."

"I don't know when it was I figured out a hundred was actually five hundred, and that he was borrowing it." She paused and glanced around the circle. By this time more people were paying rapt attention.

"Money is a strange thing. A few weeks ago my credit card was refused. I didn't know we were that badly in debt. I told my friend it was the most embarrassing moment of my life. I lied." Her last two words seemed to echo throughout the hall, as though accusing her.

"The most embarrassing day of my life was last summer. Ted went to a casino, and won – more than two thousand dollars. He decided the next day to have a barbecue, and invite everybody on the block." She shook her head and fixed her gaze on the ceiling. "Mr. flambuoyant party animal. He bought a case of Dom Perignon."

Alice's voice rose as she recalled the story. "Dom fucking Perignon! In beer cups at a backyard barbecue! I cringed every time I heard him tell some stranger, 'don't worry about it, I won it anyway.' And then as soon as his back was turned they'd roll their eyes and laugh at him. He made himself a laughing stock, trying to be something he's not!"

She paused, gripped the chair tighter, and spoke quietly again. "I cried myself to sleep that night. You see, it's not just about the money."

Lily reached over, putting a hand on hers. Alice shook it off/. "I mean, sure, it's about money. It has to be. I can't let him impoverish my kids. But it's more than that. It's about – I don't know what it's about. How it rips your soul out of you. How it turns an honest man into a habitual liar." She felt her lip trembling, struggled to speak clearly. "All the times he said he was working late, and I knew he wasn't. You know, I stopped asking him, because I didn't want to hear the excuses. I guess that's why I didn't know he was losing so much."

The words began to tumble over one another – the feelings that she could never explain to Ted, or Lily, or anybody but a room full of strangers.

"Sometimes I don't think he even knows he's doing it. I cry every time I hear him promise the kids he's going to take them to Disneyland 'soon,' and I know it's never going to happen. And you know, that's not about the money either. I mean, sure, some months are tight. And I can live with that. I married him 'for richer or for poorer.' But there are times he's swimming in it. And I know he's just going to take it to a card table someplace, and try to 'run it up.' I think that's what gamblers call it."

Alice spoke quietly, as though talking to herself. "How many times have you promised to take Robbie to his ball game on Saturday morning, and I'm lying awake until three or four o'clock, knowing you're going to stumble in after a poker game and sleep past noon? He didn't care whether you won or lost. It was never just about the money."

She focused on some of the faces in the audiences again, conscious of the fact every eye in the room was on her. "You know, he actually told me that once. Early on – we stopped in Reno on our honeymoon. He said it didn't matter whether he won fifty dollars or five hundred dollars – just winning was almost 'orgasmic!' I should have understood then what a problem it was, but I didn't." She snickered bitterly. "It would make more sense to me if he was out having orgasms - screwing around on me. I'd hate it, and I'd have to divorce him for it, but at least I'd understand it. This I just don't understand. And I don't know what to do. I don't know how to help him."

She wiped her eyes, and listened for a moment to the silence in the room. "I'm sorry. I'm rambling." She stepped around the chair and sat down, with her face in her hands.

"It's all right, Alice. Don't apologize," said Bruce. "Tonight isn't about helping him, it's about you helping yourself learn to cope."

He closed the meeting with his usual appeal for volunteers to bring snacks next week

Alice and Lily both raised their hands.

* * * *

Ted pulled a little over four hundred dollars from the till at the end of the day, careful to leave a sufficient float for the evening. It wouldn't be the first time he'd head for the casino instead of the bank.

The thought crossed his mind in the car. *How do I know somebody else isn't doing the same thing at one of the other stores? Robbing me blind?*

That's why you have bookkeeping and accounting systems in place, He squirmed uncomfortably in his seat, and glanced over his shoulder. Nobody there. *But somebody will notice.*

So what? he rationalized. *Not like I'm stealing it. It's my money, for Christ's sake. So long as I pay the taxes on it.* He snorted to himself. *Those bastards always seem to spend more time chasing the little guy than the big cheaters.*

The goal tonight was clear – to make enough money to pay for a flight to Reno. *Gotta stop going to these stupid local casinos. Twenty dollar maximum – never make any money that way anyway.*

Yeah! Gotta have a big score – pay off some of these goddammed bills. 'Course, Alice won't see it that way. She'd flip if she knew I was even thinking about it.

He pulled into the parking lot at the local charity casino. *She doesn't need to know. If I just go down for the day – fly in, fly out – don't even need to pay for a hotel room.*

He cursed as he stepped in a puddle of rain water, and tripped on the edge of the pothole, trying to step out of it. He threw his hands forward, avoiding a faceplant, but his knee barked as it hit the ground.

Somebody rushed up to him, helped lift him to his feet.

"Are you okay?"

"Yeah, I'm fine," Ted muttered. "Fuckin' pothole!"

"Did you hit your head? You could sue, you know, if you hurt yourself."

Ted glowered at the man. *Free advice is worth what you pay for it.* "I'm fine!" he repeated. *And no, I couldn't. Not without Alice finding out where I was.*

Ted felt his pant leg, obviously wet, but he couldn't tell whether it was water or blood, or both. It didn't seem to be torn. He tested his weight on the leg gingerly.

The Samaritan persisted. "You sure you're okay?"

"I think so," Ted muttered. "Thanks." He glanced at his hands, muddy and cut. *Shit. Probably left a blood stain on the pants whether the knee is scraped or not.*

He looked toward the casino entrance. "I'm gonna have to go get cleaned up." He shook off his benefactor's offer to help him walk and made his way into the building. He convinced himself he was walking without a limp by the time he reached a restroom.

He washed his hands and glanced at his face in the mirror, confirming it hadn't been damaged. He ducked into a toilet stall before he lowered his trousers to examine the knee, still bleeding more profusely than he expected. *Shit!* The pants were probably ruined. He pressed a wad of toilet paper against the cut, holding it for more than a minute in an unsuccessful attempt to stop the bleeding.

He glanced into the casino as he made his way through the lobby to the exit. It seemed dingier than usual, full of unhappy people who couldn't crack a smile if their lives depended on it.

He ignored the odd look he received from the clerk at a flower shop on the way home. He paid cash for thirteen red roses – the extra one in recognition of the fact it was February 29th.

Alice was in the kitchen when he entered the house. The knee seemed to be bleeding again; he was sure now the sock was stained as well as the pants.

"Hey, Babe. Supper smells good." In fact, Alice's cooking was predictable, but criticizing it was one mistake Ted never allowed himself to make. Unless she solicited his advice, of course. They both knew Ted was the superior chef, although she'd stopped saying it our loud in recent months.

"Hi." She turned to look at him. "What the hell?"

He grinned as he handed the roses. "I was just thinking about you today." He leaned forward to kiss her. "We have an anniversary pretty soon. Seven and a half years."

Their seventh hadn't gone well. There'd been a fight that day after a couple of spectacularly unsuccessful visits to the casino.

Alice found a vase for the flowers and glanced at Ted as he sat down. "What happened to your hands? And your pants?" She studied him more carefully.

"Had a little accident on the way to the bank."

"Jesus! Not a car accident I hope."

"No. Just took a fall. Tripped over a pothole. I couldn't see how deep it was with all this fuckin' rain."

She switched the oven off, but left her casserole in it for the time being.

"Let's have a look. Take those pants off right here."

"You know, the last time you said that to me you had something else in mind." His attempt to make light of the situation failed to produce a laugh. But he followed her instruction.

He lowered the pants to the floor.

"Jesus Christ" Alice muttered. "Here..." She pulled a clean dishrag from a drawer, wetted it, and handed it to him. "Put that leg up. We're going to have to get some peroxide onto it."

Ted heard Robbie's voice as he pulled a chair in front of him and lifted the leg onto it.

"Is supper ready, Mommy?"

"In a minute, Robbie. Not quite yet."

He'd wiped most of the blood from his leg by the time she returned from the bathroom with a medicine kit in her hand. He leaned back, allowing her to lift the cloth from the wound and pour some disinfectant over it.

"Does that sting?"

"No."

"Well, hopefully we can get away without putting iodine on it. That would hurt like hell." She produced another clean cloth. "You're going to have to hold this on it until the bleeding stops. Then we'll hit it with peroxide again."

Ted nodded.

"Stay there," she said. "I'll get you a pair of shorts. You can't eat dinner in your underwear."

Emily appeared in the kitchen, her mouth falling open when she saw her father.

"Daddy! What happened?"

"I just took a little fall, sweetheart. Not a big deal."

"Daddies don't fall down."

"Sometimes they do." He pulled the discarded pants onto his lap. "Sometimes they do."

"Mommy, Daddy fell down."

"I know baby. Here." Alice handed him a pair of cut-offs, and took the damaged pants. "We might as well throw these out. I don't think I'm going to be able to get the stain out." She tugged at the fabric. "And here – they're torn. See?" She found a rip that had somehow eluded Ted's examination.

She turned and pulled open the cupboard beneath the sink.

"Wait a minute!" Ted barked. Alice frowned at him.

"Sorry." He stood and pulled the cut-offs up. "I can probably use them for gardening." He reached for the pants. "And you don't want to throw this out." Alice's eyes widened as he pulled the remaining cash from a pocket and handed it to her.

"I never did make it to the bank. Be careful with this – it'll have to come out of my next paycheque."

Alice looked as though she was biting her tongue. She stuffed the cash into her cookie jar and turned to open the oven as Robbie entered the room.

* * * *

I wandered lonely as a cloud
   That floats on high o'er vales and hills
   When I something something saw a crowd
   A host of golden...

Dammit! Why can't I...? Alice sat in the car for several minutes, staring at her mother's garden, struggling to recall the Wordsworth poem. *Everybody knows the first few lines – but they made me memorize the whole thing in school.*

Heather's daffodils were in full bloom by early March, always the first sign of spring at the Johnson household. Vancouver doesn't experience a storybook changing of the seasons – never did, in Alice's lifetime - the city is never blanketed in white for the entire winter, waiting for the first brave shoots to peek through the snow. Rather, the daffodils would rise from the mud, flutter for a few weeks in the March winds, valiantly casting their yellow glow into the gloom of drizzle and rain, and then retreat to be replaced by the kaleidoscope of summer colours. Sure, there'd be the odd day of sunshine when you would gaze upon the flowers the way you imagine the poet did, but this was not one of those days.

Emily stirred in the back seat.

Alice saw her mother open the front door and look out curiously. She waved as she stepped from the car, helped Emily get her feet on the ground, and walked hand in hand to visit Gramma.

"What were you doing out there?"

"Just thinking," said Alice. "Trying to remember the daffodil poem, actually."

Her mother smiled. "They are nice this year, aren't they?"

"They're nice every year, Mom."

Emily ran off to the toy room – Alice's old bedroom – as soon as her coat came off, and Alice sat down with her mother in the parlour. The tea service was already set out on a silver tray.

"So, how've you been? You wanted to talk about something?""

Alice sighed, staring into her teacup. "Not so good, Mom." She'd rehearsed more than a dozen openings. *Do I tell her the whole story? Start from the beginning? Or do I just come out with it – ask for the loan?*

Heather sipped her tea, waiting a moment before she prompted.

"What's going on? Is one of the kids sick?" There was deep concern in her voice.

"No. No, it's nothing like that."

Heather's relief was palpable. "Ted?"

Alice finished a crumpet, folding and refolding her napkin nervously. "You didn't need to do all this, you know." Her mother didn't smile at the compliment.

"What's going on, dear? Are you and Ted having problems?" Heather's eyes flashed momentarily. "He hasn't started to stray on you, has he?"

Alice shook her head.

"God, no. He wouldn't do that." She swept her hair out of her eyes. "It's money, Mom." She was sure she detected relief in her mother's posture.

"Well, you know a lot of couples have those troubles sometimes. Do you have to go back to work? You're here to ask me to watch the kids?"

Alice shook her head. "If only it was that simple."

Her mother opened her mouth again, but said nothing, waiting for Alice to choose her words.

"The business is doing fine." She took a deep breath. *No point beating around the bush.* "Ted gambles." Heather looked confused. "More than I realized."

"How? What do you...?"

"He gambles a lot."

Heather's hand shook slightly as she set her teacup on the table. "You mean...? My God."

"It's not just a few dollars to tide us over. It's thousands. We're in a hole."

Alice watched the expressions on her mother's face change – shock, recognition, anger.

"And you've let this happen? Why didn't you say something before this? You must have talked to Ted about it?"

"Of course I have!" Alice failed to keep the frustration out of her voice. "Not early enough, obviously. I mean, this didn't just happen all at once. I knew he likes to play cards, but it's been getting worse and worse. We've been fighting about it for more than year now, but he hasn't stopped." Something in her throat failed and she felt like she croaked the words. "I don't think he can."

"And you want us to pay his debts." There was no question in Heather's tone.

Alice's back curled, almost into a fetal position, if one can achieve that while sitting up. She wrapped her arms around her knees. "I don't know what else to do."

"How bad is it? Are you going to lose the house? You could come home if you have to – you and the kids."

Me and the kids!? Alice's face must have telegraphed her shock. She straightened herself, turned away, and gazed out the window.

Her mother seemed to make a conscious effort to speak delicately. "Do you want to leave him?"

"I don't want to, but..."

"You need me to tell you that you have to - if he can't stop himself from self-destructing?" Heather wiped some crumbs from her fingers. "It sounds like you know that however bad it is now, it's only going to get worse."

She scrutinized Alice's face. "You don't seriously think we're just going to write a cheque and let you two carry on as if nothing happened?"

"I don't know what I think." Alice fought back tears. She added a drop of honey to her tea and stirred for more than a minute. "What's Dad going to say?"

Heather's expression softened. "Pretty much the same thing I am, I suppose. Certainly, he'll agree we'll help you, however we can. But we can't just throw good money after bad."

"I know."

"He'll also tell you what nobody ever wants to hear." She drummed her fingers on the armrest. "Probably the four most hated words there are: 'I told you so.'"

Alice sipped her tea, cold by now, and studied her mother's face.

"You know he thought you married Ted too quickly. You didn't know him well enough."

Alice pushed her hair out of her eyes again. "Do you think that?"

Heather sighed and her shoulders slumped. "You were in love. Sometimes that's enough. Sometimes it's not."

The conversation paused again while Alice added some warm tea to her cup and listened for clues to what her daughter might be up to. She heard a thump and some giggling.

"Emily! Are you all right? I hope you're not jumping on the bed!"

"I'll go check on her." The gramma left the room, giving Alice a chance to compose herself. She reappeared a moment later. "Emily's fine."

"Thank you."

"So, how are the kids taking all this? Do they see you two fighting?"

"I don't think so. Not very often. They're too young to understand."

Heather nodded. "Too young to understand what the issues are, but kids will notice it if mom and dad aren't getting along. They can't help but sense tension."

"I know." Alice raised her hands in submission.

Her mother sat down again. "I think you know what you need to do, Alice." She hesitated for a moment. "How much money are we talking about? Does he owe loan sharks, or...?"

"I don't know. I don't think so. All our credit's maxed, but I don't think he's in that kind of trouble."

"Yet."

Alice wondered if the ominous tone was necessary, but couldn't deny it was fair.

Chapter Twenty Patterson & Browne

"I take it you've discussed this proposal with your counsel, Mr. Cronkite." Ted looked at his wife's face, impassive as she allowed her lawyer to introduce the subject. "I think it's very generous. In fact, I've asked my client to sign a waiver, acknowledging I've advised her against signing it."

Bitch! But then, Browne told me to expect that from her.

He tried to focus on what the woman was saying.

The meeting was in the boardroom at Trudi Patterson's office – an informal mediation to finalize terms of the separation without the expense of fighting in court.

"Your wife keeps the house. She will pay you twenty-three thousand dollars for your share of the accumulated equity, based on the independent appraisal by Hanson and Company. Your name will come off the title immediately."

She paused as a secretary carried a tray of coffee mugs into the room.

"You understand the entirety of these funds will be applied to the line of credit, and that you will dispose of the balance, as well as all credit card debt. Mrs. Cronkite is to be released from any responsibility for any joint liability of any kind." She frowned as she continued. "Mrs. Cronkite will assume responsibility for the balance of the mortgage against the house."

Ted nodded. He addressed Alice directly. "How the hell are you going to do that? And where are you going to get twenty-three thousand dollars from?"

"That isn't really your..." Patterson tried to speak, and frowned as Alice interrupted her.

"I'll answer that question." She stared at Ted with cold stoicism. "My parents. I get some of my inheritance early. Not that it's any of your business, but Dad says it's actually good tax strategy for him. But he's made it absolutely clear there is no deal if there is any risk at all that you get your paws on a penny of it."

"Why would I want that?"

"Oh, Ted. Don't kid yourself about what you are! You know it's your gambling that's got us here!"

Ted scowled as though he'd been slapped in the face. They'd had the argument umpteen times, Ted promising to quit and Alice reminding him how many times he'd said it before.

"This time I really mean it. I really know you're serious. And I still love you."

"I know you think that, Ted. You wouldn't think I was serious if I backed down now, would you?"

"Well, maybe we just call it a 'trial separation.' Maybe we don't actually go through with the divorce. My lawyer says we can't finalize it for a year anyway."

"I don't think so, Ted."

He forced his mind back to the present, and the cold, Spartan aura of the lawyers' boardroom. "So, you told them..."

"Of course I told them! What do you think?" Her voice rose in anger.

"All right," Browne interjected. "Let's try to stay focused on what we're here for."

Alice ignored him. "If you must know, I told your mother too!"

"You what!?"

"You didn't think she'd ask me why we're separated? Even if they don't care about you and me, they want to know what kind of home their grandchildren are being raised in!" The room was silent for a moment, before Alice twisted the knife some more. "She phoned a week after you moved out, and I told her I was done making excuses for the fact you were never home. They're changing their Wills. They probably already have, so that your share goes directly to the kids."

"All right," Patterson interrupted. "We are getting a little bit off topic. Let's all cool down for a minute." She looked to Ted's lawyer for a nod of agreement.

He poured himself another coffee before speaking. "Yes. About the children..."

"About the children," Patterson repeated. She looked at Ted again. "Mr. Browne has provided us your financial statements. You earned eighty-one thousand dollars last year. Your wife believes we can resolve the issue of support without going to court." She made no attempt to conceal the edge in her voice. "Consider yourself lucky Mrs. Cronkite is only asking for temporary spousal support. Her plan is to go back to work when the youngest - Emily? – starts school in September. In the interests of round numbers, you will pay a thousand dollars a month in child support, plus the same amount in spousal support, for twelve months."

"Twelve months? School starts in three!"

"Until Mrs. Cronkite's employment is stable."

"And you want a thousand a month for the kids! For how long? How do I know that it all goes to them?"

"At least until they're nineteen. And just to be clear, you do understand this is *child* support. Your obligation to the children continues in the event Mrs. Cronkite remarries."

Ted was unable to process that thought. He heard Alice jump in again.

"You never did get it, did you, Ted? It's not just food and clothes. What do you think it costs for baseball registration and piano lessons and ballet classes? Not to mention the fact they need a roof over their heads!"

Browne put a hand up. "We're aware of the list, Mrs. Cronkite. This is a fair number, Ted, based on your income. The custodial parent is not required to account for the spending."

Patterson nodded. "That's correct. And you do agree, Mr. Cronkite, that Mrs. Cronkite will be the custodial parent. Not only will the children live with her, but she will make the decisions about schooling and extra-curricular activities."

Ted scowled. "I'm supposed to have no say?"

"Technically, that is correct."

Browne looked at his client before speaking again. "We're willing to cede full custody. Mr. Cronkite agrees the children should have a stable home."

"Yeah," muttered Alice, in a stage whisper. "Without a bunch of poker buddies hanging around!"

"All right, Mrs. Cronkite. I think that's established." Browne carried on. "Your husband will have regular visitation rights."

Patterson nodded. "We're agreeing to one day a week during the school year and up to two weeks during the summer." She took a sip of her coffee. "Do you prefer Saturdays or Sundays, Mr. Cronkite?"

Ted resigned himself to the reality. "Does it have to be one or the other? Can we decide week by week?"

The lawyers looked at one another. "That's really up to you two," said Patterson. "If you're going to be able to cooperate. You have a shared responsibility. You both have to put the children's interests first."

Ted looked at his wife. "Alice?"

She shrugged.

"I think you both know that," offered Browne. "These situations are difficult, for everybody. I actually think this meeting has gone very well."

"Very well for your client!" Patterson declared. "A lot of couples would be fighting about shares of the company."

Bitch, Ted thought again. *Still trying to throw a monkey wrench into things!*

"I don't want anything from you, Ted," Alice said. "I just want us both to start over, without hating each other."

"All right," said Patterson. "I guess that's just about it. Although there is still the matter of our fees." She glanced at Browne. "We assume your client knows we're counting on him to deal with that, since Mrs. Cronkite has no income as yet?"

Browne nodded.

"Whatever," muttered Ted. "Gimme the paper."

He scratched his signature.

Chapter twenty-one Gunsmoke

Pete Lambert's kitchen was a nightmare, with science experiments fermenting in pots on the stove as well as in the refrigerator. Fast food containers were strewn about the house, and what garbage had been collected and bagged had not been removed to the edge of the street for pick-up.

The bathroom may have been the cleanest room in the house.

Thank God for that! Ted told himself. *At least it's a roof, with a spare bedroom.* He decided to bring his own linens, rather than rely on what was on the bed. Another excuse to go back to the house. *Alice's house! Fuck.* He looked in the dresser and the closet. They appeared clean enough that he could unpack his clothes comfortably.

Lambert made no secret of the fact he was studying Ted's face. "Take what you get, kid."

"I see you've started using a cane."

"Yeah. I should have done that a long time ago. Get around better now." The cane thumped on the floor, as he demonstrated from the bedroom to the kitchen. "Problem is you have to carry it everywhere you go. You ever try to wash dishes with one hand?"

"No," Ted admitted. *And it doesn't look like you've figured it out either.*

Lambert lit a cigarette. "How come you've been such a fuckin' stranger? I don't hear from you for weeks, until all of a sudden you need something."

"I've been trying to stay away from poker. It's why Alice…"

Lambert nodded. "Fuckin' women, eh?" His face softened in understanding. "Any chance it'll blow over?"

Ted shook his head. "I don't know. I'll try. I do go over there once a week to see the kids." He started pulling dishes out of the slimy sink water. "What about Marie?"

"She's been gone two weeks this time. But she'll be back." Pete tossed his cigarette into an already full ashtray. "She always comes back when her fuck buddy goes on a bender."

"And she'll be okay with it, when she finds out I'm here?"

Lambert scowled. "I'll tell her she is." He pushed some junk off a chair in the living room and sat down. "Actually – you sweep the place up and she'll prob'ly give you a hand job!" He laughed, *too loudly*, Ted thought.

The kitchen was a multi-day project, although not as bad as appeared at first glance. Ted scraped left-over macaroni and Christ-only-knows what else into some Chinese food cartons, fired them into garbage bags, and filled the pots with water to soak. Scrubbing would be easier the second day. There was a lot of picking up and sweeping up, but he didn't volunteer to swab floors immediately.

The refrigerator was another matter. Ted couldn't bear the thought of bringing groceries home to its scum-lined shelves, *and what the hell is that smell?* Rotting oranges in the crisper.

Ted put his foot down a week into the arrangement. "You're going to have to come upstairs if you want to eat," he told Pete. "I'll cook – just as easy for two as for one anyway. But I'm not a fuckin' waiter!"

Pete grimaced. "You think you're going to tell me what to do in my own house?"

"On this one, yeah."

Pete's lawn mower ran smoothly and Ted didn't mind cutting the grass once every ten days or so. But it was frustrating to know that he was doing it more to keep dandelions down than anything else. "You want me to pick up some Killex?" he suggested. "Your place could look so much better if we got rid of the weeds."

"No point," said Pete. "I used to try. But they just blow in again from the neighbours' anyway." He took a slug of his beer. "Nobody around here gives a shit."

There was tension over the telephone. Ted was home most evenings, consciously avoiding casinos, racetracks, and poker tables. Friday nights were the exception, when he'd make sure to be at the bridge club rather than anywhere near Pete's game. If it wasn't Friday night it would be the weekend when he was out with the kids, that there'd be a crisis at one store or another that somebody thought required the boss's attention. And Pete soon tired of taking the messages.

"I told your kid I don't give a shit the debit machine is down!"

"You what?"

"I thought she was gonna bust out bawlin'!" He laughed uproariously.

That will not fucking do!

He brought it up with Alice. "Do you think maybe I could tell them to go back to using this number? I'll check in with you for messages when I drop the kids off."

"You are kidding, right?"

Ted sighed heavily. "You know, it was embarrassing enough when I had to tell a bunch of teenagers I'm not living at home anymore. But now this is affecting the business!"

Alice had her back to him, leaning into the car to check Emily's seatbelt. "Why don't you just carry a pager? Everybody in the real estate office had one ten years ago." She stood upright and turned to face him. "You've got, what, five stores now? You want to be a mogul you've got to learn to act the part."

The electronics shop had an even better idea, steering him to the brand new notion of cellular technology. "Well, not *brand* new," said the rep. "They've been around since 1985, and they've gotten better and the price has come down quite a bit."

Down!? That's as much as I pay Alice and the kids in a month. And the fuckin' thing's heavier than my briefcase! But it was a status symbol. And a legitimate tax deduction.

* * * *

His visitations were often frustrating, trying to think of activities that would work for both a seven year old boy and a four year old girl. Sometimes he took them to the swimming pool at the rec center, but even there he found one-on-one tended to work better. It seemed the kids needed an occasional break from one another as much as time visiting their dad. He brought Emily her first bicycle – no training wheels! - on her fifth birthday in September, and spent most of the morning with her at a nearby park, teaching her to ride.

Alice was civil that day. "Are you going to stay for lunch and some cake?"

He looked at his daughter. "What do you think, sweetheart?"

"Yeah!"

"Sure." He nodded to Alice. "Thank you."

Ted assumed responsibility for barbecuing the hot dogs. There were greasy cobwebs to wash off the grills first, which of course led to a water fight with plenty of wrestling for control of the garden hose. Even Alice laughed when she was sprayed liberally. Ted couldn't help noticing how good she looked in a wet tee-shirt.

Emily blew out her candles on the first try.

"Did you make a wish?" said Ted.

"I wished you would stay home with us!"

Shit! I can't tell her wishes don't come true when you tell what they are. She'll think it's her fault.

The pain on Alice's face made it clear she had the same thought. She broke the silence.

"Why don't you come inside and get some dry clothes on, Ted? I think you've still got some stuff here."

"That sounds good." He stood up.

"Look in the cabinet over the washer. Some of your old gardening scrubs."

He ducked into the bathroom while Alice changed the kids into fresh clothes. Robbie was showing his sister how to use her new Etch-a-Sketch when Ted stepped out of the bathroom.

"Where's Mommy?"

"In her bedroom."

Alice reappeared, in a dry top. "Let's sit outside for a minute, while they're quiet."

"So," he began, "Emily's liking kindergarten?"

"Pretty early to tell. She doesn't fight about going."

Ted nodded. "And what about you? You working again?"

"Not yet." Her expression hardened. "They didn't exactly keep my old job open. But I've got some irons in the fire." She looked away for a moment. "Don't worry. You stop paying me next June either way."

"That's not why I..." He tried not to sound defensive. "I just wondered how you're doing."

"I'll be fine."

Ted gazed around the familiar patio and garden, his eyes stopping on the rhododendron bush that he and Alice had planted together. Alice had chosen the location and Ted had been on the end of the shovel. It was supposed to be the one project they would maintain themselves, without Heather's help, although it hadn't quite worked out that way. The mother-in-law's heart was in the right place, and when she showed up with gloves and pruning shears *who could say no?*

He studied the lawn, thinking about the one job he was allowed to do without benefit of female supervision. It looked as though nobody had kept up the edging that summer; grass was encroaching onto the patio again.

He turned to look at Alice. "You mowing the lawn yourself? I guess Robbie's a little young yet." His weak attempt at humour fell flat.

"You want me to put the barbecue in the shed? The hose? Or do you think you'll need them again this year?"

"Maybe next weekend." She hesitated, and spoke carefully. "How are you doing, Ted?"

"I haven't played cards since we signed the papers, if that's what you mean. Well, except for the bridge club sometimes."

"Yeah. Lily says she's seen you there a few times."

Ted found the quiet more comfortable than awkward, listening to the laughter of the children inside. He was thinking about asking for a beer when Alice shattered his reverie.

"I think you should go pretty soon."

That's a hell of an about face. What did I do wrong?

"For your sake, Ted. Mom and Dad are coming to visit. They're bringing supper – for Emily's birthday."

"Oh. Of course."

She called to the open back door. "Emily! Robbie! Come say good-bye to your dad!"

He exchanged hugs with the kids, and reached for Alice. She allowed him a perfunctory squeeze, but turned her face away when he tried to give her a peck on the lips.

"Ted, I don't think..."

He walked around the outside of the house to his car.

* * * *

Ted completed the purchase of his condo at the end of October. Two bedrooms, or more correctly, one and a den, but the plan was to furnish it with a captain's bed, in the hopes Alice would allow some overnight visits. She would have flipped had Ted ever raised the subject while bunking at Lambert's.

He slipped Pete five hundred dollars the day he moved out. "I know it wasn't part of the deal, but you've been a good friend and I just wanted to say thank you. I'd have gone crazy if I had to spend all this time in a motel."

Pete dropped his tough guy façade for just a moment. "It's been nice having the company, kid. You're okay."

"I'll look in on you once in a while. I haven't given up poker forever, you know."

What the hell did I say that for? It had been a productive few months, with the monkey off his back. Some bills were paid, his new address suited his station in the community, and he had every intention of spoiling the kids rotten with gifts at Christmas. He even planned to try to reconnect with his own parents in Penticton over the holidays.

* * * *

Christmas was harder than he imagined, with visions of Alice and the kids, Connie and Dean and their little monsters, all gathered around the table at Bob and Heather's house. *Traditional family Christmas. Yeah right.* Alice ensured the kids made their obligatory phone call to Penticton, to thank Grampa and Gramma for the new toys, and to talk to their father. The conversations were stiff and too short.

Ted called Pete the day he arrived back in the city, inviting himself to a Friday night poker game. Marie was home again and had agreed to keep the potato chips and beer coming.

It's not hard to play cards self-destructively. What is hard is to do it without everybody else at the table knowing it.

Ted was half aware he was embarrassing himself the third time he made a ridiculous re-raise. One of the guys peered at him over his glasses. "Just call," he said. "If you want to. I don't want any more of your money than that."

"Fuck you!" Ted blurted. "Chicken! You know I got you beat!"

The man shrugged and called Ted's bluff, pushing another fifty into the pot. He showed a queen-high flush and claimed the pot without bothering to look at Ted's holding. Ted folded his cards, tossed them onto the top of the deck, and stared blankly into space.

"You wanna sit one out, kid?" said Pete. "Maybe get your head back in the game?" He looked around for his wife. "Hey! Marie! You wanna bring us another couple of beers?"

Ted knew what was she going to say. *Sure, Hon,* he sneered to himself. *Sure, Hon. And he soaks it up, even though he knows she'll fuck anything with three legs.*

Ted leered obnoxiously as he took the bottle from her, chugged a third of it, weaved, and almost fell off the chair.

Pete got up and pulled Ted to his feet. "Come on, kid. You're not driving anywhere tonight."

"Sur'z hell am. We gotta finish zhe game first."

"You are finished." Ted was in no condition to judge the meaning behind the other guys' stares. "Hey, Joe. Gimme a hand here."

The two men wrestled Ted to the spare room and dumped him on the bed. Joe pulled his shoes off before he switched out the light and closed the door.

Ted managed to roll over in time to heave onto the linoleum floor rather than the bedding.

* * * *

Pete and Marie were at the table drinking coffee when Ted shuffled into the kitchen in the morning. Pete looked up and laughed. "I don't think I've ever seen anybody get so pissed on so little."

"I don't drink a lot," Ted mumbled

"Good thing, since you can't handle it!"

"I have to mop up the bedroom. Cleaning stuff where I remember it?"

Marie pointed without looking at him.

Ted avoided gagging as he scrubbed up his mess. He felt a little better when he helped himself to coffee and sat down with his hosts.

"Thanks for the bed. What a night!"

"Fuckin' right, what a night! What the hell came over you? I've never seen you play that stupid!"

"How much did I lose?"

"I dunno. Check your wallet. At least you didn't write any IOU's." Pete lit a cigarette and blew smoke in Ted's face. "We put you to bed before it got that bad."

"Did you win?"

"Some." Pete stared at his friend's bloodshot eyes. "What the hell were you thinking?"

"Thinking about the kids."

Pete sighed. "Yeah. They say Christmas is the worst." Marie nodded in agreement.

"I get Robbie all day on his birthday in a couple of weeks. I've gotta come up with something that'll knock him on his ass!"

Marie got up for another coffee. "How old is he?"

"Going to be eight."

Pete pointed at his mug and sat back with a thoughtful expression. "What if we take him to the range?"

Marie frowned as she poured Pete's refill.

"What?" said Ted. "Driving range? I don't golf. And you sure as hell don't."

Pete blew another cloud of smoke. "Gun range."

Ted's eyes widened. "Can we do that?"

"You can't. But I'm a member." Pete was in his element. "You'll have to bring proof of age. Eight's the minimum. And you do have to be there with him, of course."

Ted nodded thoughtfully. "I'll have to get his birth certificate. What does it cost? Do they rent guns?"

Pete gave him a bemused look. "You've never done this, have you? Have you ever fired a gun?"

Ted shook his head.

"I've got six of them. A .22 rifle and pistol; you and I'll use the big bores. You pay for the ammo."

* * * *

"Where are we going, Daddy?"

"Put your seat belt on." Ted smiled at the boy. "We've got something special planned today. We're going to see my friend, Mr. Lambert."

"Mr. Lambert? Is he a teacher?" In Robbie's world teachers were the only adults who expected kids to use the title.

"No, not really. But he's going to teach us some fun stuff today."

Robbie stared curiously as Pete loaded his gun cases into the trunk.

Rifle and pistol fire could be heard as Ted pulled into the parking lot. Robbie's eyes lit up.

"Do you know what that is?" said Mr. Lambert.

"Sounds like TV!"

"It's not TV. It's real!"

The front end staff was efficient. "Which target package do you want?"

Ted, with no idea what the man was talking about, deferred to Pete.

"Standard, I guess. Probably shouldn't encourage the kid to shoot at profiles."

Lambert made sure his guests wore their ear protection correctly, and instructed them both how to aim, breathe, and "squeeze the trigger. Don't pull on it!"

The excursion proved to be one of the biggest victories of Ted's life. Robbie couldn't have been more thrilled. He didn't complain when Mr. Lambert told him he couldn't use the adult rifles. "You're a little small for that yet. The kick would break your shoulder."

Ted was more interested in the boy's target scores than his own.

"You're a natural," Pete declared. "You, not so much." He looked at Ted and laughed.

Ted almost cried when his son told him, "This was the best birthday ever!" He tousled the boy's hair. "We're not done yet. You ready to have some cake?"

Pete dug out some old photographs back at his house, and told stories that Ted hadn't heard before. Robbie soaked it up for hours. "You were a real soldier?"

"Used to be, yup."

* * * *

"Thanks, Pete. I owe you, big time."

"Hey! I had fun. Let's do it again sometime."

Ted pulled up in front of his estranged wife's house ten minutes before Robbie's school-night bed time. He walked with the boy to the foot of the front steps and watched him scurry up to the porch. Robbie turned and waved before reaching for the door handle, only to have it pulled open from the inside. Ted waved as Alice put an arm around the boy's shoulders and ushered him in. She must not have noticed him standing in the shadows.

Or was it a slight? Either way, he wasn't about to let it ruin his day. He was still patting himself on the back on the drive home.

The telephone rang insistently in his kitchen as he stepped from the elevator, waltzed down the hall, and unlocked his front door. He stopped in the entrance to hang his coat, sensing no obligation to hurry.

She launched into it the instant he picked up. "Are you *out* of your fucking mind!? Of all the fucking hare-brained..."

He chuckled, set the receiver on the counter, and answered a call of nature in the bathroom while she ranted at the toaster.

Chapter twenty-two Crystal

Ted was confident the first time he strolled into the casino at the Aladdin Hotel in Las Vegas, well rested and congratulating himself for not ordering any booze on the flight. He turned his nose up at the sea of slot machines, ignored the craps, roulette and even the blackjack tables, and kept walking in search of the baccarat pit. The idea of an exclusive table for the high rollers, set apart from the crowd, captured his imagination.

Not that he'd ever seen the game in action, much less played it, but the handbook he'd read on the airplane made it seem so simple. *Always wondered why there's so much mystique around it in the Bond movies. I guess it's a European thing.*

The book explained how only two hands are dealt, no matter how many players are at the table. You bet on one or the other of them to win. They call the hands "bank" and "player", but that's just show-biz. They could just as easily be A and B, or black and red. *Might just as well be flipping a coin,* Ted thought. *Although there is something weird about the way the rules favour the "bank" side* – about fifty-one and a half per cent, it said. *I'll figure out the mathematics later.* Whichever hand is closer to nine wins, and tens don't count. *Simple.* The author recommended betting on the bank all the time and paying the house's five per cent commission on winnings.

The acrid odour of American cigarettes assaulted his nose. *What the hell makes them so much different from ours?* Cocktail waitresses buzzed around in tight tops and ultra-short mini-skirts.

Ted reflected on the events that made his vacation possible. A well-considered bet on Calgary to win the Stanley Cup had paid for the trip and the expiry of his spousal support obligation to Alice left him enough cash to be a player. He tried not to think about what she would say about it. He'd arranged for child support to flow directly from the company account so that it wouldn't be in his face every month.

He straightened his tie as he approached the roped off area, and stood outside it for a moment. *Dammit, I wish Alice could see this with me.*

The table was huge, elongated with rounded corners. He counted twelve sway-backed arm-chairs, ten of them empty, *for the players, obviously,* and two utilitarian seats, side by side, in the middle of the far side of the table, occupied by tuxedo clad staffers. A third employee, apparently some kind of a supervisor, sat on a chair on a dais at one end, overlooking the proceedings.

A tall man in a Stetson hat and bolo tie was sliding cards out of the shoe, one to the "player," one to the "bank." One more to the "player," one more to the "bank." Ted could see the player hand was a six; the bank's a four. The dealer pulled another card without waiting for instruction. A nine was added to the bank hand, reducing it to three.

"Fuck," snarled the cowboy, as the staff cleared his bet from the table. The sore loser shoved the shoe to his right without looking. The attractive young woman two seats over put her hand on it without comment, and pulled it in front of her. Ted noticed she had a minimal pile of chips, and bet just one of them.

"Bets down," announced a croupier. "Mr. Cullen?"

The Stetson twisted back and forth as the man shook his head. "Not this fuckin' time!"

The woman dealt the cards, a win for the bank side. A chip was added to her collection.

Ted shrugged and entered the pit, deliberately choosing a seat to the woman's right, away from the loudmouth. He thought he could play despite the uncomfortable vibe.

"Welcome, sir," said one the croupiers. "Minimum bet's twenty, maximum four thousand."

Ted counted out a thousand dollars. "Just give me hundreds." He received his ten chips and placed one of them on the bank side. The obnoxious man placed a five hundred dollar player bet.

The pretty blonde dealt the cards: a queen and a nine to the player, a four and an eight to the bank. "Player wins!" announced the croupier. "Natural nine!"

"Well done, baby!" blurted the loudmouth. "That's what we like to see!"

She remained expressionless as she slid the shoe in front of Ted. "I have to deal?"

"The shoe passes after every player win." The formal-sounding employee waited a moment. "You can't deal if you don't place a bet, sir."

Ted picked up a chip and hovered it uncertainly over the table.

"It's customary to bet on yourself when you're the dealer, sir."

Ted nodded and placed the hundred dollars on the bank square.

"Kid doesn't know what he's doing!" sneered the lout. He waved at the thousand dollars in chips on the player side in front of him. "Let it ride!"

Fuck you, pal! Ted placed another hundred in his bank square before he reached for the first card, his heart pounding. Nerves or anger? *Never needed to win one so badly in my life.*

"Player wins! Natural eight!"

Fuck!

"Way to go, boy!" Cullen sneered.

A croupier took the shoe from Ted and slid it in front of the mouth. Ted didn't look at him.

"I dunno," mumbled Cullen. "I think it's time for a break." He stood and stretched. "Why don't you let me buy you a drink, baby?"

She ignored him as he stuffed his winnings into his pocket and strode toward the bar.

The woman placed another twenty dollar bet on the table and looked at Ted. He shook his head. She dealt the player a king and a four, a ten and a five to the bank. The fifth card was a five, to the player.

"Player wins, with nine!"

Shit. That's three times in a row. Ted accepted the shoe. *But I'm not supposed to jump on the train.* He put a hundred dollars on bank. Win! *It's not supposed to flip one at a time.* He pressed his bet with another hundred. Win! Six hundred dollars on the table, and two thirds of it the house's money. *This is what they call getting on a roll!* The woman smiled at him and placed a chip on her bank square.

"All right. You're my good luck charm." He dealt the cards, a pair of aces to the player, a jack and a four to the bank.

"Baccarat! Bank wins with four!"

Ted grinned at the blonde woman. "One more?"

Her narrow shoulders rose in a shrug.

The second card was red, flagging the fact the shoe was nearly finished.

"Last hand," declared a croupier.

Ted slid the cards onto the felt and turned them over by flicking them confidently in his fingers. "Yes!"

"Bank wins! Natural eight!"

Ted felt like the king of the world. He turned to speak to the young woman, but she was already getting out of her seat. She walked away wordlessly, leaving her meager capital on the table.

The croupiers spread all the cards face down on the table and began mussing them. Ted watched curiously. "It's actually the best way to randomize them," one of them explained. "Eight decks. We can shuffle each one of them over and over again, but we'd never mix them with each other. This way anything can happen."

"So..." Ted tried to raise the subject casually. "What's her story?" He nodded at the empty seat.

"Toni?" One of the men laughed. "She works for the house. We can't deal the cards if nobody puts a bet on the table, and you might want to sit one out, right?"

"Ahh..."

"This your first time in Vegas?"

"Yes."

"Where from?"

"Vancouver."

"Canadian! You like baccarat?"

Ted offered a friendly grin. "So far I'm doing better at it than anything else."

It dawned on him what was going on. *Be friendly. Keep the customer engaged so that he doesn't walk away with his winnings.*

He stood up. "I'd better go get checked in. I'll probably be back."

"Busier in the evening, sir. More lively."

Ted began to step away.

"Sir?" He looked back. "Your commission?"

"Oh, yeah. How much?"

"One hundred ten dollars." He hadn't seen anybody making notes of his wins, but he knew their number was correct.

* * * *

Ted played some five dollar blackjack after dinner, rather than risking his winnings with the big-leaguers in the baccarat pit. He allowed himself a couple of drinks at the table. *What the hell! They bring 'em to you free if you're playing!* He didn't consider the option of jumping in a cab to the airport and getting out of town early, with his profit.

He wandered outside and strolled a portion of the strip, alternating his gaze between the gaudy neon above and the advertisements for escort services on the sides of taxis on the ground.

He checked out Caesar's Palace, *the granddaddy of them all, right?* He wandered through the casino to find the baccarat pit. *Twenty to two thousand. Not as good as Aladdin's!* He stuck his nose into a souvenir shop, full of tacky busts purporting to be various Roman gods and emperors. He picked out a model chariot for Robbie, a Caesar's Palace snow globe (*snow in Las Vegas – yeah right*) for Emily, and stood in front of a rack of togas, thinking about Alice. *Would she ever wear it? There is Hallowe'en. I have to talk to her about that. Maybe she'll let me take the kids out while she stays home and hands out the candy.*

He sauntered into a bar back at his own hotel. It suited his mood – dark and almost deserted. He took a seat at a table, four over from the nearest other patron, a winsome woman in a svelte dress, with one stiletto dangling from her toes in what Alice used to call "that fuck me look." *Catty? Maybe. But not intentionally. Alice is just the most honest person I know.*

Ted snapped out of his reverie when he realized the woman had locked eyes with him and smiled. He watched her push her chair back, stand, and sashay toward him, hips swaying as though well practiced in the art. As she came closer he could see she was obviously braless, her nipples marked by enticing bulges in the fabric of the dress.

"Buy a lady a drink?"

"Sure." He pushed a chair out for her just as a waitress appeared.

"Manhattan," said the woman. "Little on the sweet side." She licked her painted lips.

Ted nodded. "Might as well make it two."

"You here alone?"

Ted nodded.

"I'm Crystal."

Really? You expect me to believe that?

"Ted."

She put out a hand, holding on to his longer than necessary.

"You got a room here?"

He nodded. "What about you?"

She threw her head back and laughed. "Yeah. At least one." She lit a cigarette. "What's your number?"

"My number?" For some reason Ted was focused on the crack about 'one.'

"Your room number."

The drinks arrived, giving him a chance to think about how to answer. He showed his room key to pay for the drinks, and noticed Crystal's eyes go to it.

"Eleventh floor! My lucky number."

Ted frowned. *Jesus Christ! Can it get any cheesier?*

"Where you from, Ted?"

"Vancouver. BC, not Washington."

"I know Vancouver. I been there. Back when I was a dancer."

"You were a dancer?"

"Number Five Orange!" She twisted her shoulders and pushed her chest forward

"You looking for some company, Ted?"

This is the part where I don't know what to say. She's obviously a hooker, but on the one in a million chance she's not, I don't wanna end up wearing a drink.

Crystal leaned forward. Her breasts rested on the table, accentuating her cleavage. Ted took it as a signal the actual negotiations were about to begin.

"How much?"

"Two hundred for a bj. Four for full service. A thousand if you want sugar all night long."

"A thousand! That's way too much."

She allowed a scowl to peek through the practiced smile. "I don't have to spend the night. Four hundred. You get an hour."

Ted shook his head. "Sorry. I don't have that kind of money."

Crystal swirled her drink and put her lips to the straw. "What kind do you have?"

He thought about it, thought about Alice's warm body and how it used to feel so right, in bed beside him.

"Five hundred – overnight."

"Half price! Are you fucking kidding me?"

Jesus, she's not worried about discretion, is she? Ted sensed everybody in the bar looking at him. Or her. He shrugged, expecting the hooker to get up and leave, not at all sure he wanted her to.

"You got a wife at home, Ted?"

"Sort of. We're separated."

Crystal nodded. "I hear that a lot." She took a generous swallow of her drink. "Tell you what. I know you're a nice guy. Nine hundred."

Ted shook his head again. "Can't do it, Crystal."

"Oh, well. Your loss." She flounced out, leaving her cigarette burning in the ashtray.

* * * *

He was sitting up on the bed, two pillows behind his back, studying the television movie options, when the phone rang. It was the security desk at the base of the elevators.

"Crystal's here, says you're expecting her. Should I send her up?"

"Sure."

There was a discreet tap on the door two minutes later. The creases in her face were more visible in the hallway light than they had been downstairs but her figure was just as good.

"I do need a place to stay tonight. Seven-fifty?"

"Six."

"Seven."

Ted waved her into the room.

She dropped her handbag on the table beside the television and turned the volume down.

"Money first."

Ted counted out the bills.

"You gonna offer the lady a drink?"

"Whatever you like." He pointed to the mini fridge. "I guess you know where it is."

She helped herself while Ted stowed his wallet and jewelry in the safe.

"So, how do we do this? Just hop into bed, or can I undress you...?"

"Whatever you want. I can do a strip tease."

She sat on the bed beside him and pulled his hand to her chest. He squeezed and stroked while Crystal unbuttoned his shirt.

Half an hour later Ted was nearing the end of his self-control.

"Come on, big boy!" She thrust her hips up one final time. "Oh, yeah! Oh, yeah! That's it! That's my big boy!"

Ted rolled to the side, gasping, as she got up and sat in the chair, apparently comfortable in her nakedness. "So, you here on a junket, Ted?" She lit a cigarette.

"A junket? You mean like some sort of tour group?"

Crystal laughed. "You are new at this, aren't you?" She blew a smoke ring. "A junket is where the casino comps your stay. They'll pay for your room, and meals, and even your flight, if they think you're going to lose enough money at the tables."

"How do they know?" He was too intrigued to be embarrassed at having to ask.

"You have to deposit your money with the casino bank before you come down. Usually ten thousand. Do you play that kind of money?"

"I haven't. But I suppose I might." He slid his lower half under the sheet as he spoke.

"Good! When you come back look me up."

"How? You're going to leave me your phone number or something?"

She laughed at him again. "No, silly. Ask for Taylor at the bar. He'll know whether I'm in the hotel. He looks out for me."

* * * *

Ted slept well, dreaming of an earlier, simpler time, skinny dipping in the warm summer water of Okanagan Lake. He knew he was swimming, but he wasn't immediately conscious of the water, except between his legs. Probably because his equipment wasn't accustomed to being untethered in public. The waves slopped over him softly as he floated on his back.

It was dark. Late night beach party. Who was there? He could hear voices, laughter. He strained to make out the words. Faces were blurred in the darkness. High school! That's what it was! The old gang together again. Is that – Neil? He struggled to focus on the face. And Joanie! He was sure it was Joanie, swimming twenty or thirty feet away. Some guy was hanging around too close to her. "*Fuck off, Mac. That's not what you do when you're skinny dipping. You give everybody their space.*"

He kicked toward her, but he wasn't moving. *I have to rescue her.* "Ted!" He heard her call to him, and she swam toward him. A light appeared miraculously from the bottom of the lake and he was able to see Joanie breast-stroking in his direction, the globes on her chest half hanging, half floating, just below the surface. Her face morphed as he watched. It wasn't Joanie at all, it was Alice. And she seemed to be drifting away from him even as she swam.

He groaned and opened his eyes in time to see Crystal lift her face from his manhood, long enough to mutter "it's about bloody time!"

"Who's Alice?" she asked, when she was done. "Your wife?"

Ted shook his head.

Chapter twenty-three Brian

Ted took the souvenirs to Alice and the kids on Saturday.

Alice was stone faced. "Say thank you to Daddy."

Emily jumped into his arms for a hug. Robbie was more restrained.

Alice frowned at the package he extended to her. "You really shouldn't do this, you know."

"Just open it."

"What the hell? It's a dressing gown?"

"A toga."

"A toga! When am I going to need a toga? "

"I was thinking maybe Hallowe'en."

Alice's expression was more baffled than angry, until she examined the label. 'Caesar's Palace, Las Vegas, Nev.' She grimaced and pushed it back at him. "I can't believe you think this is appropriate."

Ted's face fell. "It's not a big deal," he mumbled. "I was just there, and I was thinking about you, and…"

"You mean you were thinking about party girls back in college!"

"No! I mean, not at all. I just wanted to get you something, and…" He dropped into a chair. "There are no other girls. Never have been. Not since we got married, anyway."

She sat across the coffee table from him, with the garment still in her hands. "I know." She spoke softly and the hard lines faded from her face. "I haven't either." She glanced at the kids. "Go get your shoes on. Daddy's just about ready to go."

"We haven't heard from your lawyer about finalizing the divorce."

"I haven't told her to go ahead," she said. "I don't need to yet."

'Does that mean…?'

"Don't ask me that right now, Ted. This doesn't help." She dropped the gimmicky apparel on the couch beside her, and sighed. "You should come for Hallowe'en. Come early, for supper. Then you can take the kids trick-or-treating, and I might try to figure this thing out." She held it up. "Which is the front, anyway?"

He took Robbie and Emily to Playland that day. He wondered if the toga was in the trash before the car pulled out of the driveway.

* * * *

Alice surprised him with a telephone call early in December.

"Ted, do you think you could take the kids overnight on Saturday?"

"Sure, if they want to. What's going on?"

"It's our office Christmas party. I think it might go pretty late and my usual babysitter can't stay past eleven." She paused. "Normally I'd ask Mom and Dad, but his party is the same night."

"What time do you want me to pick them up?"

"Can you make it before supper? Feed them at your place? The party starts at five and I've got to get dressed for it."

"Hey," said Ted. *Might as well ask.* "If you've got a regular babysitter, why don't we go to the bridge club one night? Maybe Friday?"

The pause at the other end seemed interminable. "Alice?"

"I don't know, Ted. You know I haven't played in more than two years."

"Yeah, I know. So what?" He cajoled. "It's not a date. It's just a bridge game."

Only one of their opponents pried. "Hey! Haven't seen you guys in forever. This mean you're back together again?"

Alice looked down at her cards and shook her head. Ted didn't say anything.

****

Ted was in his lawyer's office in the spring of 1990, signing the transfer and mortgage documents to acquire his sixth location. It was a landmark achievement, the first one where Ted would actually own the property. Leases were fine for the stores, but somehow it felt renting the corporate headquarters wouldn't do. Ted thought he was ready to establish some permanence.

Browne handed him a newspaper, open to the business section. "Did you see this?"

Blockbuster Video, the monster chain that started in Dallas just five years earlier, was making noises about coming to Canada. Ted scowled.

"You sure you don't want to think about buying a franchise?"

"Absolutely no fucking way!" Ted threw the paper down. "Pardon my French."

Browne looked at him quizzically.

"I'm sorry, Aaron." He watched Browne slip the signed documents into a file folder as he tried to collect his thoughts. "I was supposed to be the guy selling franchises. There is no goddammed way I'm ever going to think about buying one! I didn't have this idea to make somebody else rich."

Browne nodded slowly. "I can understand that. And I think you've done well for yourself." He produced a bottle from a desk drawer. "Would you like a drink? Little celebration?"

Ted shook his head.

"You know," said Browne, as he poured himself a shot, "if you asked a hundred people in the street, ninety-nine of them would say they want to see independent Canadian companies do well. But will they be there for you when Blockbuster opens up right across the street from you? That's the question."

The office was silent for a moment.

"Do you think I could have done it, Aaron?" Ted rubbed his fingertips together in front of his chest. A nervous tic? Or a sign he was thinking? "Did I ever have a chance? A kid from a little town that nobody outside of BC has ever heard of?"

"Ray Kroc was from Chicago." Browne drained his glass before he carried on. "But I don't think that's the issue. The United States is just a way bigger market, way more opportunity. And for all their chest-thumping about 'free market' they're really very self-protective. They're never going to let somebody from Canada go down there and tell them how to do things, whether it's hamburgers, videos, or fighter jets." Ted recognized Browne's reference to the Arrow debacle.

"So, no," the lawyer concluded, "I don't think you were ever going to be any bigger than a hundred or so stores across Canada. And that would have taken some doing."

Browne seemed uncomfortable, shuffling papers aimlessly on his desk. "Maybe if you'd put every last cent back into it." He studied Ted's face. "Don't look so beaten up about it. You're still young. How old are you?"

"Thirty-one."

"Yeah, see? You keep growing at this rate you'll be a millionaire before you're forty."

"Maybe."

Browne cleared his throat and poured another shot. "Sure you don't want one?"

Ted shook his head again.

"You still see Alice every week?"

"Just about."

"She hasn't said anything about increasing child support? She could, you know, if she gets wind of how well you're doing."

Ted shook his head. "She seems to be doing all right on her own. She's working for the TD."

Browne opened his mouth, as though to ask another question.

"She's not a teller," Ted elaborated. He smiled. "They've actually put her name on her door."

"And neither one of you is in any rush to finalize the divorce? You can, you know. It's been well over a year."

"I know." Ted took a sudden interest in the condition of his shoes. "I'm still hoping she won't."

* * * *

"I might be late bringing the kids back tonight. I thought we'd run out to Cultus Lake. If they're having a really good time, and you never know what the traffic might be like on the freeway."

"All right. But phone me when you get in the car, so I'll know to look for you in an hour." Doors and windows were open all over the house, allowing a fresh summer breeze to flow through, and Alice seemed to be in a good mood. "And keep a close eye on Emily! I know she's had swimming lessons, but she's not very advanced. Don't let her try to keep up with her brother unless you're right there."

Yeah, yeah, yeah. I know.

They were past Langley, nearing Abbotsford, when Emily said something completely unexpected, from the back seat. "I think we been to Culdush Lake before."

"I don't think so, Emily."

"I 'member this road." There was a squeal. "Daddy, Robbie's hittin' me!"

"Robbie! What's going on back there?" Ted glanced in the mirror. Robbie had his hand over his sister's mouth. "What's going on!?"

Emily twisted her head out of her brother's reach. "We went to a lake, with Brian."

Robbie rolled his eyes. "Way to go, dummy. You weren't supposed to say anything about that!"

"Daddy, Robbie called me 'dummy.'"

"I heard. That's enough, Robbie!" Ted tried to keep his attention on the traffic. "Who's Brian?"

"Mommy's friend."

"And he took you guys to Cultus Lake?"

"Mom came too," the boy mumbled. "And it wasn't Cultus Lake."

"It wasn't? Where was it?" Ted struggled to keep the anger out of his voice. *Not the kids' fault!*

"There was a lake, but we didn't go swimming in it. We went in the hot pool, at the hotel."

'Hot pool?' "You mean Harrison Hot Springs?"

"I think so, yeah."

"And you stayed in the hotel?"

"Yeah."

"All in one room?"

"No." Emily piped up again. "Me and Mommy had our own room. Robbie stayed with Brian."

Ted's blood boiled. *I don't know whether I like that more or less than the alternative!*

Robbie was muttering at his sister again about telling secrets.

"It's okay," said Ted. "I won't tell Mommy that you told, and you don't tell her either. We'll just keep it our secret, okay?" He realized his hands were gripping the steering wheel too tightly. "Let's just try to have a good time today and forget we ever talked about it. I don't think you've ever been to Cultus Lake. It's a really fun place for kids." *More than fuckin' Harrison is!*

He made a point of leaving in time to have the kids home for supper. *Maybe cut short the afternoon delight.*

Ted controlled his tongue when they arrived at the house. But he looked at Alice differently. *She's always been beautiful.* She'd kept her figure into her thirties. From fifty feet away she looked as good as a twenty-year-old swimsuit model, and in close quarters he found her even more striking. There was a depth in her eyes, no sign of the pouty lips that so many young Bambis seemed to cultivate, and the highlights in her hair were natural. *There's no way in the world guys wouldn't hit on her!*

* * * *

"Lily? Ted."

"Ted! How are you? Don't tell me you're ready to buy another building already?"

"No. Don't want to disappoint you." He cleared his throat and tapped a pencil on his desk nervously. "But this is a social call. I thought we might be able to get together for dinner or drinks one of these nights, just for old times' sake."

"That sounds great. You know what? I'll buy. It's not like you haven't steered enough commissions my way."

Dinner conversation revolved around Ted's plans for the new location and how much he liked the condo Lily had found for him, and moved through Frank's bridge career, how he was moving up the list of top masterpoint winners on the continent.

"How often does he get home?" asked Ted.

"Not very. A lot of times it makes sense to go straight from one Regional to the next, there's only one day in between." Lily set her fork on her plate and wiped her mouth with a napkin. "He did come home for a couple of days after Seattle last month, but then he was off again."

Ted pushed his cutlery onto his plate. "You want to look at a dessert menu?"

"I'm stuffed," said Lily. "But I could use another wine."

Ted signaled for the waiter.

"You don't travel with him much? I'd think that would be a fun thing to do."

"I've seen most of the stops at least once. After a while one convention center looks the same as all the others."

Ted nodded. "And you're busy with your own work, of course?"

"Of course."

"How often do you see Alice?"

Lily thanked the waiter for the new round of drinks, and took a sip before responding. "I wondered if that was the reason for this."

"I was just curious – whether you think she's doing all right."

"Seems to be."

Ted tried a more direct tack. "I hear she's been seeing somebody."

Lily seemed to cogitate for a moment. "Ted, I don't want to get in the middle of anything."

He tried to speak lightly. "You are kind of in the middle. You did introduce us, you remember."

"That was ten years ago, Ted. A lot of water under the bridge since then." She squinted at him. "How did you hear she's got a boyfriend?"

The word was like a punch in the gut, even though Ted knew he should have expected to hear it.

"You got a private eye watching her or something?"

Oh, come on! Ted was on the verge of snapping at her when he remembered the promise he'd made to the kids. "What if I have?"

Lily set her glass on the table and leaned forward. "You can't do that, Ted. Alice is trying to move on. She's entitled to. And you've got to do the same. Brian's been good for her."

"Brian? That's his name?"

Lily scowled and drained half her glass. "I've already said too much."

"Are they sleeping together?"

She shook her head.

"Is that a 'no?' Or do you just not want to tell me?" Ted sensed his voice rising, but pressed on. "Lily, if there's some other guy living with my kids I think I've got a right to know!"

"They're not living together. Yet, anyway."

"But they are sleeping together? At our house?"

"It's not your house anymore Ted." She waited a minute for the heat to dissipate, and lowered her voice when she spoke. "Look, Ted, Alice is a young woman. She's got most of her life ahead of her, and she deserves to be happy. So do you."

Ted glanced around at other tables. Nobody seemed to be eavesdropping. *If I say this to Lily I'm sure Alice'll hear about it.*

"I can't. I love her more now than I did when we got married."

Lily's mouth fell open.

"We were so young, we didn't really know what we were doing. You know the story." He hesitated for a moment. "Did you know Frank tried to talk me out of it? He wondered why Alice didn't just have an abortion."

"No. He never told me that."

"He didn't try very hard, but you know Frank - he doesn't usually poke his nose in at all."

Lily nodded in agreement.

Ted carried on. "You know, she hasn't asked for the final divorce yet. I have to wonder if that means..."

"She's confused, Ted. She wanted it to work, but..." Lily shrugged.

"I know. And I'm trying to change."

"Can a leopard change its spots?"

* * * *

Alice met him at the door when he showed up to collect the kids Saturday morning.

"They're not here," she said.

"What? Why...?

"I shipped them to Mom and Dad's last night." She took a step back and waved him through the door. "Come on in. We need to talk." Her demeanour seemed calculated; neither friendly nor combative.

Ted slipped his jacket off as he entered the house.

"Let's go in the kitchen," said Alice. "I've got coffee on." She poured him a cup as he sat down at the table. Ted nodded his thanks without a word.

Alice sat at the far end of the table, and they stared at one another for nearly a minute. Ted saw she was in a button-up blouse and her hair was brushed, but she wore no make-up.

She finally broke the silence. "So, you know."

Ted still didn't speak.

"Lily phoned the other night, told me about your dinner date."

He acknowledged her with a nod.

"She thinks you've had somebody spying on me."

Lily can think whatever the fuck she wants. Ted refused to dignify the remark with an answer.

"How did you find out, anyway?"

He noticed her glance at the counter, where a coffee mug sat on top of a couple of dirtied side plates beside the sink. *I guess I know why those are there.*

"No," said Alice. "Don't tell me. I don't need to know. But I told her you wouldn't do that."

"Thank you." His sarcasm wasn't deliberate, but he made little effort to conceal it.

Ted looked around the kitchen for more evidence of a male presence, and beat down an urge to jump up and snoop in the bedroom before he spoke again.

"How long has it been going on?"

"We met last fall."

"Last fall! And you're just telling me about it now?"

Alice sighed heavily. "We are separated, Ted. It's not really any of your business who I'm…"

"Have the kids met him?"

"Yes."

"Then it is my business!"

She didn't seem taken aback by his anger.

Another several seconds passed in silence.

"How often are you sleeping with him?"

"That is none of your business," she snapped. "But I will tell you this. It's more often than it was six months ago." The anger faded from her voice and she became pensive. "I didn't want to make that mistake again."

"Mistake!?" Ted felt like he'd been slapped in the face.

"What else do you call it when you end up divorced?"

There it is! Fuck!

Alice finished her coffee and set the cup on the table more carefully than necessary, before she looked at him again. "I talked to Patterson yesterday. You'll get the papers next week."

Ted slumped in the chair, his hand shaking as he tried to take a swallow of coffee.

Alice spoke softly. "You knew it was going to come to this, Ted. We can't go back to the way it was before."

"Why the hell not?"

Her only answer was a shake of her head and another lengthy silence.

"Do you love this guy?"

"He doesn't gamble."

Ted banged his fist on the table. "That's not what I asked you!"

"I know." Alice got up for a fresh coffee. "He wants me to marry him."

"And you're going to?"

"I don't know, Ted! I told you – I'm taking it slower this time." She carried the pot to the table and refilled his cup.

"Thank you." He hesitated. "This used to be my favourite time of the day. But you know that." Was he kidding himself, or were there tears in her eyes?

She turned back to the counter and slipped the dirty dishes into the sink.

Seriously? You think I didn't see that? He chose not to pick a fight over it. "I do love you, you know."

"I believe that, Ted. At least, I believe you think it. And you need to believe this isn't easy for me either." She picked up a dishrag, holding it under the water tap for a moment.

"Is it about the money? I can pay it back, you know. Keep your father happy, and we can start over."

Alice grimaced. "You don't want to hear what Dad would say about that." She sighed as she sat down again, aimlessly wiping the table in front of her. "And no, it's not about the money. I've told you that too many times already. I just can't live on a roller coaster."

Ted sighed heavily and looked around the kitchen again. "What does this guy do?"

"He's a building contractor." She paused, seemed to consider how much to tell him.

"He's working on plans to finish the basement."

Shit! "So that means he thinks he's going to move in here!"

"Ted..."

They looked at one another for a moment, and then away, as though on cue, both pairs of eyes drawn to the clock on the wall.

"They'll be dropping the kids off in ten minutes," said Alice.

Ted pulled himself up, trying not to appear unsteady on his feet. "I'd better go, then. I don't feel like seeing them today. Tell them I'm sorry."

Alice remained seated at the table while he let himself out.

Chapter twenty-four The Junket

Ted booked his first junket to Sin City for the weekend of the wedding. He made the decision the instant Alice gave him the news.

"Ted, I think you need to know I am going to marry Brian." She spoke with her back to him, washing the kids' breakfast dishes.

He tried not to react. "When?"

"Next month." Alice turned to face him, wiping her hands on a dish towel. "It's not like there's a lot of planning involved. It won't be big. I think that ship has sailed."

Ted took a seat at the kitchen table and used his bare hand to wipe some crumbs into a pile. He studied the effect rather than looking at her. "I guess I'm not invited."

"Seriously?"

"Of course not." He looked up. "What the hell else was I supposed to say?"

"You could say you're happy for me. Or at least good luck, or something." Alice frowned. "You won't be able to see the kids that weekend."

"You know you can't just decide that arbitrarily." By this time his rights were more than a signed agreement. They'd been codified by the court. "You could ask."

"Oh, for Christ's sake, Ted. Grow up! You miss half your dates anyway!"

Half? "I do work, you know."

"We all do!" Alice flung the towel aside and threw her hands up in the air. "I don't want to fight with you about this, Ted. It's out of your hands."

Ted glanced at the kids, obviously listening. Robbie was motionless, with a Ninja Turtle figure in his hand; Emily had dropped her crayon and appeared on the verge of tears.

That was the image he forced himself to keep in his mind as he boarded the plane. He couldn't bear thinking about his daughter scattering flowers for some other guy. The pictures of Robbie stuffed into a tuxedo and Alice beaming in a wedding veil were harder to ignore.

"Anything to drink, sir?" A stewardess was a welcome interruption.

"Absolutely! CC. Make it a double, and keep them coming!"

The young woman frowned as she poured one mini bottle and handed him a second, unopened.

"Ice?"

"No. No, thank you." He made a point of speaking more politely. *Not her fault.*

He thought about the fight they'd had the day Alice served him the divorce papers. At least she'd had the courtesy to have them delivered via Browne rather than dumping them on him in front of a bunch of kids at one of the stores.

That had to be Alice. Patterson would have wanted to embarrass me as much as she could.

Supper hour had been the worst time to call her about it. *That was stupid!* It had been too easy for her to use the kids as an excuse. *"I can't talk now, Ted. I've got to go."*

He hadn't intended it to turn into a fight. He bit his tongue, hard, rather than making some sarcastic remark about how long she'd hidden the affair from him. *I'm not the one who lied here. And I'm willing to forgive her.*

He knew it was too late but he couldn't resist trying to tell her otherwise. *"Why can't we go back to the way things were?"*

"Too many things have happened, Ted. And we can't just pretend you're not still gambling."

"It's not like I can't afford it."

"Ted, I can't..."

"Yeah, you can. You just have to want to." He was sure the pause on the other end was real. *But did it mean anything?*

"Ted, the kids are waiting for their supper."

He tried one last Hail Mary. *"It's your parents, isn't it? Daddy's girl, gets divorced just to keep peace in the family."* He heard the click on the other end of the line.

Ted thought about the day his in-laws had learned of Alice's pregnancy – how furious Bob had been. Alice had stood by him that day, assuring her father over and over again their love was real. Yes, the baby was earlier than planned and it might be inconvenient, *"but we're going to make this work."*

God knows what would have happened if she hadn't been steadfast.

He opened his eyes when he felt a splash of liquid on his shirt. His clenched fist had crushed the plastic drink cup.

* * * *

Ted played like a man who was distracted, making one bad decision after another. The first night at the baccarat table cost him more than five thousand dollars. Day two at blackjack was a saw-off. By the second night he decided to fall back on the old standard, poker.

They can't all be pros just because it's Las Vegas. He invested too much energy thinking about the guys who seemed to know what they were doing, and not enough on the mom and pop types. Ka-ching.

He phoned his manager at home Sunday afternoon.

"I missed my flight back. Have things been okay this weekend?"

"Oh, yeah. No problems."

"Well, I'm going to stay down here another day. Maybe two."

Ted didn't know it was a pattern the casinos had seen often. Winners jump the next flight out of town, no matter where it's going. Losers get desperate and dig themselves a deeper hole.

By Monday night he was reduced to pulling out the credit card and musing about how to cut costs at a couple of the shops for a few weeks. He'd have to pull more shifts himself to catch up.

With his ego badly in need of a boost, he made a beeline for the lounge at the Aladdin and perched uncomfortably on a barstool. The place felt seedier than the last time he'd been there. More of a scent of spilled booze in the air?

The bartender turned to him.

"Taylor around?"

"Taylor?"

"I understood he was a bartender here."

"Maybe was. Not anymore. What can I get you?"

"Nothing, thanks," Ted mumbled.

He left the bar feeling oddly dejected. *Why? Girls in Vegas are a dime a dozen. Not like I owe Crystal anything.*

But the leap had been made, he'd made up his mind he was going through with it. He felt empowered, the first time all weekend he was actually committed to a plan of action. He headed for the front door.

Ted figured there were two basic choices on the strip. A streetwalker, or call one of the agencies that advertised openly. *I know they're legal. I guess the girls outside are too.*

He wandered in the direction of the nearest corner, and didn't cross the street when the signal flashed "walk."

"Hey hon. You lost?" The voice behind him was inviting enough. He turned to look.

"Nah, I'm just looking at the sights."

"Looking for some company?"

He eyed the girl up and down. "How much?"

"Five hundred, full service."

"Three." He didn't think before he blurted the counteroffer, in a voice he was sure wasn't his own.

The smile left her face and the goth make-up lost any hint of appeal. "Fuck you! Five. Take it or leave it."

"I'll leave it, thanks." Ted crossed the street. *This could almost be fun.* But the hormones demanded action, not research.

Trixie – *yeah right* – was a shapely girl, maybe on the high side of twenty-one. She asked for four hundred.

He studied her bustline, wondering how much of it was tit and how much was artificial padding. "You worth it?'

"Primo pussy, baby."

"Lose the gum."

She pouted, but spat it into a gutter.

The encounter served an immediate need, but it wasn't Trixie or Crystal that Ted was thinking about.

Chapter twenty-five Monica

Ted prospered despite himself. There was some licking of wounds following the Las Vegas debacle, but he gave himself a raise and restructured his personal debts. The company was performing well enough and a line of credit against the condo made more sense than credit card interest rates. The void in his life had little to do with money.

Pete Lambert remained his closest confidante, despite their obvious differences. Ted dropped in to visit from time to time, over and above poker games, feigning an interest in Pete's model railroad hobby. But he longed for the innocent comfort of Neil's company.

Neither of the children seemed interested in spending a Saturday at their dad's apartment or hanging around one of the stores, and visiting with them at home was uncomfortable with Alice's new husband in the picture. Ted found it harder and harder to come up with fresh ideas for appropriate outings. It wasn't long before Alice's hyperbole was truth.

And what of Alice? Ted had to admit Lily was right. *She's moved on. And I should too.*

A thirty-two year old divorced man. Makes a good buck. He scrutinized himself in the mirror. The face that stared back at him looked its age. Not embarrassingly cherubic, but not an old man either. He ran a comb through his hair. *Has to appeal to somebody, right?*

He thought about Lily, and the fact she was alone most of the time while her husband was off playing bridge for a living. But she'd never shown the slightest inclination, *and a guy shouldn't do that to Frank anyway.*

An advertisement for an event called 'speed dating' caught his attention. A room full of women on the prowl – it sounded as though the odds would be in his favour.

Ted had his hair styled and invested in a new pair of patent leather loafers prior to the gathering. He recalled Alice telling him more than once how a man's shoes are the first thing a woman looks at.

* * * *

The venue was less than up-scale – a banquet room at the Elks community hall. Ted chose to look at the bright side. *At least there's nobody here outside of participants. Wouldn't want it to be in a restaurant someplace with a bunch of strangers listening in.* In fact, the room was spacious enough to set tables comfortably apart for privacy. The more Ted thought about it the more sense it made.

He stood near the bar with a glass of whiskey in his hand, sizing up the competition. Half the guys were in jeans and sneakers. He wrote them off immediately. A couple of men were in business suits, most of the others wore sports jackets with shirts open at the neck. Ted thought about slipping his tie off, but decided it might pay to stand out from the crowd, particularly since his was the only one in the room perfectly shaped in a Windsor knot.

One of the well-dressed fellows sidled up to him.

"Your first time at one of these things?"

Ted nodded. The guy seemed to be studying the women more than the men.

"Me too," the man said. "An actual meet market – no need for the quotes around it." He chuckled at his own joke and offered Ted a hand. "Charlie."

"Ted." The handshake was firm and friendly.

"You a single guy, Ted?"

"Divorced, actually."

"Me too," said Charlie. "I hope I don't run into anybody that looks like my ex. Definitely don't wanna do it all over again with that..."

The thought was interrupted by the tinkling of the coordinator's bell.

"Thank you all for coming," called the woman. "It looks like everybody's here, so we can get started in just a couple of minutes. My name's Belinda, and I'm going to make sure this evening goes smoothly for everybody." Her voice projected confidently.

"I think you all know the basic format. Each lady will have a mini date with each gentleman – a few minutes to get to know something about each other, and decide whether you'd like to arrange another meeting to take it further. We only have a couple of rules. Be polite. Put your best foot forward. And, gentlemen, please do not ask for any identifying information. Don't ask for last names or phone numbers. We don't want anyone to have to feel uncomfortable saying no." She paused to let that sink in. "Keep notes on all your dates, particularly the ones that go well." She smiled brightly. "We'll collect them at the end, and pass your information on to the people you are interested in seeing again." She looked around the room. "Simple enough, right?"

"Now, we have sixteen ladies and sixteen gentlemen. By my arithmetic we can allow five minutes for each date, and we'll all get home at a reasonable hour." She rang her bell. "When you hear this bell again, it's time for the gentlemen to move on to the next table. Don't dilly-dally. We all need to respect one another's time."

People were already gravitating to their assigned tables. "You've all been given a table number to start – if you'd take your seats, please. We'll add a minute for the first date..."

Belinda was drowned out by the hubbub of voices and scraping chairs.

Ted waited behind his chair for the young woman assigned to his table to arrive and they shook hands before sitting down.

"So," she smiled at him. "Did you bring a list of conversation starters?" Ted judged her to be several years younger, but with a confidence in her bearing. She was attractive without an excess of make-up. Her paste-on name badge read 'Monica.' Ted put a finger to his lapel, unconsciously checking his own.

"I jotted a few things down, but I'd rather just wing it."

"Well, how about we get the obvious business out of the way first? Are you married, how old are you and do you have a job?"

Ted laughed out loud, but stopped when he realized Monica didn't seem to get the joke. "No. Thirty-two. And yes." He continued grinning. "I guess you have a reason for asking?"

"You might be surprised," said Monica.

"I take it you've been to these things before?"

"Couple of times. Haven't found Mr. Right yet." She tapped her fingers on the table and glanced down at her scoresheet. "But we're not supposed to talk about other dates."

"Well, what else can I tell you?" Ted spoke lightly. He decided he liked the woman's direct approach.

"What do you do?"

"I run a small business." He grinned. "Well, maybe it's a medium size. I don't know one definition from another."

Monica appeared suitably impressed. "What sort of business?"

Ted hesitated. "I don't know if I can tell you that without breaking a rule. It might be an identifier."

Monica leaned back in her chair and fixed him in her gaze.

"Is it a parking company?"

Ted pursed his lips and shook his head, choking down another guffaw.

"Is it legal?"

This time he did laugh again. "Yeah, it's legal. I have signs up and everything." He rubbed his chin. "I'm sorry. I don't mean to be sarcastic. I thought we'd talk about our favourite movies and favourite bands and stuff."

It was Monica's turn to chuckle. "Yeah. The small talk portion of the evening."

Ted learned that she liked to work out at the gym, played mixed-league softball once a week with her cohorts from work, and had no idea that bridge was a card game. "But I could probably learn it. We did like to play hearts sometimes when I was growing up."

"Were you good at it?"

The bell tinkled during her shrug, before she had a chance to say anything in response. Ted stood up and offered her a hand. "Thank you. This has been nice."

She nodded, and surprised him with another question as he was stepping away. "So, who is your favourite band?"

Ted turned to look back at her. "Rolling Stones. Always been the Stones."

* * * *

He stepped forward nervously when one of Belinda's assistants called his number at her table alongside the bar afterward.

The woman glanced at his feet, and then his face. She held a sheet of paper in her hand.

"Here's a list of the ladies who say they'd be interested in having a call from you." She didn't hand it to him immediately.

What's wrong? "How many?" He gulped, worried the answer might be embarrassing.

"All of them." The young woman sniffed. "You wearing some new cologne I haven't heard of, or something?"

Ted took the paper. *Jesus! What would Alice think?* He tried to force the question out of his mind.

* * * *

Dinner dates with Cindy and Laura were pleasant enough. One of them actually invited him in for a nightcap afterward but the evening ended disastrously when she kicked him out of her bed for uttering the wrong name at the penultimate moment.

He called Monica two weeks after the faux pas.

"Ted! Jeez, I was starting to wonder if I wasn't going to hear from you."

"Yeah, I'm sorry. I..." *What the hell do you say that doesn't sound like boasting?*

"I get it. I wasn't number one on your list, right?"

Ted didn't answer.

"It's okay. I know how these things go."

"I didn't want to call a bunch of girls at the same time." Ted mumbled his explanation. "I'm actually new at this. I didn't think it would be fair to..."

"That's really sweet."

Awkward pause.

"So, I thought maybe we could go out for dinner or something on Friday?"

"That won't work. I actually have another date."

"Oh."

"But what about tonight?"

"Tonight?"

"It's our store's ball night. You could watch the game, and join us for drinks afterwards. Bring a glove, just in case some of our players don't show up."

Ted didn't play that night, but watched the game from the rickety bleachers. Monica sat beside him while her team was batting. There were no dug-outs at the public school playing field.

"So, how come you're new at this?" She spoke to him with her eyes on the field. "Way to go, Billy! Hustle!"

Ted joined her in applauding the base hit. She turned to look at him.

"I was actually married, for just about eight years."

"Was?"

"Yeah. We were separated for two, and then we got divorced a year ago."

"Ah. Kids?"

"Two. A boy and a girl."

"And they live with your ex?"

"Yeah, I see them as often..."

"Oops," Monica interrupted as the batter popped out. "I've got to get up. I'm on deck." She put a hand on Ted's arm. "We'll finish this later, okay?"

Monica stepped to the plate after her teammate stroked a single to right field. Ted watched the defence make its usual beer-league adjustments – fielders move in when a woman's at the plate. He bet himself it would be a mistake this time, and nodded in satisfaction when he was proved correct. Monica cranked a flyball over center field's head for a three-run home run. There were high fives and hugs around home plate, and then the team was back out on the field before Ted had a chance to congratulate her. But he smiled and waved from his seat in the stands.

"You're a hell of a ball player," he told her later, in the bar.

"I guess." She shrugged with what seemed unusual modesty. "Sometimes I surprise the guys." She chuckled. "Sometimes I think I intimidate men!"

Probably why you haven't found Mr. Right, Ted thought. But he decided to leave the personal questions for a less public setting. He knocked back the last of his beer.

"Well, I should get going. This was fun. Do you think maybe we could get together next week sometime, for dinner?"

"I'm not doing anything on Saturday."

Ted shrugged. "Do you want to give me your address? Or should we meet someplace?"

She seemed to study him carefully. "I suppose you could come by and pick me up."

It was a little after nine when he got in the car, too early to go home on an adrenaline-charged evening. The local blackjack table beckoned.

* * * *

"Wow!" It was a sincere reaction, when Monica met him at the front door of her apartment building Saturday night. She wore a hip-hugging short black dress, with a stylish sweater on top, a completely different look than the ball shirt and track pants four nights before.

She smiled and did a quick spin for him on the sidewalk. "Just in case you decide to take me dancing later."

"It's not in my usual bag of tricks, but it could be fun."

"You and your wife didn't go out dancing?"

"No. Not much."

She waited until she was seated in the car. "You don't want to talk about her?"

"It's not that. I just didn't think you'd want..."

"You know a lot of guys can't shut up about their exes. They're either still in love with them or they've got a hate-on for women that makes you wonder why they're dating anybody." Monica's hands were moving almost as fast as her mouth. "I guess they're just looking for an easy roll in the hay."

Ted tried to dismiss the memories of Alice "in the hay."

"So, why'd you get divorced? Did she have an affair?"

"No. She wouldn't do that."

"Did you?"

"No." *God, she is direct.* "It was just – what do they call it? – irreconcilable differences."

"But you still see her from time to time? You must, if you visit your kids."

"Yeah. Supposedly once a week, but it doesn't always work out. What about you? You've always been single?"

His attempt to change the subject wasn't immediately successful. "You know," she said, "the shrink on the radio says you have to wait at least six months before you introduce me to them."

"Yeah, I think I've heard that too," he mumbled. Monica was quiet for all of about fifteen seconds, allowing Ted to concentrate on his driving.

"Yes," she said, suddenly.

"Yes, what?"

"Yes, I've always been single. Well, legally, anyway. Did live with a guy for a few months when I was young and stupid. Thank God I didn't marry him! When he wasn't toking up he was playing video games twenty-five hours a day. Usually both. You know, he..."

"So, what do you do now?" Ted felt justified interrupting her. "Your ball team looked like a hardware store?"

"Yeah. I'm a cashier, mostly, but I do have to help customers sometimes. Some people are so helpless you wouldn't believe it. Took me the longest time to get it straight in my head what a ratchet wrench is. Thank Christ for metric sizes. All the old guys still bitch about it – they'd rather talk about three eighths and five sixteenths and Christ knows what else. We were lucky to grow up after all that nonsense. You know, somebody complained to me the other day that another customer dinged his door in the parking lot. Like there was something I could do about it!"

Ted nodded, unsure what he was agreeing with.

* * * *

Nothing was quite perfect at dinner. The ice chips in the water glass made it difficult to drink from it and the refrigerated butter was too hard to spread on the potato. Ted might have lived happily ever after, oblivious to such common failings, but he thanked her, under his breath, for drawing them to his attention.

The music at the techno dance club was God-awful but served one purpose. Monica didn't try to talk over it. There was no denying she looked fabulous on the floor, bumping and stepping in time with the beat, and it felt magnificent when she'd grind against him. Then she'd be off again, writhing in the middle of a crowd of people, none of whom seemed to have any idea who was dancing with whom.

Ted didn't think he'd ever felt so old.

* * * *

He pulled up in front of Monica's apartment building at almost two o'clock in the morning, too tired to accept an invitation inside had it been forthcoming. She leaned across the console between the seats to give him a peck on the cheek, offered a spritely "Thank you! Call me, eh?" and popped the door open without waiting for him to be gentlemanly about it. Ted hadn't thought that far ahead.

He drove home with the window open to the elements in order not to fall asleep at the wheel, and fell into bed thinking about the good night kiss after his first date with Alice. It was that memory that compelled him to call Monica again a few days later. *Have to do something!*

He didn't take offence when she giggled at him.

"It took you that long to recover?"

"It was a pretty long day," he mumbled. "I'm sorry I kind of faded."

"Not to worry."

Short awkward pause.

"What if we try to do something earlier next time?" she suggested.

"Like in the daytime? We could go walk around Stanley Park or something."

"I was thinking maybe the racetrack," she said. "Saturday afternoon."

Ding-ding-ding. "You like to go to the races?"

"Yeah. Usually with a bunch of girls, but I don't have to hang out with them."

Ted put in a call to the ex to switch his date with the kids for that weekend. He was careful not to snarl at the receptionist who picked up the call. "Is Alice Holman in please?"

Alice's tone was cool. "You're not going to see them on Saturday?"

"Something's come up. I thought Sunday instead."

There was no mistaking the aggravation in her voice. "That's going to be complicated. Robbie's started soccer – his first game's on Sunday."

"That's perfect! I could take him to that."

"That won't work, Ted."

Awkward pause.

"Brian's taking him. He has to. He's the coach."

Fuck! She knows she can't do that! I don't wanna have to get Aaron involved in this.

"I suppose you could take Emily for a few hours, so I can go watch the game without worrying about her."

Ted glanced up as one of his front counter kids tapped on the door. It was in that split second, when he didn't click off, that he heard Alice's post-script.

"Can you make it to Robbie's parent-teacher conference Monday night? I've got a late meeting at work. Brian says he can go but I think you should take an interest."

"I'll do it." He made no effort to disguise the edge in his voice.

* * * *

Saturday dawned cloudy and cool, but with no rain in the forecast it looked to be a perfect day for horse racing. Ted bet fifty dollars on the favourite in the first race and doubled his money. Monica was looking ahead to the fourth race.

"My mother knows the guy that owns Yellowknife. Says he's really fast if he can get a good start. Hasn't won a lot of races but they're trying a different jockey today."

"Yellowknife? That's an unusual name."

Monica shrugged. "Why don't we get some lunch while we wait for his race?"

They were seated in the clubhouse when the windows closed to betting on the second race. *Just as well,* Ted thought. *Might have got that one wrong.* His date's advice was the closest thing to inside information he'd ever had about a horse race and seemed better than a random guess.

Monica was more interested in digging out personal details. "I think it's time you told me what business you're in."

He set his drink on the table and looked her in the eye. "I rent videos. You know – movies..."

Uncertainty flickered on her face for just a split second. "Cronkite? You're the Cronkite at Cronkite Video?"

Ted nodded. "You know us, then?"

"Well, yes, although..." She trailed off.

He took a sip of his drink and looked at her curiously.

"I usually rent from Blockbuster."

"Oh, well." Ted shrugged. "C'est la vie."

"They let me pay with my credit card. Can I do that at your place?"

"Oh, yeah. Same rules, same prices, same selection. Pretty much the same everything. We just hope people will prefer to boy local."

"Yeah – I've heard the ads."

Monica wagered twenty dollars on the feature race, and stood aside as Ted approached the window. "A thousand dollars on the five horse."

"A thou....!?"

"I'm counting on you."

"Yeah, but..."

Ted smiled to himself. *Glad I can actually surprise her!*

Yellowknife went off at eight to one. *A nice win if it happens.* Ted was far more confident than he should have been. The gambler's ebullience had his head in the clouds.

They stood at the rail to watch the start of the race, to hear the thundering of hooves on the way to victory. Monica squeezed his hand in anticipation. Ted imagined himself lifting her off her feet and swinging her around in celebration. The grandstand behind them was abuzz.

"And they're off!" The uniquely nasal, high-pitched voice of the track announcer blared through the loudspeakers.

At the clubhouse turn it was Dark Knight, Giza Point, and on down the line to Yellowknife, bringing up the rear.

Shit. Ted clapped his hands without knowing why. Monica was still screaming encouragement. "Go Yellowknife!" She jumped up and down in excitement as the horse found its stride on the back stretch.

"Giza Point by a nose, Dark Knight is fading on the outside, Thundercloud, and Yellowknife is moving up on the inside ..."

Ted forgot for an instant who was beside him, and reached over to squeeze her backside. Monica glared at him. "Sorry," he mumbled.

By the time they both turned their attention back to the race their horse was running third but losing ground to the leaders. The cheering and screaming around them swelled as Thundercloud and Giza Point battled on the home stretch. Yellowknife held on to a comfortable third.

Ted ceremoniously tore his ticket into eight pieces and scattered them in the breeze.

"I guess I've got to go collect a few bucks," said Monica. She didn't say anything about Ted's indiscretion. He looked at her in surprise.

"I bet him to win, place, or show." She looked away from him, at the horse prancing toward the winner's circle. "You know, you could have done the same thing. For a thousand dollars – at least you'd get most of your money back."

Ted tried to force a smile. "Yeah. I suppose. But go big or go home, right?"

Monica frowned as she turned to lead him up the stairs to the pari-mutuel windows.

Chapter twenty-six Ms. Cheevers

Robbie pointed down the hall to his fifth grade classroom before he ducked into a restroom. "I'll catch up with you."

A blonde woman seated at the teachers' desk looked up as Ted entered the room.

"Can I help you?" There was a hint of impatience in her demeanour.

"I'm Ted Cronkite. I have an appointment to talk about Robbie?" Ted glanced at his watch.

"Mr. Cronkite?" The woman appeared confused.

"Are you Ms. Cheevers?"

"Yes."

"And Robbie's in your class? I am at the right place?"

"Yes, but..." She stood to give him her full attention. "I was expecting to see Robbie's mother and father."

"His mother can't make it tonight. I'm his father."

"But..." The teacher seemed to be scrambling for an excuse. "I'm sorry. I thought I knew his dad. Robbie's on the same soccer team with my son, and I've seen him come to practice with Brian."

Ted was in no mood to forgive the misunderstanding. "Brian's my wife's second husband." He refused to utter the word 'stepfather.'

"Oh." Robbie entered the room. "Hi, Robbie!" She tried to use the boy as a diversion from the awkwardness.

Ted wasn't having it. "Has he claimed something other than that?"

"No. Yes. No. I don't know whether he's actually said anything." She pushed her hands down the sides of her jacket, trying not to look flustered. "He acts like he's Robbie's dad, and I guess I just assumed..."

There's going to have to be a chat with Mr. fucking wonderful!

Cheevers assumed an air of importance, picking up some papers from her desk.

"Robbie's grades are fine, Mr. Cronkite. All his marks are above average. He's particularly strong in reading and writing." She handed Ted a list of test scores. "All these quiz scores are out of twenty." Ted couldn't help conjuring up a picture of a blackjack table, looking at the column of nineteens and twenties. He tilted the page so Robbie could see it.

"What happened here?" He pointed to a lone twelve. The teacher frowned as though biting her tongue.

"I didn't know all the different kinds of words."

"Do you know them now?" asked Ted.

"Yup."

"Good!" Ted noticed the look of relief on the teacher's face. "That's what tests are for, right? Just a check-up, nothing to be scared of."

The boy shrugged.

Ted turned his attention to Ms. Cheevers again. "So, he's doing fine, then? What about friends? Does he get along with everybody in the class?"

"That's where we do have a bit of an issue."

Ted glanced at his son before he focused again on the teacher.

"There was the tobacco episode."

"The what?"

"Your wi – his mother didn't tell you? They were certainly notified."

Ted shook his head.

"There was a group of boys caught smoking on school grounds. Not in the school, but on the property. None of them would own up to bringing cigarettes or tell us where they got them from and we could never prove anything, but we had to suspend them all for a day." Her voice took on a stern tone, as though she was speaking for the boy's benefit. "There've been some accusations against some of the boys – stealing lunches and that sort of thing. Not Robbie specifically, but we're watching all of them. We'd rather that group didn't hang out together."

Ted studied his son's face, impassive, not cowed in the least by the warning.

"I'll have a talk with him." He couldn't think of anything else to say.

"Good." Cheevers nodded. "And Mr. Cronkite? I'm sorry about the misunderstanding." She waved vaguely at a stack of file folders on her desk. "I should have known about you and Robbie's mother."

"Her name is Holman."

* * * *

Ted armed himself with his copy of the Separation Agreement before driving the twenty-three blocks to the ex's house Saturday morning. He couldn't recall having decided to count them; maybe he was asleep when he did it? Four traffic lights en route, three of them red, as always. *Figures.* Anything to keep his mind off the pending confrontation. He'd rehearsed it often enough over the past week. *No point sweating it. Maybe they'll be half-assed reasonable.*

Brian's truck was backed crookedly into the driveway, and the tailgate was open – hints that Ted should listen for the sound of power tools inside. The noise seemed to be coming from the basement. He remembered the arguments he'd had with Alice about how to finish it. It remained one of his regrets that they'd never sorted it out, *but we would have. Every marriage has disagreements – some of them matter more than others.* Obviously there'd have to be a plumbing element – *you need a bathroom on both floors.* Ted had thought they might as well tie it in with a wet bar in the rec room; Alice couldn't see the point. *I hope Dickhead doesn't fuck it up. Or, on second thought, maybe I'd rather he does.*

Alice pulled the door open. "You're early. They're just finishing breakfast." She seemed flustered. "You can wait in the car. I'll tell them you're here, they'll come out when they're ready."

"Actually, I have to see Brian for a minute."

Alice frowned.

"You might as well come outside too." *Better if the kids don't hear this.*

She hesitated, studying his face. "All right." She turned and waited for a pause in the sawing. "Bri-an," she sang. "Can you come up here, Luv?"

"What!? Right now?" The voice that drifted up the stairwell didn't sound happy.

"Yes, Luv. Right now."

Ted pushed a pair of fingers into his throat, mocking a gag reflex.

"What's going on?" Brian was brushing sawdust off his clothes as he reached the top of the stairs. His right hand balled into a fist when he caught sight of Ted standing in the doorway.

Ted felt his muscles tense. *Stay calm*, he ordered himself. *Don't back down to this guy.*

"You called this meeting, Ted," said Alice. "What's going on?"

He decided to answer her, put Brian in third person. "I want to know why Robbie's school teacher thinks he's his father."

Brian's laugh morphed into a sneer. Alice tried to keep the peace. "I'm sure you must have misunderstood, Ted. She wouldn't..."

"She was pretty sure."

Brian raised a hand, shushing his wife. "Where the hell would she get that idea?"

"You tell me," said Ted.

"I have no idea."

Ted had a flashback to a poker game, years ago, in a sleazy east end gambling joint, the only time in his life he'd seen a smile as phony. "What are you telling the parents on your soccer team?"

"I tell them that I'm coaching their kids." Brian scowled. "Something that you never bothered to do."

Stay calm.

"That's your issue, Ted? That Brian's coaching Robbie's soccer team?" Alice stepped forward, placing herself between the two men.

He shifted his focus to her. "I think you know there's more to it than that."

"Like what?" Brian took a step forward.

"Like you have no standing here!"

"Ooh – big man..."

"Shut up, Brian!" Alice turned to face her husband. "Ted is the kids' father. One day a week."

"I'm always their father!" he barked. "The fact I only see them once a week was to keep you happy. Not this guy."

"What do you want me to do, Ted? Withdraw Robbie from soccer? He shouldn't have a life because he doesn't know when you're going to show up and when you're not?"

The boy appeared in the background, obviously listening.

"No," muttered Ted. "He should play some sports. I just don't want there to be any more misunderstandings." He looked pointedly at Brian. "Any."

Brian shuffled half a step closer.

"All right," said Alice. "I'm sure it's all an innocent misunderstanding. From now on Brian will be sure to tell anybody who needs to know that he's the stepfather." She glanced at Robbie. "Come on kids – get your shoes on. Your dad's ready to go."

* * * *

Ted leaped to his feet along with the rest of the Canadians in the bar, at the sound of Joe Carter's bat on the ball. It was a satisfying crack, the kind that leaves no doubt the baseball is not coming back. Ted's cheers were the stuff of pure joy, for the Blue Jays' second World

Series victory. He wasn't thinking about the wager as he danced around his chair, exchanging hugs with random strangers – men and women alike.

. In fact the historic win for the maple leaf produced a comparatively small profit for Ted. The 1993 Blue Jays were a team of destiny, with a line-up stronger than the one that had won it all the year before, and the Vegas oddsmakers knew it. The march to the title had been more antiseptic than thrilling. Even so, Ted knew the stadium in Toronto would be sold out, and Les Vegas seemed the second most exciting place to be part of the action.

The only thing that could have made it better would have been a main squeeze to share the moment with him. With nothing happening on that front for more than six months, he'd called Bobby – first time the brothers had spoken in years.

"Las Vegas?" said Bobby. "I dunno..."

"Have you ever been there?"

"No."

Ted could hear his sister-in-law in the background. "Somebody wants you to go to Las Vegas?"

Bobby didn't cover the mouthpiece before he answered her. "It's Ted."

"Ted! Your brother Ted? Tell him you're working, or something. You're not actually thinking of going!?"

Ted wasn't sure if it was his name or the mention of the gambling mecca that got Lexi's back up. Nor could he be sure whether his brother might have joined him had he not been forbidden.

The party started on the airplane. Ted purchased his ticket rather than asking one of the casinos to approve a junket. *Probably turn out cheaper this way*, given that he had every intention of consuming a considerable quantity of alcohol. One man smuggled a bottle on board in his carry-on luggage, markedly reducing the wait time between drinks. All the chatter seemed to be about baseball rather than blackjack. Somewhere over the mountains Ted was on a first name basis with more than a dozen of his fellow passengers. Unfortunately, none of them was a single female.

"You've been down before?" somebody asked him.

"Oh, yeah. Couple of times." Ted knelt in his seat, chatting over the headrest with the fellows behind him.

"So," the guy said, "Are the women as easy as I hear?"

Heads turned to look at the source of a thump and rattling noise – one of the happy travelers had crashed into a service cart in the aisle.

"Sorry," the man muttered, stepping on somebody's foot as he tried to squirrel himself into a row of seats, out of the flight attendant's path.

"It's Dale," Ted observed. "And the stewardess doesn't look happy."

"Wonder if they're going to cut him off?" Howie chortled. "You were saying?"

"Oh, yeah. I don't know what you hear." Ted chuckled. "But you don't have to go looking very far."

Howie guffawed, spilling some of his drink. "Oops. Don't tell my wife that!"

A woman seated across the aisle glanced at her husband and frowned. The husband stared straight ahead, expressionless.

The excursion was a saw-off, financially. By the time Ted collected his winnings he'd already spent them on air fare, a round of drinks for the house, and his personal entertainment, including limo rides to and from Glitter Gulch. In scenes reminiscent of who knows how many Hollywood movies, he'd stood with new-found friends through the car's sunroof, screaming and waving Blue Jays colours. *What the hell? Nobody down here knows that we're supposed to hate Toronto!*

Chapter twenty-seven Blockbuster

Saturday, January eighth, 1994, a little after eleven p.m. First day of the year that it didn't rain.

"Which house?" asked the cabbie.

"Huh?" Ted was lost in thought, unable to believe Pete had been so dismissive. *Alice'll get it. I know she will, even if nobody else does.*

Addresses were invisible in the suburban darkness, not that that was an issue for Ted. *Guy probably thinks he's driving me home.*

"Right 'ere!" he declared. "Juss pull over – no need to go in the driveway."

He handed the driver a twenty for a nine dollar fare, told him to keep the change, and staggered slightly as he stepped out of the car. He fumbled in his overcoat pocket for a half empty bottle of rye, stood on the sidewalk watching the taillights vanish around the corner, and contemplated the stillness for another moment before weaving up the sidewalk to Alice's front porch. *Correction – Alice and Dickhead's.*

He didn't count the times he rang the bell before he gave up and banged on the door. The light flicked on over his head and he was sure he detected angry whispers on the other side of the door, followed by a moment's silence, before Alice threw it open.

"For Christ's sake, Ted! You'll wake the kids up."

"Hi tuh you too."

"What the hell are you doing here, Ted?"

He weaved and stared stupidly. Alice grabbed his lapel to rescue him from falling backward down the stairs. She glanced up and down the street for his car, a pointless exercise in the blackness.

"You'd better come inside. You're in no condition to drive anyway."

Ted took a pull of whiskey before he stepped across the threshold. Alice tugged her housecoat tighter around herself and eyed the bottle.

"You've been drinking."

"No shit, Sherlock." He reconsidered. "Mrs. Holmes." He laughed, too loudly. "No shit Mrs. Holmes! Ishat your name now?"

"If that's what you're here to go on about – do you want me to call Brian and have him throw you out on your ass?" She steered him to a chair in the living room. "What's going on, Ted? You can't just come barging in here whenever you want."

"I juss came tuh see if you heard the news."

"What? What's so important? Did somebody die?"

He looked up, squinting against the light. "Who died?"

"Nobody," snapped Alice. She took a step back, glaring at him. "Just tell me your news."

Ted took another generous gulp of rye. "Blockbuster sold out."

Alice's eyebrows went up. "You mean...?"

Ted spread his arms theatrically. "Eight point four billion dollars!" He tried to stand, but fell back into the chair. "U.S.! Eight point fucking four fucking *billion* dollars!" He peered into his bottle. "I thought I'd celebrate uh little."

"Jesus H. Christ," Alice muttered.

"Eight point four – not uh penny more!" His singing was hopelessly off key, but enthusiastic.

Alice stared at him.

"I shoulda bought shares. I never shoulda bothered working. I shoulda juss waited fer these guys 'n' bought shares." He shook his head.

"You couldn't possibly have known, Ted."

"Couldn' I?"

"Daddy?" There was another voice, from the hall.

"Go back to bed, Emily," said Alice.

"Wait uh minute." Ted struggled to his feet. "Come give Daddy uh hug." He reached for her. "You're turning intuh quite the little lady." He staggered but was careful not to spill any booze on her. "You know you coulda bin rish? All the diamon's in the world!"

The child looked confused. "Akshilly, I think you're more uhn em'rald girl."

"All right, Ted."

"Are you going to stay here, Daddy?"

"I dunno, sweetheart. I don' think so."

"Yes," said Alice, firmly. "Just for tonight. Go back to bed, Emily. You can visit Daddy in the morning."

"Come on, Ted. You can sleep on the couch downstairs." She tried to take the bottle away from him.

He pulled his arm back, playing a game of keepaway. "Where's Brian? Maybe he wants tuh have uh drink with me."

"I don't think so, Ted." He allowed her to strip him of his overcoat and watched it fall to the floor.

"Eight point four – not uh penny more. Eight point four – don'cha dare be sore!"

The Boss could sing it better. I'll have to send him an email. He let himself be led downstairs, and passed out with the rhyme repeating in his head.

* * * *

Alice met him at the top of the stairs eight hours later. "Since you're here you might as well stay until the kids are ready to go."

She added a mild edge to her voice, signaling acquiescence to practicality more than a sincere invitation.

Ted nodded.

"This is a one-time thing, right? You can't get in the habit of showing up here in the middle of the night. Brian's not going to tolerate it again." He'd made his feelings about Ted's presence crystal clear last night in bed. "And neither am I." Alice spoke just loudly enough to be sure she'd be heard in the kitchen, sharply enough, she hoped, to pacify an angry husband.

Her ex nodded again, and she studied him sympathetically. "You look like hell." He was unshaved, uncombed, and his clothes were rumpled. "Whaddaya think you need first? Coffee or Tylenol?" She knew she was dancing in a minefield when she said it.

"Coffee'd be great, thanks." Ted followed her into the kitchen. Brian didn't look up from his newspaper. The headline "Blockbuster Sale" was visible on the back of the page he was reading.

"Are the kids up?"

"Yes. But I don't think they're dressed yet." She watched her husband as she poured Ted's coffee, wary of the signs of a pending eruption. She'd seen it before – the tensing of the shoulders, the way his fingers would curl into his palms and then release, over and over again. Alice flashed him her "Don't say a fucking word" look.

She glanced into the hallway. "Robbie! Emily! Come on – it's time to get moving! Your dad's here."

She handed Ted his coffee. "Why don't you wait for them in the living room?"

Emily appeared first, running to Ted for a hug, clutching a Barbie doll in her hand. "Can you help me with this, Daddy?"

Ted fiddled with the gown, that always seemed at least one size too tight even for the impossibly skinny figurine. Emily beamed with delight when he handed the doll back to her, fully clothed.

"Look, Mommy!" She ran to the kitchen.

Alice turned away from her pans of hashbrowns and bacon on the stove, smiling and nodding to her daughter.

Robbie sauntered into the kitchen.

"Hey, Buddy!" said Ted. He'd got up from his chair and was standing behind the boy. "How 'bout we go out for breakfast this morning? Then maybe we can go shopping for a birthday present."

Robbie looked to his mother for a nod of approval. "I think that's a good idea," she said.

Ted pulled a cell phone from his pocket. "I've got to call a cab. I'll tell them to get here as quick as they can."

"Where's your car?" asked Alice.

Ted seemed to think about it for a moment. "Pete's place."

Shit. She frowned. "You don't have to go in, right?"

"Maybe just to say hi." Ted completed his call and turned his attention back to the kids. "Where do you guys think you want to eat?"

"McDonald's!" Emily bubbled. Robbie shrugged.

Alice switched off the stove and went to supervise the donning of coats and boots. Brian folded his paper, looking as though he was ready to spit bullets, but he waited until Ted and the kids were on their way out the door before he said anything. "When do you plan to have them back?"

Ted didn't answer him directly, although his expression telegraphed what he must have been thinking. Something along the lines of *When we're fucking good and ready, pal!*

Alice hugged the kids and turned to Ted. Her arm must have had a mind of its own; she couldn't help running her fingers through his hair. His crop didn't look any better for it but his half smile was an improvement. "Call me later, okay? Let me know what you're doing today."

"Okay. Sure."

She closed the door behind them and turned to face the inevitable cross-examination.

"How the hell did you ever marry that loser?"

Chapter twenty-eight Emily

A Clark County Sheriff's Deputy found Ted at the baccarat table at the MGM Grand.

"Mr. Cronkite? Ted Cronkite?"

"Yes."

"Could we speak privately, please?"

Ted got up, surprised.

"I think you'll want to bring your chips." The unflappable table staff didn't pester him about his outstanding commission. There was plenty enough in his cashier's account to cover it.

"What's going on?"

"I think we should go to your room, sir." The cop's face was grim.

Ted's sense of foreboding mounted aboard the elevator but he couldn't speak, for want of privacy.

"All right," he said, as he unlocked his door. "What's this about? Am I in some kind of trouble?"

"No, sir. Please sit, Mr. Cronkite." The deputy cleared his throat. "I'm sorry sir. I've been sent to relay some very bad news."

Ted's body tensed more than it already was.

"We've been asked by the RCMP in Coquitlam to inform you your daughter – Emily Cronkite - has been in an accident. She didn't survive."

"What!?" Ted slumped in the chair, his face in his hands, the room spinning around him. "That can't be! She's only ten years old!"

Emily! Who loves running and swimming and Barbie dolls.

"That has to be a mistake!" The words came breathlessly, as though he'd been punched in the gut.

"I'm afraid it's not a mistake, sir. I'm very sorry."

Beautiful little Emily! Whose smile is even brighter than her mother's!

"What happened? What kind of accident?"

"Some sort of traffic accident. A Mr. Holman was driving. Her stepfather, I gather."

"Stepfather!? I hate that fucking word!"

"I'm sorry, sir."

"I knew that fucking guy was no good!" Ted forced himself to look at the officer.

"What happened?"

"I don't know, sir. That's all we've been asked to pass along."

"What about Robbie? Her brother?"

"I have no information, sir. I'm sure they would have told us if anyone else was involved."

The deputy waited for Ted to compose himself. "I presume you'll want to go home immediately? I'll drive you to the airport if you like."

Ted nodded, numbly.

The uniform helped expedite his check-out. There wasn't a lot to say in the car.

"When did this happen? "

"Today, sir. About three hours ago. I'm very sorry for your loss, sir." The officer didn't take his eyes off the road.

Why the fuck wasn't I there? Why was that moron driving her anywhere?

He thought about the day Emily was born, how happy Alice was to learn she was the mother of a little girl. They'd told each other a hundred times the sex wouldn't matter, "so long as it's healthy." Ted had meant it, and never held Alice's little white lie against her. Her joy at having the perfect family had trumped all else, for a time. *Healthy! Why the fuck couldn't she have been home with the measles or something today?* He remembered the first time he'd held her, tiny and helpless in his arms. *Fuck! It must be even worse for Alice.*

The lead weight in his gut was as real as the one pressing on his chest. The cop frowned but didn't protest when Ted released his seat belt so he could breathe. Memories cascaded through his mind, jumbled together into a single deluge that seemed hell bent on drowning his very soul. Bird-watching in the park down the street – the four of them together, Alice trying not to laugh at Emily flapping her three-year-old arms, not understanding why she couldn't fly. The time some self-righteous woman gave him a dirty look in the family change room after one of Emily's swim lessons – as though a dad wasn't supposed to be there. The way Emily tried so hard to stem the tears when she couldn't get the hang of riding a two-wheeler, and the euphoria when she finally mastered it. The first time she sang at a school Christmas pageant, Alice seated beside him in the audience, giving rise to fleeting hope the children might yet bring the parents together again. He recalled the day he'd probed, as mildly as he knew how, Emily's belief in Santa Claus. "Oh, no, Daddy," she'd said. "I know he's not real. Mommy and Brian already told me." *Fuck!* The innocently earnest look on her face when she told him, "You know the Easter Bunny and the Tooth Fairy aren't real either, right Daddy?"

"I guess you found me through the company?" He fought to maintain his stoicism. "My ex doesn't know I'm down here."

"I don't know, sir. The RCMP instructed us where to look for you."

There was no problem transferring Ted's ticket to another airline, with space aboard a flight departing immediately. He barely heard the clerk's explanation that there would have to be a stop in Seattle, and her whah-whah'ing some instructions about finding the correct gate at Sea-Tac for the second leg of his trip.

He phoned Alice during the layover, praying she would have no idea what he was talking about. He steeled himself for the torrent of abuse that would no doubt be her reaction to his shocking her needlessly with his nightmare.

"I don't know how it happened," she blubbered. "The car was broadsided. They say Emily died instantly. She probably didn't see it coming."

Ted felt his knees turning to rubber. "I'll land in less than three hours. Where do you want me to go?"

"Come to Mom and Dad's house." He could hear her crying. "You probably have to take Robbie. Mom's taking me back to the hospital."

"Brian?"

"His leg was pretty smashed up. I have to be there when he comes out of surgery."

Like I give a shit? At least I don't have to look at him today. I'd probably fuckin' kill him!

His next call was to Penticton.

"Mom, are you sitting down? I've got some really bad news. Emily's..."

He froze, unable to utter the words that would make it real, the words that would force him to come to terms with the fact he would never see his little princess again.

"Emily's what? Ted?"

He held the receiver away from his ear and wiped his eyes.

"What's happened? Ted!?"

"She's dead, Mom." He closed his eyes and pictured his mother dropping the phone and clutching her heart.

"How? What?"

"A car accident. I don't know very much about it. I've been out of town, I'm just on my way back now."

"Is Robbie all right? Alice?"

"Neither of them was there, thank God."

She can put two and two together. Don't ask me the obvious.

* * * *

Connie's face was cold when she answered the door. She waved Ted into the house without a word.

He could see his ex father-in-law rise from his seat in the background. He'd gone gray since Ted last saw him, and his face was drawn. He looked ten years older.

Go ahead! Say it! Where the hell were you?

"Ted."

"Bob."

Bob stood in front of him, put his hands on Ted's shoulders.

"I'm sorry, Ted. I'm so sorry."

It was the first time in eight hours Ted allowed himself to cry. He fell into a chair with his face in his hands. He looked at Bob, and watched Connie set a coffee on the table in front of him.

"Or would you rather have a drink?"

Ted shook his head helplessly. He tried to speak, but the words wouldn't come. Bob sat down again, beside Connie on the couch.

Breathe, Ted commanded himself. *Be strong.* "Does anybody know what happened?" His voice cracked. "I take it he was driving her to school?"

"Actually, no. It was a school field trip. Brian was a chaperone." Bob hesitated. "There was another girl killed too."

What?

"I guess a truck hit them in the intersection. The entire passenger side of the car was destroyed. They say neither girl suffered."

Like that's supposed to make me feel better.

* * * *

Brian had an easy excuse for not attending the funeral. He was immobilized in the hospital. Ted counted it a blessing. *Christ only knows what I might have done if he showed up here.* He could only guess at Alice's thoughts on the matter. He didn't need to be psychic to know everybody was avoiding any mention of the name.

Ted sat in the front pew, to Alice's left, with her father, mother, and Robbie to her right. She didn't squirm free when Ted put his arm around her, weeping into his shoulder throughout the service.

The Cronkite family was in the second pew, along with Connie and Dean and their kids. Lily and Frank and a handful of other friends and acquaintances from the bridge club were near the front. A significant number of Emily's classmates attended, most of them escorted by one or both parents, interspersed with several of Ted's employees and Alice's co-workers from the bank.

Pete and Marie chose seats in the back.

An open casket was not an option.

Chapter twenty-nine Robbie

For Brian, it wasn't so much that his wife rebuffed his advances. It was that she did it with her *fist*.

He was laid up at home for weeks after being released from the hospital. In point of fact, the cracked ribs were more painful than the shattered leg, but either way he wasn't going anywhere. Slinging tools and scrambling up and down ladders were out of the question.

For the first week, Alice brought him meals in front of the television.

"Thanks, Babe." He massaged her backside as she turned, and she swatted his hand away.

"Don't fucking touch me!"

"I'm sorry." *How many times do I have to say it?* "I know you're mad."

She glowered at him. "Mad!? You know I'm 'mad?'"

"What do you want me to say?"

"There's nothing you can say. 'Mad' doesn't begin to cover it."

Robbie stared coldly.

Brian wheezed. "I know. I should have seen that the truck wasn't going to stop." He winced as he shifted his good leg. "How about you bring me a glass of water, son?"

"I'm not your son! And I never will be!" Robbie stormed out of the house.

Alice recoiled as the door slammed behind him, and turned to the kitchen. She supported herself with both hands on the counter for a moment before she reached into a cupboard for a water glass.

Brian watched her carry it into the living room, looking for all the world as though she wanted to throw it on him. Instead, she set it on the table and stood over him, chewing her lip.

At least she's not bawling her eyes out. I guess we're past that part. "I want to make this right between us. I know it's a tragedy. But we'll get through it together."

"Get *through* it!? Get through to what? She's not coming back!"

"I know." Brian set his plate aside, appetite gone. "I'm just sick about it. She was a wonderful kid."

"Don't call her a kid! She was a child. My daughter."

I don't know if I'm going to be able to fix this.

"I'm going back to work tomorrow. Homecare will send somebody to look in on you. Get lunch and help you get to the bathroom."

* * * *

Ted found Robbie sitting on the floor of the hallway, with his back to the door, when he stepped off the elevator in his building.

"Hey, Buddy!"

Robbie looked up through bloodshot eyes. "How come you're so late?"

"Work." Ted unlocked the door as the boy stood up. "How long have you been here?"

"I dunno."

"I'll have to get you a key," Ted promised. An afterthought. "How did you get in the building?"

"Somebody was just leaving."

"You hungry?" Ted dropped his mail on the kitchen counter, noticing there was something from the MGM. *Looks like it might be a cheque?*

"I guess so."

Ted pulled another pork chop out of the freezer. "Maybe the microwave will do a fast thaw on this." He began cutting salad vegetables into a bowl as the machine whirred. "Does your mom know you're here?"

Robbie shook his head.

"Do you want to phone her?"

"Can you?"

Ted opened his mouth to speak again, but he was interrupted by the ringing of the telephone.

"That might be her."

Robbie looked away.

"Ted. It's me." He recognized Alice's voice instantly. "Have you seen Robbie today?"

"Yeah, he's here. We're just going to have some supper."

"You couldn't have called to let me know?"

"I just got home five minutes ago, Alice. We were going to phone you."

There was no response to that.

"We'll see you later, all right?"

"All right." A pause. "Thank you."

Robbie was seated at a far corner of the table, fidgeting nervously, as Ted hung up the phone. He studied the boy curiously.

"Can I stay here tonight?"

"Sure. If it's okay with your mom."

"How come it has to be okay with her?"

Ted sighed. "Let's sit down." He led Robbie to the living room. "I guess we're overdue to have this talk." He paused, thinking about how to explain it to a thirteen year old. "When your mom and I – separated – we agreed that you and Emily would live with her. It never meant I loved you any less, but you needed to know that you had one home, that you could always rely on. Does that make sense?"

"Nobody asked me." Robbie sat on the edge of the couch, one knee bouncing anxiously.

"Robbie, you were seven years old. It was up to your mother and me to know what was best. And then later on, when we asked a judge about it, he said we were right."

"It's not best anymore," the boy mumbled. His leg ceased twitching. "I don't like Brian. Mom and him fight all the time."

Oh, boy. Am I cut out for this?

"They're just going through a really hard time right now."

"No – I mean even before the accident." The nervous twitch reappeared.

Ted stared in amazement as his son paused.

"He's always telling her what to do. She cries all the time. Sometimes it's about Emily, but I don't think it always is." Robbie twisted his hands together. "Sometimes he tries to tell me and Emily too."

What!

Ted spoke carefully. "When did this start?"

Robbie shrugged.

"Does he ever hit you? Or Mom?" *I'll fucking kill him.*

"I don't think so."

Ted's blood pressure dropped a notch.

He waited until he thought Robbie was asleep before he picked up the telephone.

"Alice. Ted. Robbie's in bed. He's going to spend the night here."

"I figured. Thank you." She spoke softly and seemed sincere.

"I'm gonna get him a key, so he can come any time."

The silence was deafening. Ted felt his pulse throb against the handset. "Alice? Is that all right?"

"Yeah."

"What's going on over there? Are you okay?"

"Yeah." Her voice was barely above a whisper.

"Are you sure? You don't sound very good."

"As good as I can be."

The telephone line transmitted her pain as clearly as if she'd been in the room beside him. "I know." Ted was overcome by a wave of helplessness, unable to fill the vacuum in his chest, the void that had been his constant companion for a month. "I wish it could have been me." *Please believe me when I say it.* "I wish I could trade places with her."

He straightened up the kitchen, loading dishes into the automatic washer, and turned his attention to the mail. Junk flyers and routine bills were tossed aside. He paused over a notice from the strata council before he tore open the envelope with the casino letterhead and studied the cheque - what he left behind when he departed Las Vegas abruptly. *Minus those chips I left in the room. Wonder if housekeeping's ever had a fifteen hundred dollar tip before?*

He dug in a drawer for a cigarette lighter. Time stood by with infinite patience while he held the paper over the sink. He jumped at the sound of gunfire and screeching tires from some cops and robbers drama on the forgotten television.

He flicked the lighter.

* * * *

Brian eventually admitted fault. There was little point denying it, given the number of witnesses who told police they'd seen him try to beat a light, entering the intersection more than a second after it switched red. He didn't contest the two hundred-fifty dollar fine and six demerit points for driving without due care and attention.

Ted was beside himself. A traffic cop reiterated the explanation patiently when he tried to argue the point.

"There's no evidence of any criminality. No alcohol, no drugs, no witnesses say there was anything unusual about his driving prior to the accident." The constable seemed to speak from the heart. "Believe me, Mr. Cronkite, we checked. That's why it's taken so long. Labs don't work as fast in real life as they do on TV."

"Nothing unusual about running a red light?" *You've got to be fucking kidding me!*

"People make mistakes. Sometimes they have tragic consequences. To meet a criminal standard we'd have to be able to show there'd been a pattern of behaviour."

What the fuck does that even mean?

Ted forced himself to speak calmly. "What the hell was his excuse? Did he say anything to you guys?"

"He said he was part of a convoy – he just followed the car in front of him without thinking. He didn't notice the light had switched."

"Un-fucking-believable," muttered Ted.

"I understand your anger, sir." The cop sighed. "We're all very sorry for your loss. But it is believable. It happens all too often." He pointed to a chart on the wall, where the Mounties kept track of 'the deadly dozen' intersections with the highest crash rates in their jurisdiction.

"I know it doesn't help, but it was an accident."

* * * *

The other family took the lead on the civil liability question, asking for a million dollars in punitive damages. The Insurance Corporation of BC offered ten thousand in its opening effort to make the case go away.

"I have to sue," Ted told his ex. "I know you can't, or won't. But this is ridiculous."

"Go for it!" she muttered. "Nail his hide to the wall."

Chapter thirty Napoli

The mid 1990's were a golden age in home entertainment.

Cronkite Video was reliably profitable, expanding regularly until 1997, when Ted faced an important decision – whether to open yet another store, or re-trench. Just about the time that it seemed every household had two video cassette recorders, Digital Video Disc players appeared on the scene.

I can't not keep up, he realized. *Question is, do we dump the old to bring in the new? Or do we have to make room for both?*

"What do you think, Alice? You going to throw your VCR in the garbage?"

She laughed.

God, it's nice to hear that again.

"Why on Earth would I?"

It was getting easier to be comfortable in Alice's company, notwithstanding the fact her surname remained an irritant. Ted knew enough not to rush her on that matter. It was enough, for the moment, to know there were times she seemed to need his counsel as much as he hers.

They hadn't planned to make love the first time they slept together following Brian's departure. Ted had been privy to some of the details – what Robbie had been able to tell him – about the way Brian and Alice had cohabitated as virtual strangers for the better part of three years. It was consistent with what little he gleaned from Lily. They made their peace at the bridge club, where they formed a semi-regular partnership that lasted for more than a year.

"Provided," said Lily, "You don't pester me about Alice. I'm not allowed to talk about her." Then she let something slip. "My matchmaking days are done. Forever."

It wasn't a complete shock when Alice herself revealed, as casually as if she was discussing the weather, that her husband had walked out, nor was it a particular surprise when Ted was invited to supper on a Saturday night.

Robbie stayed in that night to kick his dad's butt at chess, several times.

"How the hell did you get so good at this?" Ted's game relied entirely on wits, while Robbie demonstrated some of the conventional tactics that a conscientious student can learn.

The boy shrugged modestly. "Just playing in the school library, I guess."

"Maybe you ought to think about starting up a club?"

"Maybe." Robbie packed up the game pieces and stowed the box on a bookshelf. "G'night Dad. Thanks for the games."

Ted gazed through the front window, ruminating partly on Alice's reflection and partly on the darkness beyond. "There still aren't enough street lights in this block," he mused. "Wonder if they're ever going to do anything about it?"

She looked up from her book. "Mmm. I suppose I should talk to the neighbours about starting a petition. Squeaky wheel gets the grease."

Ted checked his watch. "I guess I'd better go – it is getting late."

Alice swung her legs off the couch and set her novel on an end table, with a bookmark placed carefully between the pages. "Do you have to?"

This time Ted was surprised. Stunned in fact. He glanced at the stairwell to the basement.

"I don't mean downstairs."

Ted was putty in her hands.

Alice sighed. "I don't know whether I want to do anything. I just want you to hold me." Not bedroom eyes, exactly, but the corners of her mouth curled into a coy smile. "All night."

"I did hear it might get chilly tonight." He wasn't sure she heard him correctly, through the frog in his throat.

She looked at him as though he was daft, and then laughed openly. "Give me a minute to get changed before you come to bed."

He closed the drapes, moved chairs and chess table back to their stand-by positions, and carried empty glasses to the dishwasher.

* * * *

The kitchen looked different in the morning light than he remembered, but the feeling was familiar and comfortable. There'd been new appliances and a dinette suite over the years, but the little things – the placement of the clock and the calendar on the wall, and the organization in the cupboards and drawers - were unchanged. He found a bag of ground coffee right where he expected it to be.

"Decaf?"

"Yeah. Brian always said caffeine made him edgy."

Blame it on whatever you can, pal.

"I just ran out of the real stuff. Would you prefer tea instead?"

"No, this'll do." Ted sniffed the package through a scrunched nose. "Robbie still likes his eggs scrambled?"

"Just like you." Alice sat at the table, watching him start the coffee and open the fridge. "I remember the first time you made us breakfast."

"Me too." He stepped toward her. They were locked in an embrace when their son entered the kitchen. Ted smiled as Robbie discreetly backed out of the room.

"He wants you to take him driving again today," said Alice.

"Yeah. I figured. Hey. Buddy," he called. "Ready to try some real roads this time?"

"Yeah!" They'd practiced turning and stopping and parking in vacant parking lots often enough.

Alice's brow furrowed as father and son left the house an hour later. "Be careful!"

"You might as well take it from here." Ted tossed Robbie his keys and climbed into the passenger seat. He watched the boy settle himself behind the steering wheel. "Don't forget to adjust your mirrors."

Robbie turned and looked over his shoulder correctly as he backed down the driveway.

"Hold it!" Ted barked, just before he reached the end. "Did you make your left side shoulder check? You have to make sure there's nobody on the sidewalk."

"Oh, yeah." Robbie entered the street safely and shifted into drive. "Which way do we go?"

"Head out into the Valley to start. Let's stay away from traffic as much as we can."

The lesson was uneventful for the first thirty minutes. Robbie applied the accelerator and brake smoothly, made his shoulder checks, and used turn signals appropriately. But he showed signs of impatience, batting his hands on the wheel, when they found themselves behind a bus on a rural highway. Twice, he stopped and waited while passengers stepped on and off.

"Why the hell can't he get off the road?"

"A lot of roads are too narrow to have bus pull-outs," said Ted. "Don't sweat it. We're not in any hurry."

The bus pulled onto a slightly wider shoulder, with its rear end only two or three feet into the travel lane.

"Finally!" Robbie muttered as he jerked the steering wheel and accelerated to drive around it. The car was almost parallel with the bus driver's side window when a sports car appeared from the around the bend ahead, obviously speeding, in the oncoming lane.

"Look out!" Ted shouted. "Get over!"

Robbie swerved at the same instant as the other driver leaned on his horn, pulling back into his lane without checking to confirm he'd passed the bus.

"What the hell is that guy's problem? He's obviously speeding!"

"Yes," said Ted. "But if you hit him it would have been your fault."

"My fault! How can it be my fault when he's doing twenty over the limit?"

"You were in his lane. A head-on can only happen when one of the cars is on the wrong side of the road."

"Well, I've got a right to go around it when somebody's blocking my lane! People do it all the time!"

"Yes, they do. And no, you don't. You never – ever - have a 'right' to be in the oncoming lane. You're allowed to, in exceptional circumstances, when you can see that it's absolutely safe – when you're sure there's no-one coming."

"But..."

"I don't care that everybody else does it!" Ted allowed his voice to rise in exasperation. "There are a lot of idiots on the road. You have to look out for them. That's what makes driving so hard." His eyes clouded as he thought about the split-second error that had shattered their lives. "Pull over!"

Robbie stopped the car and looked at his father.

"What if you'd been the guy coming the other way?"

"I wouldn't have been doing eighty," the boy insisted.

"Doesn't matter," said Ted. "You hit somebody head-on at one-twenty you're probably just as dead as if it had been one-forty." He forced himself to speak calmly. "The fact is, you couldn't see far enough ahead, because of the curve. There are times when it makes sense to take a risk – driving is not one of them."

Robbie muttered something unintelligible.

"It's the same argument you get from idiots who think they have a 'right' to turn right at a red light," said Ted. "When you're looking at a red light you do not have the right of way. Period. You might be *allowed* to make your turn if it's not going to interfere with anybody else, and that means pedestrians and bicycles as much as cars."

He studied his son's face. "Are you okay to keep going? Or do you want to take a break?"

"I'm okay," Robbie muttered.

"You sure?"

"Yeah."

"All right. Let's turn back toward town. I've got to check in for a minute at one of the stores."

* * * *

Alice put a hundred dollars' worth of Lotto 649 tickets in Ted's birthday card several weeks later.

He was incredulous when he opened it.

"Jeez – Ted, I didn't even think..." She paused, her face slightly reddened. "It's not really like gambling, is it? It's a shot. Either you win a million or you don't."

The inscription was in Alice's handwriting but put the boy's name first. "Happy 39th from Robbie and Alice."

I'd rather the card said 'love, Alice.' That would be worth more than the million!

Robbie was delighted to see his parents together. Part-time was better than nothing. "Why don't you guys go out for dinner? I could drive you," he hinted.

"You don't want to have supper with your dad on his birthday?"

Robbie shrugged.

Alice deferred to Ted. "Where would you like to go?"

"Napoli?"

She stopped in her tracks. "Napoli? Is it even still open?"

"We could check it out."

Robbie nodded. "We hang out there sometimes. What's so special about it?

Ted and Alice shared a look.

"Okay. Whose car do you want me to take?" Robbie caught the keys his father tossed him.

Alice let Ted take her hand as they walked from the car. "I can't believe you remember our first date."

"I remember everything, Alice. I've never stopped thinking about you."

He felt her hand tighten on his.

"The place has changed," she remarked as they entered. What passed for old country decor seventeen years ago now appeared trite, almost shabby. The place seemed to reverberate with the sound of giggling teenagers.

"Oh, come on," said Ted. "I bet the pizza's still just as good." He looked around. "We were that young once, you know." He reconsidered. "Almost."

They overheard the debate one table over as they sat down – somebody being ID'd for drinks.

"Ask me! Ask me!" Ted joked as a server appeared. He smirked at the young woman and pulled out his driver's licence.

"Oh, Ted, stop it!" Alice chuckled.

"Would you like a drink before you order?"

He glanced at the drink menu – fifty varieties of something called a Bellini. "I don't suppose you make a Harvey Wallbanger?"

"A what?"

"Har-Vey Wall-Banger."

The girl frowned at Ted as though he was setting her up for an obscene joke.

"I wonder if she's coming back?" mused Alice, as the server walked away.

She was back a minute later. "I'm sorry. It's not on the menu, but the bartender says he thinks he knows how to make one."

Ted held two fingers up in the air.

"Can I take your food order now too?"

"Large Hawaiian? Extra cheese."

"No problem."

Alice lowered her hand from her chin and spoke first. "So, here we are again." She twisted a lock of hair. "What? What are you looking at?"

"The prettiest girl in the place."

Alice blushed. "I didn't notice you even sizing anybody else up."

"Didn't need to." He reached for her hand, rubbed her fingers gently.

"People are looking at us, Ted."

"See? They know it too." He changed the subject abruptly. "Do you still have your charm bracelet?"

Alice appeared flabbergasted. "You remember? Jeez, I haven't worn it in years. I haven't even thought about it."

"I told you. I remember everything." He laughed. "We got the ketchup bottle problem solved, but they still put too much glue on the toilet paper."

"And the commercials are even louder now than they were then." They both laughed as she finished the thought.

They sat in silence for a minute, paying no attention to the giddiness around them.

"You told me you were going to open six or seven stores. You've got, what, twelve?"

"Fourteen."

"How many people do you have working for you now?"

"Mmmm – more than a hundred, if you count the part-timers. Some high school kids, some are at SFU."

"What about Robbie?"

The question was a bolt of lightning. Ted thought about it as the drinks arrived. Alice tasted hers first.

"Just the way I remember them!" she told the girl. Her expression was serious when she turned back to Ted.

"He hasn't asked me. I didn't know he's looking for a job. I mean, I am still paying..."

"Are you? Cheques have been coming from the company for years, I don't know who signs them. Do you even know about them?"

"Of course I do."

Alice averted her eyes, looking down as she unwrapped the napkin around her cutlery. "You're right. I'm sorry." She hesitated before she looked at Ted again. "You never did cut the amount after Emily..."

Died. She still can't say the word. "I know."

Alice composed herself, swiping hair out of her eyes. "He hasn't been looking. Truth is, he doesn't worry about money. He wouldn't need to anyway," she said vaguely. "But a kid does need to start learning some responsibility."

Ted nodded thoughtfully. "From me? I'd put him in touch with Adrienne – personnel. I mean, I can have her hire him, but then it's out of my hands. If he doesn't work out I can't have a bunch of people complaining about favouritism."

"He's your son, Ted. Can't you take him under your wing? I mean, you do still work on the front counter once in a while?"

"Oh, yeah. There's always a hole to plug – somebody's sick, or writing exams - or getting married." He said it deliberately, to test the waters. Alice's face told him he struck a nerve. She sat back and crossed her arms.

The pizza came, breaking the tension. They ate in silence for a minute.

"You know," said Alice, "he wants to join the gun club."

"Yeah, he mentioned that. Are you going to let him?"

"What do you think? Should I?"

Ted shrugged. "There was a time when you freaked out about it."

Alice pulled another slice of pizza to her plate. "Yeah. I guess I did kind of go off on you that day. I'm sorry."

Ted didn't speak, and didn't touch his food for at least a minute.

"What's wrong?"

He shook his head.

"Come on, Ted. Is there something wrong with the pizza? I think it's okay."

"I don't want to sound like I'm complaining, and I certainly don't want to start a fight. But I don't think you've ever said that to me before."

"What? What did I say?" The look of confusion left her face. "I'm...Really? I mean...Are you sure?"

Ted nodded. The blood drained from her face. "I – that – I didn't know. I'm sorry."

Ted gripped her hand in his. "It's okay. It's not like you have anything to be sorry about. I'm the one that destroyed this family." The kids at the next table were quiet, as though listening.

He pushed the remainder of the pizza aside. "Let's get Robbie to take us to the cemetery before dark. I want to visit her for just a minute."

Chapter thirty-one Bobby

Bobby Cronkite was in the observation lounge at Calgary airport a year later, in time to watch Ted's flight land before making his way downstairs to await the parade of passengers.

Will I even recognize him? He tapped his foot nervously. *Don't be stupid. It's only been ten years.* Ten years since he'd seen his only brother! *Except for the funeral of course.* And that hadn't been the right time to catch up. *How the hell did it come to that?* He tried to forget the bitterness, the nasty things Ted had said when Bobby took their father's side in the fight over the Will. But it replayed in his mind.

Bobby had been hearing it for months, from everybody whose opinion mattered: Lexi, Mom. Dad, the one child who was old enough to understand; friends – even his secretary hadn't been shy about weighing in. "Get over it. Make this right before it's too late."

The invitation was extended and accepted, for the elder brother to spend his fortieth birthday in Alberta. Ted was aloof on the phone at first, but came around quickly enough, accepting the offer willingly if not eagerly.

He appeared, striding amidst the crowd of travelers, towing a carry-on suitcase and with a satchel slung over one shoulder.

Bobby smiled as he extended his arms for an embrace. Ted reached out for a handshake, and then stepped in just as Bobby lowered his arms.

"Okay. Which is it going to be?" Ted's smile was less than radiant but there seemed to be trust in it. Their arms went around one another and they patted each other's backs, the way brothers do when the absence is measured in weeks, not years. Bobby reached for the suitcase, knowing it was a redundant gesture.

"Have you got more luggage?"

"No, I generally travel pretty light."

"I guess we're ready to go, then."

They picked their way through the bustling crowds, walking side by side through the sliding exit doors. "How's work?" said Bobby.

"You know – same shit, different day. How about you?"

"Oh yeah, same thing. Oil has its ups and downs." Bobby chose not to open the trunk as they approached the car. "Might as well just throw these in the back seat, eh?"

Ted nodded.

"Too bad we can't take in a football game while you're here," said Bobby, as they settled into their seats. "The Stamps are in Regina this weekend." He glanced at Ted apologetically. "Might have been a chance for you to see a real game. How do you live with those bloody Lions?"

"I don't pay a lot of attention any more," Ted mumbled.

"I wouldn't either." Bobby chuckled. "What were you – last place again last year?" He gave his brother a playful punch in the arm. "And the Canucks sucked wind too. What the hell is it about Vancouver sports?"

Ted grinned. "Yeah, well the Flames weren't much better."

"At least we won one Stanley Cup this century."

Bobby stopped laughing. "So, is there anything in particular you do want to do while you're here? I've got the rest of the week off work. Thought we might go nose around the Badlands for a day." He slowed and stopped for a red light. "Have you ever been to Drumheller?" *Just don't say you want to go to a casino.*

Ted nodded noncommittally.

"I hope you're okay with being in for dinner tonight. Lexi baked a cake for you."

"Yeah, that's fine," said Ted.

"All right!" Bobby stepped on the gas again. "And if it's okay, we thought we might make a guinea pig of you. We'll throw some bison burgers on the barbecue." He glanced at his brother. "Unless you want to stop and pick up some steaks?"

"No," said Ted. "Bison's fine. We've – I've – actually had it before."

"Oh, yeah? Is it popular out there?"

"No, it was a specialty thing. At Expo, 1986. They had it at one of the pavilions. I don't think it was Alberta..." Ted's voice trailed off.

"Twelve years ago," Bobby mused. "And it hasn't caught on yet." He cleared his throat. "I don't know why not. It should be cheaper than beef, you'd think. I don't know a lot about ranching, but from what I understand they're hardier than cattle, easier to run up north."

Ted nodded. "Alice looked for it in the stores a couple of times, but didn't find it."

The car was quiet for a moment as Bobby made his shoulder check and pulled onto the crosstown expressway. "So, how is Alice? You must still see her from time to time? If that's not a touchy subject."

"Not at all," said Ted. "She's doing better, since she got rid of that useless tit of a husband."

Bobby glanced over in surprise. "I hadn't heard that."

"No. I suppose there's no reason why you would." Ted paused, seemed to be thinking about how much to say. "I guess they were doomed when she blamed him for Emily. Weird thing is, he divorced her. What a fucking idiot!" He spat the final sentence.

"I guess I'm sorry to hear that. We always liked Alice."

Ted turned away, gazing out the side window.

"So, can I ask? Did they ever figure out what happened? We never heard anything from you after the funeral."

"Yeah, I'm sorry about that, Bobby. I should be doing more to stay in touch."

Bobby studied his brother for a moment, concluding the apology was sincere. He was trying to decide what to say when Ted spoke again.

"Dickhead's fault. He ran a red light." He was quiet for a moment. "You know, you see it just about every day. Most times the idiot gets away with it, but..."

"Shit. I guess you sued the bastard? How'd that turn out?"

Ted pulled a package of cigarettes from his pocket and glanced over, asking wordlessly for permission.

"I suppose so," said Bobby. "Just keep the window wide open."

"Sort of," said Ted. He pulled out a cigarette and put it in his mouth, unlit. "It never went to court. The insurance people actually weren't too bad but the law is brutal."

"How so?"

Ted took the smoke from his mouth. "They paid for the funeral and pretty much wrote us blank cheques for counselling, but there's not much else. I mean, it would have been a slam dunk win, but you can't prove any damages for loss of a child. It's not like there was any evidence she was going to support me in my old age." He broke the unlit cigarette in two and flung the parts out the window. "I wouldn't have got enough to pay the lawyer."

Bobby didn't know what to say.

"You wanna know the really fucking stupid thing?" Ted withdrew another smoke from his pack, and produced a lighter this time.

"Mmm."

"Dickhead took them for more than I did! He and Alice were in marriage counselling for months." Ted inhaled deeply from the cigarette and scowled at the unpleasant memory. "And that was over and above getting his vehicle replaced and the grief counselling for both of them – and Robbie too, of course."

He was quiet again for a minute. Bobby waited to hear whether he wanted to open up more. *What the hell else do you do?*

"I lose a daughter, and he's worried about a fucking truck!"

"I'm sorry, Ted. I shouldn't have brought it up."

"No. It's fine. It's supposed to be good for me to talk about it." There was a faraway look in Ted's eyes. He tried to blow a smoke ring.

"Never did learn how to do that."

He shook his head. "I still think about that day. I don't believe in any of that meta-physical horseshit, but I can't help wondering if there wasn't some kind of Karma in it. Like, why was I a thousand miles away when it happened?"

"You can't blame yourself, Ted. If you'd been at home, or at work, or whatever, you still wouldn't have been driving. You couldn't have made any difference."

"I know that!"

Bobby was taken aback by his brother's vehemence.

"But I also know that if I'd never started Alice wouldn't have divorced me, and everything would be different."

The car was quiet again, for more than a minute.

"So, have you been back there since? I mean, are you still...?"

"Gambling?"

"I was going to say 'recreation.'"

"Call it what it is. I'm an adult. I know nobody..."

Bobby hit the brakes and leaned on his horn as an oversized SUV veered in front of him, jumping to an exit ramp from the left lane. Ted extended his arm out the open window, exchanging birds with the other driver.

"Ass hole," Bobby muttered.

"Yeah," said Ted. "I guess you get them in every town."

"So, are you still playing? It's not like you have to go to Vegas anymore, with casinos springing up everywhere."

Ted butted out his smoke and lit another one immediately. "I haven't bet a nickel on anything in more than four years."

"Good for you! Is it hard? Do you miss it?"

"Not like I miss Emily."

There was another extended silence.

"How's Lexi?"

"She's good," said Bobby. "Getting back into work. Was going to wait until all the kids are in school but it was driving her crazy, so we're doing the daycare thing." He made his turn onto an exit ramp.

"You're a lucky man, Bobby. Don't ever take it for granted."

He decided not to tell Ted about the occasional tryst with his secretary. *We're not quite that close yet.* "Still no special women in your life?"

"Yeah," said Ted, after a moment's pause. "Alice."

"I know that, but I mean..."

"I know what you mean." Ted took another long drag from his smoke and butted it in the ashtray. "I think I'm going to ask her to marry me again."

"What? I mean – really?" Bobby smiled broadly. "Whaddayou think she'll say?"

Ted shrugged. "I don't know. Obviously I hope she says yes."

That's better. The upbeat sound in Ted's voice was welcome.

"We see each other pretty much two nights a week. I mean, we don't – you know – every time, but I'm sure there's a connection." He swiped at a fly, buzzing around the windshield in front of him. "It's funny, you know, dating somebody you've been that close to. I guess you call it dating. I mean, you can't pretend like you're just getting to know each other, but..."

"Well, I'll be damned! I wish I'd known that. We would have invited her to come with you. I mean, you hear stories like that sometimes, but I've never known anybody."

* * * *

"Did you have a nice visit with your brother?"

Breakfast was on Alice's patio the following Sunday.

"Oh, yeah. It was great." Ted gave up trying to spear a piece of bacon and picked it up in his fingers. "He asked about you. They all say 'hi' – well, at least Lexi. I'm not sure how well the kids remember their Auntie Alice."

She seemed to look past the trees into the sky. "Let's see – Jamie, Darren, and Elizabeth, right?"

"Exactly! Well done!"

Alice smiled thinly.

"I think they miss having you as part of the family." *That was a stupid thing to say. Two of them weren't even born yet.*

Alice didn't point out his excess glibness.

Ted finished his coffee and wiped his mouth with a napkin. "You know, our anniversary's in less than a month. Do you think maybe we should celebrate it?"

Alice frowned and seemed to take an interminable time thinking. She squeezed the collar of her blouse tighter around her throat before she finally spoke. "I know where this is going, Ted, and the answer's no." She dropped her napkin onto her plate. "I'm sorry. I'm oh for two, I'm not getting married a third time."

"But I thought..." His face fell and his shoulders slumped.

"Don't get all sad about it, Ted." She looked him in the eye. "Things have been" – she searched for the word – "pleasant, for a while now. Can't we just go with that?" She squeezed his hand. "I mean, last night was amazing."

Alice got up, her hips swaying as she carried the breakfast dishes into the kitchen, leaving him alone to ponder the songbirds and the mid summer foliage. *Maybe this was your chance to get it right.* His hand shook as he reached for a cigarette.

"When did you start smoking again?" Alice reappeared, carrying a pitcher of ice water and a pair of matching cut glasses.

"I don't. Just the odd one now and again."

"Well, not in the house, all right?"

She set the glassware and a handful of unshelled peanuts on the table and bent to give him a peck on the mouth. Ted tapped one of the glasses curiously with his forefinger. He heard the satisfying ring of crystal.

"A wedding gift," said Alice, before she sat down. "I can switch them for kitchen stock if you like."

Ted shook his head. "Whatever."

Alice filled the glasses and drained half of hers immediately. "It's getting warm already." She gazed into the back garden.

Trying to change the subject. But Ted persevered. "You hear anything from Brian at all?"

"Not since the divorce. Why would I?" She still didn't look at him.

"Because he knows he's an idiot for letting you go?" Ted tried to speak lightheartedly.

"He didn't have much choice." Alice brushed some crumbs from the table and picked up a peanut. "It's true, he left me. But it was because I wouldn't sleep with him for more than a year." She turned and tossed the peanut to a squirrel, foraging in the grass. "If that's any of your business."

"But you kept the name."

They watched the animal pick up the peanut in its front paws, stow it in its mouth, and scurry away.

"I wonder if he'll ever actually come up on the patio to get one?" Ted mused.

"He will." Alice pointed at her small pile. "As soon as we go in the house, he'll come and take them right off the table."

Her face darkened as she returned to the subject. "It's only because I haven't got around to it yet. It's going to make for a pain in the ass at work."

"That's a good excuse. Maybe you don't know what you want to change it to." He leaned down to stub out his cigarette and picked at some crumbling concrete in the patio, rather than looking her in the eye. "You think you can keep the place up on your own?" He dropped the butt into his shirt pocket.

"I was okay before Brian and I'm okay after him." Her back stiffened and her eyes narrowed. "Johnson. I'm a Johnson. I'll fill out the papers this week if it makes you happy." She swatted viciously at a wasp. "Fucking bugs!"

Ted pretended to admire the garden, not letting it be obvious he was devastated by the rejection. "Your roses seem to be doing well." He didn't ask who'd actually planted them. "How are your mom and dad doing?"

"They're fine. Dad's talking about maybe retiring soon, so they can spend more time on the boat. Robbie's out with them this weekend."

"Mmm. I wondered why he's not around." Ted pushed his chair back. "I'm going to head out," he announced,

"I thought you didn't have to work until this afternoon?"

"I've got some paperwork to catch up, and I've gotta check the mail at home." He wondered if she caught the emphasis on the last word.

He left Alice sitting alone on the patio, tossing peanuts to the squirrel. *Dammit! Doesn't matter whether she believes the excuse or not. She wants her independence, but does that mean I'm supposed to just let that be enough?*

But he berated himself in the car. *Idiot. Forty years old and you still don't know the first goddammed thing about women. When to shut up!* The couple in the car next to him at a light jumped when he cut loose a primal scream.

Chapter thirty-two Christine

Four times over the next five days Ted picked up the phone and began to dial her number. Four times he hung up before the final digit, not knowing what he wanted to say. Or how to say what it was he wanted to. *Dammit!* He sought out ads for the singles clubs that had failed to interest him in the past. He studied himself in the mirror, noting the first sprinkle of gray in his hair. *Not going to do a goddammed thing about it! They say Bambis like an air of distinction.*

He lapped up the attention that would come his way when he bought drinks for groups of women in hopes of bedding one of them. *Doesn't much matter which one.* It was a no-lose scenario for several weeks - whether he scored on Friday night or not, he was expected in Alice's bed on the Saturday, until she learned what he was doing and cut him off. She seemed to think 'friends with benefits' should be an exclusive arrangement. *Whatever.*

It was probably Robbie who told her. He showed up unannounced at Ted's condo on a Saturday morning, before the one-night stand had left. She was insatiable – wanted it again the morning after, and the sounds were unmistakable the instant Robbie walked in the door.

* * * *

Ted met Christine at a popular singles hang-out on Richards Street.

"I'm sure I've seen you before, but I can't place where."

She sniffed and tried to brush him off. "Why don't you just say it the usual way - 'haven't we met somewhere before?'"

"No, seriously." Ted addressed her sincerely, wanting it to sound like more than a stock pick-up line. "I don't think we've met, but I'm sure I've seen you around."

She turned away from her girlfriend at the bar and studied Ted more closely. "Y' know, maybe you're right. You do kinda look familiar."

"Buy you a drink?"

"My friend needs one too."

Ted made light of studying the girl from all angles. She giggled when he asked her to stand for a moment and show him her walk. "Wait a minute! I know! You work at a gym, don't you?"

"Yeah! Do you go there?"

"No." He laughed. "I'm not into pumping iron. I have a shop in the same mall. I guess we've seen each other coming and going."

He thought he could hear the wheels grinding in her head. "Yeah." A look of actual recognition swept over her face. "The video place! I been in there. I rent movies all the time."

"Well! I thank you for your patronage." He paid cash for the drinks.

* * * *

From Christine's point of view Ted seemed an ideal catch. Dad-bod, not bad for its age – *how old is he, anyway?* – dressed well, and always seemed to have a wad of cash in his pocket. The first time he pitched the notion of a whirlwind visit to Las Vegas there was no need to ask whether he planned to rent one hotel room or two. The relationship they stumbled into may not have been deep enough to drown a housefly, but it seemed more promising than anything else that was going on in Chris's life at the time. None of the muscle-bound meatheads who made passes at her every week at the gym offered anything beyond inflated opinions of their own sexual prowess. Ted showed her some pleasures that those guys either didn't know existed or didn't know a girl was entitled to expect.

There were lavish gifts. He presented her the first on board a flight to Nevada.

"What's this?"

"Open it." She couldn't know he was as eager to see what was inside as she was. His personal assistant had done the shopping.

Chris tore the paper and lifted the top of the box. Two sparkling gems, affixed to the ends of stud earrings.

"My God," she breathed. "Are they real?"

"Of course they're real," he laughed. "Nothing but the best for my pretty."

Not all the gifts were of a material nature. There were his-and-her massages, pedicures, and even a bikini wax, in preparation for a sun-spot/swimsuit vacation.

"Jesus Christ!" Ted howled. "How often do women do this!?"

Chris stopped laughing long enough to whisper wetly in his ear. "I got you something special this time." He turned his head to look at her face. "A heart shaped bush!" He put his arms around her and pushed his tongue into her willing mouth.

The Luxor Hotel on the Vegas strip became a second home. Ted talked about the Aladdin, but it had closed in 1997 and was demolished the following year. And he said the MGM reminded him of work. Christine selected the Luxor based on its pyramid architecture and the mock-up Sphinx in front. She actually knew more ancient Egyptian history than Ted had given her credit for, and reminded him of it at every opportunity.

She held her tongue when she would watch him leave several thousand dollars behind on a bad night at the baccarat table. There were some wins, of course, but Christine privately preferred to see her sugar daddy lose money. She found the sex was more aggressive at the conclusion of an expensive evening.

* * * *

Adrienne was promoted to the office of General Manager, reflecting her ever-increasing responsibility for day-to-day management of the company. But even she would have been surprised to learn how vulnerable it was to the owner's excesses.

Ted was asked – no, it was demanded of him – that he sign personal guarantees in order to secure renewal of a pair of leases. Within months the line of credit against his condominium was extended to the point he was unable to satisfy a third lender's requirement, and he was forced to shutter one of his less profitable locations.

That was the day he received news his father had died of a massive and unexpected heart attack.

There was a strained telephone conversation with his mother.

"I want you to speak at the funeral, Ted. The eldest son should give a eulogy."

"What? You want me to stand up in front of the entire town and tell them what a wonderful guy he was?" He flung his pen across the kitchen, with Chris looking on, dumfounded. "The guy that disowned me? Cut me out of the Will the first excuse he had?"

"Maybe you should stop for a minute and be thankful for the fact Robbie won't have student loans."

There was an angry pause. It took all of his willpower not to bang the phone down.

"He was your father, Ted. Can't you set your pride aside for one day?"

"Why don't you ask Bobby? He's better in front of crowds than I am anyway."

Another awkward silence.

"You are coming."

"I'll be there." Ted sighed.

* * * *

He resisted a temptation to wipe a smirk off the clerk's face when he checked into a motel with Christine. Bobby and his family stayed at the house with their mother, and escorted her to the funeral chapel.

Ted selected seats near the back, feeling like an outsider behind the rows of civic dignitaries, a Chamber of Commerce delegation, and other professional colleagues and friends. Although his plan to maintain a low profile was doomed. Christine's one black dress was the kind of short cocktail number that everybody notices for the wrong reasons, given the setting.

Bobby button-holed his brother following the graveside service. "You are coming to the house, aren't you? It would kill Mom if you don't show up."

"Christine, this is my brother, Bobby."

Bobby's eyes were frigid as he took her hand.

His mother greeted Ted at the house with a perfunctory hug, just long enough for somebody Ted didn't recognize to interrupt her before the necessity of introductions. *So that's the way it's going to be!* Christine didn't appear perturbed.

"Let's get a drink," he muttered. Chris seemed to fade into the background as people Ted half recognized grabbed his hand or rubbed his shoulder, offering the obligatory kind words. "You must be Ted." "I'm so sorry for your loss." "He was a great man, wasn't he?".

The crowd thinned within less than an hour. "I guess you want to go soon?" he said to Chris.

"I think you should stay to the end, shouldn't you? It is your family." She nibbled his ear gently. "I'm going to go to the bathroom."

Mom pulled Ted aside as though she'd been waiting for the opportunity.

"Who *is* that woman, Ted?" she hissed.

"My girlfriend."

"Good God, she's young enough to be your daughter! I can understand a mid-life crisis, but can't you see you're embarrassing yourself!"

Ted felt his face redden, but it was the wrong time and place to argue about it.

"She could be dating Robbie, for Christ's sake!"

"I don't think so, Mom."

Robbie heard his name and turned away from his conversation with his Uncle Bob.

Barbara's expression softened. She grasped Ted's lapels, tugged gently and patted his chest, the way she used to when she was buying his clothes. "You are looking good. I like your suit. It's nice material." She looked up. "And you've still got all your hair." She ran her fingers through it. "A few grays, but you're going to keep it, you know. You're lucky - you've got good genes. Your dad had a full head, right up to the end."

His escort appeared.

"Christine, this is my mother. Mom, Christine."

The young woman smiled politely. "Mrs. Cronkite."

"Oh, call me Barbara."

Ted spent the required couple of minutes chatting with each of his nieces and nephews, and hugged his sister-in-law. Bobby followed him to the door.

"You know, Dad was proud of you. For the business." He seemed to be searching for the words. "He finally saw how right you were. He just couldn't get past – you know..."

"I know." Ted scuffed the ground with his shoe. "I guess I can see his point."

"So, how are you doing?"

"I don't know. It's not going to last forever. Technology changes every five minutes. I don't know how long I want to keep fighting it."

"No. I mean, how are *you* doing?"

Ted's eyes followed Bobby's to Christine, standing a few feet away, but he thought of Alice. Alice, who would have understood his mixed feelings about his father. Alice, who would have grieved sincerely with him. Alice, who was so much more than a good-time girl.

"I dunno."

* * * *

"Where are we going?" Christine asked.

"Gotta make a stop before we go back to the motel."

"This is the road to the graveyard, isn't it? Weren't we just there?"

Ted parked the car in a different section of the cemetery.

Chris was confused again. "I thought..."

"Not Dad. An old friend." She was taken aback when he told her to wait in the car.

What am I supposed to do, Neil?

What was it that sighed in response? The wind whipping through the trees? Or the leaves, rustling in the face of the wind? He knew what a physics textbook would have to say on the subject, but the answer held no meaning that day.

* * * *

The affair fizzled like a spent firework. Ted realized he was tired of Chris's incessant vanity, just about the time she tired of being asked why she was out with her father. The break-up wasn't entirely cordial, but there was no screaming row. Ted sensed they both felt cheapened by the experience. Christine packed her things and left the condo with a handshake that reminded him of buying a used car. *You don't like the guy but you go through the motions because he's given you the best deal you could get.*

Chapter thirty-three Surf 'n' Turf

Ted knocked tentatively on the front door of Alice's house. It took him three months to screw up the courage to face her and her birthday seemed a logical excuse. He held a bouquet of flowers behind his back, shuffling his feet anxiously on the porch.

The door swung open. "Ted!"

"Lily!" The speech he'd rehearsed a hundred times was blown out of the water.

"I – uh – I just came – um – Is Alice home?"

"She's getting dressed." Lily didn't offer a welcoming smile. "We're just about to go out for dinner."

"Oh – well, uh..."

"Who's at the door?" He heard Alice's voice a few seconds before she appeared in the hall. Lily turned and looked over her shoulder.

"Ted!" Alice's hairbrush slipped from her fingers and thumped on the floor.

He stepped past Lily into the hall, pulling his arm forward to reveal the flowers. "I just came to say happy birthday. I brought you these." Alice didn't rush forward to accept the gift, gaping at him incredulously.

"Do you think we should put them in some water?" Ted tried to encourage her with a smile.

"Ted, I don't..."

"I should go," said Lily.

"No!" Alice selected a coat from the hall closet. "You owe me a dinner, and we're going to go out. Ted, you can let yourself out. Do whatever you want with those."

Ted searched just about every cupboard in the house for a vase large enough for the bouquet. He finally found one in a pile of junk on a corner of the patio. He set the flowers in the middle of the kitchen table, and sat down to open the envelope containing the card he'd written. "Love always, Ted."

He stared at it for a long time before he slipped it back into the envelope, and pulled it out again. He studied the handwriting – not as pretty as his secretary's, but it wasn't a job to hand off to somebody else. *Wonder how long I can keep her? The way things have been going...*

He leaned the card – sans envelope – against the vase and examined the effect. *Which'll she see first? Depends whether she comes straight into the kitchen or sits down in the living room first. Is Lily coming back here with her?*

Goddammit! He thought about taking the card away, taking the flowers and card – *No!*

He left it, in the envelope, flat on the table beside the vase, and slipped out of the house, but not before retrieving the forgotten hairbrush from the hallway floor. He set it on the kitchen counter rather than entering her bedroom.

Alice phoned three days later. "Ted. It's me."

"Hi! Listen, I'm sorry I..."

"Thank you for the flowers. They're lovely."

"Happy birthday."

Awkward pause.

"Did you and Lily have a nice time at dinner?"

"Oh, yeah. It was nice. We try to get together at least once a month, special occasion or not."

Awkward pause.

"Listen, Ted. Do you want to come over for coffee?"

* * * *

Alice wore a weekday suit, make-up, and hair style, rather than a casual Saturday look. Ted's attention went to the charm bracelet on her wrist.

He held out a brown bag. "I brought coffee, just in case. Freshly ground." That produced the desired effect, a gentle laugh to break the ice.

"It's already on. Come on in."

They sat at ninety degrees to one another at a corner of the kitchen table. Nothing was spoken for at least a minute. Ted could see the birthday card standing on the table, near the flower vase. He thought he noticed Alice's eyes go to it as well.

"So...?"

"Let me start, Ted." She sat ramrod straight on her chair. "Did you get it out of your system?"

Jesus Christ! No beating around the bush. He fished a package of cigarettes out of his shirt pocket.

"Not in the house, Ted. Do you want to sit outside?"

"No." He tossed the smokes aside and glanced at his wet coat, slung over the back of a third chair.

"Did you?"

"Alice, it was just a fling. She didn't mean..."

Alice put up a hand. "You don't have to make any excuses. I don't want to know anything about her. More than I already do. Except that it's over."

Ted spoke as solemnly as he knew how. "It's over." He shifted his chair closer to her. "Look, Alice..."

"Stop!"

"I love you, Alice. I always have. I loved you before I met you. I couldn't know it then, but I know it now. You are the most perfect woman in the world and I was lucky to find you. You're beautiful and smart and funny and – I'm not good at this." He looked down at his hands, wringing them together as though it would help summon his confidence. "Waking up beside you in the morning is what makes the day worth living. And I know that I'll never feel that way about anybody else."

She assumed a more natural posture, body slightly slumped, with her arms resting on the table, her right hand twisting the fingers of her left. "I believe that. And in a perfect world..." She looked up from her hands, glancing briefly at Ted before she gazed out the window. "I loved you too. Maybe I still do. I never stopped caring about you."

"Then why...?"

"You know the answer to that! Because I can't rely on you!" Alice seemed to choke on a swallow of coffee. She banged the cup down, splashing dark liquid onto the table. "I can't go through that again."

The conversation paused. Ted added some milk to his coffee, stirring it far longer than necessary.

"I have stopped, you know."

"Again! How long this time?" She pointed an angry finger at him. "I've got a pretty good idea how much time you spent in Las Vegas with your little fling. I hope the casinos paid for her tickets too!"

"How...?"

"You didn't think somebody'd notice when you disappear for a week at a time? Your son, Lily, I've got other friends. People care about you, whether you know it or not!"

She got up and dumped the remainder of her cold coffee into the sink, replaced it with a hot cup.

"What would you like from me, Ted?" Her back was to him when she asked the question. "How often do I need to jump in the sack with you?"

I guess that's a fair question. But he gaped at her in stunned silence.

She spun to face him. "Once a week's not enough? Twice? Seven times?"

"Alice, it's not about that." He held his hands palms upward, pleadingly. "I want you in my life. Full time."

At least half a dozen expressions crossed her face before she turned to the sink again. She picked up a dishrag and wiped the spill from the table, along with a small handful of dropped flower petals.

"These are beautiful," she mumbled.

"I didn't know how long they'd last."

Alice sat down again, wiping her eyes. "You've got a good heart, Ted. You've been a better father than I gave you credit for." She hesitated and forced a chuckle. "You're a lousy dancer. But you cook and did your share of the house work." She smiled thinly. "And God knows you have other skills that a woman needs. But I can't be married to you."

Ted glanced outside as a gust of wind drove sheets of rain against the window. Alice reached into a pocket for a tissue and blew her nose. He pushed a hand slowly across the table to touch her. She recoiled, briefly, and then seemed to reconsider, allowing him to wipe a tear from her cheek. Ted slid off his chair and knelt before her, resting his head in her lap. He felt her fingers stroke his scalp, the side of his face, the back of his neck.

"Mmm. I remember when you used to do that." He extended his arms around her waist.

He shifted when his knees became uncomfortable, lifting himself to his feet. Alice looked up through damp eyes and choked. Ted couldn't tell if she was trying to avoid crying or laughing. It might not have been one or the other. And then she was in his arms, her lips on his, her tongue seeking his with a frantic energy.

She withdrew from his embrace. "Let's sit in the living room," she whispered.

"Okay." He lowered a hand from her breast. "You want me to bring your coffee?"

"Sure." But she looked at him as though he was witless.

Ted took a seat in an easy chair. Alice didn't ask his permission before she doffed her jacket and settled in his lap, with her legs extended across an armrest and her chest turned to press against his.

"Mmm." He squeezed her tightly. "You are the most beautiful woman in the world. You know that?"

"Oh, Ted. Stop it."

Ted drew a fingertip slowly, sensuously, down her arm from the shoulder to her wrist.

"You're wearing your charm bracelet."

"That's not a coincidence. I dug it out because I knew you were coming."

"You knew? Before or after you phoned me?"

Her laugh was genuine. "You know, if you'd brought me a charm from Caesar's I might have had to keep it. At least I'd've had a harder time throwing it out." She put a fingertip on the end of his nose. "I mean, a fucking toga? What the hell were you thinking?"

He toyed with a couple of the pieces he'd added to the bracelet, remembering the special occasions. "I'll have to take it and get it cleaned for you."

"Not today."

How can two people while away an entire afternoon in one another's embrace, whispering nothings? A couple of teenagers, finding they suddenly have the house to themselves for the first time, would seize the moment, lacking the patience to give the wonder its due.

She nuzzled his ear. "You're going gray."

"Am not." A few seconds later, "Ouch!"

"What's this?" She waved it triumphantly in front of his face.

She leaned away from him for a moment, reaching for her shoes. Ted pulled them off for her and massaged her feet.

"How many pairs have you got now?"

"Way more than I did when we were married."

"Way more than you need, you mean."

"No more than every other woman." She crouched to slip his off as well, before settling in his lap again, laying her head on his shoulder

"I hear you're a honcho at the bank now."

"Mmm. I suppose." Her lips brushed his cheek. "Why?"

"Well, there's something you might be able to explain to me."

"Mmmmm. What?" She worried his earlobe between her lips.

"Why is it that tellers always want to give me a receipt when I make a withdrawal?"

"So what?" She didn't seem perturbed about it.

"I need a receipt when I give somebody money, not when they give it to me."

She withdrew her tongue from his ear. "I suppose some people just want a record of every transaction."

"Yeah, but why call it a 'receipt?'"

"Really?" She lifted her head and gave him her 'are you daft?' look again. "You want to think about that instead of where my hand is right now?"

Ted's eyes glazed over and he tipped her head forward for a kiss. "Maybe we'll come back to it."

Alice rolled aside and spoke seriously at one point. "You know, I would have gone to your father's funeral. I would've liked to have seen your mom again. I always liked her."

"I know. You'll get other chances."

"Robbie said it was big."

"Yeah, I guess Dad was a pretty important man in Penticton." Ted startled. "Where is Robbie? Is he going to walk in on us?"

The music of Alice's laughter filled the room again. "No. He's gone up to Whistler with some friends. He didn't tell you that when he asked for the weekend off?"

"He didn't talk to me about it. I guess I didn't get the memo."

"Mmmmm. That's okay." She slipped a hand inside his shirt.

"Wait a minute!" Ted smiled broadly. "What friends? Girls?"

"Mmm, some of them, I suppose, yeah." Alice seemed more concerned with Ted's buttons than with what she was saying.

"Well, I'll be damned! Do you think they're doing this?" He pasted his mouth to hers again.

Alice came up for air. "No. I think they're skiing." She pulled his head forward for more. "They'll be doing this tonight."

* * * *

The room darkened as the late afternoon sun faded from the sky.

Ted checked his watch. "You think we should go out for dinner? It is getting on." He grinned. "And we haven't had any lunch today."

"Nope." Alice got up, straightened her remaining clothes, and stretched. "I want you to cook for me. Like you used to. I'm going to take a bath."

Ted snooped in the kitchen for ideas.

Damn! She did plan this before she phoned.

He called down the hall to the open bedroom door. "I've never actually cooked lobster, you know."

She must have heard him; he heard her call back. "You'll figure it out. And don't forget how I like my steak!"

Chapter thirty-four Aaron

In 2002 Blockbuster Inc. reported record world-wide revenues of (US) 5.57 billion dollars through 85 hundred stores in the United States and twenty-eight other countries, including Canada. (Report to US Securities and Exchange Commission, file number 001-15153). The report cited industry estimates of more than twenty-four billion dollars in total consumer spending on home viewing of movies in the United States alone that year.

Cronkite Video was not on anybody's radar.

The shift to the DVD format had provided a boost to the industry overall, but increased consumer interest in purchasing rather than renting opened the door for even larger retailers, Wal-Mart among them, to seize a slice of the pie. Pay-per-view cable and satellite services already represented ten per cent of the market. Ted foresaw that would be the wave of the future, whether Blockbuster knew it or not.

The industry that had literally been invented by Ma and Pa operators just a quarter of a century ago had gone corporate, and it was a game the small independents were ill-equipped to play.

With responsibility for a payroll swollen to two million dollars annually, plus leases, mortgages, and other overhead, Ted felt the pressure. He knew his market share was dwindling, and the year spent entertaining a sugar baby had been costly. He decided to address the problem by cost cutting at the top. He reduced his own draw, laid off his assistant, and decided the notion of "head office" had to go.

He made the announcement at a farewell party for Adrienne, the Chief Operating Officer.

"We love her!" he declared, in front of the gathering. "We wish her well in her new role at RBC. We know she'll do well. Adrienne's been an integral part of this team for eleven years, and we cannot replace her!" He paused and looked into as many faces as he could. "We're not going to try."

Reaction was mixed, judging by the murmur in the room. People whose livelihoods depended on the firm were either worried or outright shocked. University students, who viewed the job as a stopgap on the way to better things, shrugged. High school students, working their first jobs, had no idea what to make of it.

* * * *

By the turn of the century most British Columbians didn't need to travel outside the province to experience the thrill of gambling. A plethora of small scale casinos had sprung up as far back at the mid 1980's, including the one in Ted's back yard of Coquitlam. But 1999 was a landmark year. With the full blessing of the provincial government of the day, the Royal City Star opened its doors aboard an old paddle-wheeler moored in the Fraser River at New Westminster, billing itself BC's first Las Vegas-style casino. The first so-called "destination" casino, with over three hundred hotel rooms and a theater, playing host to a revolving card of has-beens and B-list performers, would open just a few years later, in nearby Richmond.

Ted scoffed at the self-congratulatory spin-doctoring. The official government line insisted that gamblers would flock to British Columbia from as far away as Japan, Korea, and China, filling public coffers with easy money. Ted put himself in the overseas shoes. *If I was going to go to North America to gamble, why on Earth would I go anywhere other than Las Vegas?*

He wrote numerous letters to politicians, pointing out the dangerous absurdity of their presumption, how he was sure those millions of dollars would never emigrate from faraway lands, but would be sucked from the homes and families of struggling locals. None of his letters was ever mailed. Ted always retreated from the embarrassment of telling his own story.

"You should," Alice told him. "Let them know how shorted-sighted this is. Personal stories matter."

"Aw, they wouldn't read it anyway. They don't give a shit. So long as they think it'll get them votes they're going to keep doing what they're doing."

The deliberate dishonesty of the promoters annoyed him. "They could at least call it what it is. It's *not* fucking 'gaming!'" He thought about his childhood games of Parcheesi and Yahtzee and Scrabble. "Dad would roll over in his grave if he could see what's going on now!" *Where would we be if I'd played Snakes and Ladders with Robbie and Emily instead of playing so much poker?*

"Well, if you're that mad about it, change it. Get yourself elected." Alice was curled up on the couch in her housecoat, with a glass of imported wine in her hand. "I really think you could. You're a smart guy. People should listen to you."

"Do you know how many hours I work already?"

Politicians never openly admitted their folly, but Ted noticed when the spin eventually took off on an interesting tangent. With the proliferation of Internet gambling the argument in favour of live casinos became, "At least it's a way to *keep* the money in BC."

Ted's disdain for bullshit probably served him well. It wasn't a gut-wrenching struggle to keep his promise to Alice – and to himself – that he would never set foot in any of the province's new monuments to risk-taking.

* * * *

Alice was half dressed when Ted rolled out of bed on a cool autumn Friday morning. "Do you want me to put the coffee on?"

"No. I'll grab one at the office. I'm running late." She gave him a peck on the mouth. "You kept me up too late last night. Too late for an old lady."

Ted made a show of glancing around the room. "What old lady?"

"Here." She turned her back to him. "Can you help me with this?"

He planted a kiss on the back of her neck after he connected the bra straps. "I think I'll stay at my place tonight. Give you a break."

Alice looked at his face in the mirror as she brushed her hair. "How come?"

"We've got a little poker game arranged."

She stopped what she was doing and turned to face him.

"A 'little' poker game?"

Ted shrugged. "I haven't seen Pete for almost a year. He called the other day, and..."

Alice hesitated, choosing her words carefully. "Well, I guess you should stay in touch with your friends. How's he doing, anyway?"

Ted shrugged again. "Getting older. Like all of us."

"I hope he's getting wiser." She resumed brushing. "I mean, he knows he can't afford the kind of stakes you got used to, right?"

"No." Ted watched her apply powder and make-up. "We're not going to do anything that any of us can't afford."

"Well, I guess a nice game with ten or twenty dollar pots doesn't hurt anything. And hopefully at the end of the night everybody breaks even. Do you think you can do that?"

"It'll have to be a little more than that," Ted mumbled. He sat on the edge of the bed in his underwear, watching her.

"You know that I'm not going to wish you good luck." Alice reached for her blouse. "What are you looking at?"

"You. I still can't choose, you know."

"Between what and what?"

"Tits or ass. They're both fantastic!"

She was still chuckling when she left the house.

* * * *

Alice let herself into the building with the key she borrowed from Robbie, but she rapped on the door of Ted's third floor suite rather than walking in unannounced. The murmur of male voices and laughter was audible in the hall.

She knocked a second time before she recognized Ted's voice.

"Yeah!" He pulled the door open, and broke into a broad smile. "Alice!"

"Can I come in?"

"Yeah – of course." He took the two grocery bags she was carrying and led her into the kitchen.

"I just thought if you're going to do this, you should do it right."

Ted peeked into one of the bags – the one with a package of bacon-wrapped scallops on top. "Holy shit! Thanks." He stood uncertainly for a moment before he reached for her coat. "I guess you should meet the guys."

She followed him into the living room.

"Guys, this is my – girlfriend, Alice." He pointed clockwise around the table. "Pete, Trevor, Aaron, Joe."

Girlfriend? Wonder how many of these guys know the truth? She smiled and nodded to each of them in turn. Pete didn't say anything.

"Don't fill up on potato chips, gentlemen. I've got some treats coming."

"All right!" somebody declared. "Bonus!" A couple of the men clapped their hands.

Alice carried two ashtrays to the kitchen and emptied them before she switched on the oven.

The apartment was tidy and spacious enough, but the décor showed no sign of a woman's touch. Furniture was mismatched and the living room drapes looked as tired as the carpet. A big-screen TV sat against the feature wall, with a pair of Bateman prints hanging above it – the ones Robbie had given his dad for Christmas several years ago, with some significant help from the Bank of Mom. There was a framed eight-by-ten of Robbie in his high school graduation gown, and a business association plaque, recognizing Ted's contribution to youth job creation. Alice knew that was more about finding affordable labour than community service, *but whatever. Can't deny he did do it, no matter what the reason.*

She knew his kitchen would be fully equipped. "You sit down," she told Ted. "I'll find everything." She heard somebody ask him why his girlfriend didn't seem to have been there before.

"She hasn't." She could hear the shrug in his voice.

Alice was sliding a tray of appetizers out of the oven when she sensed one of the guys enter the kitchen behind her. It wasn't his presence that startled her as much as what he said.

"Mrs. Holman? Can I help you with those?"

She jerked upright. "It's Ms. Johnson now."

"Sorry. Ms. Johnson. Alice. May I call you Alice?"

"Well, yes, but you do have me at a disadvantage."

The man spoke quietly. "We met when you were Mrs. Cronkite." Alice was still baffled. "I'm Aaron Browne. Ted's lawyer."

"Oh." She didn't put a hand out to him.

"I must say I'm surprised to see you here. Pleasantly surprised, but surprised."

Alice didn't comment.

"I just wanted to tell you I think you did the right thing when you divorced Ted. I understand why you did it."

She sensed it was more than a platitude. "I had no choice."

"No. You can't allow a gambler to drag you down with him. And you had the children to think about." He looked directly into her eyes. "I was very sorry to hear about the little one. Ted was badly broken up about it."

"We both were."

"Yes, of course."

She made room for a second hot tray on top of the stove.

"You said you understand."

"I do." He held a plate, watching as Alice began transferring hors d'oeuvres onto it. "My father." He lowered his voice even further. "Ted doesn't know that, and I'd rather keep it that way." He paused before he elaborated. "There is a stigma, as you well know."

"Yes, there is." Alice stopped what she was doing. "Don't take this the wrong way, but why are you here? I mean..."

Browne shrugged. "A small game. Hundred dollar buy-in, no skin off anybody's nose. It was going to happen whether I'm here or not."

"You think Ted can...?"

"Truthfully, I'm not optimistic. I take it he's been doing better, if you're seeing him again. But if he's an addict, any betting at all is like 'just one drink' for an alcoholic."

They were interrupted by a guffaw and curses from the living room. "Full boat! Queens over tens!"

"If you care for him you won't enable him."

Alice nodded at the food. "I'm hoping this'll put more attention on socializing – less on the cards."

"Maybe."

Browne carried two plates of snacks, Alice brought side plates and napkins. She made a point of distributing them on the card table, interrupting the game. Ted frowned slightly when Joe slapped the cards onto an out-of-the-way side table.

Chapter thirty-five The Donald

The implosion of Cronkite Video was less spectacular than its rise, despite the fact it happened an order of magnitude faster. Decisions were made out of necessity more than on the basis of volume. Ted closed locations as leases expired, regardless of which store was turning a profit and which wasn't. His objective was to wind down without declaring personal bankruptcy. After all, Donald Trump had done it. One of the loudest braggarts in the world had managed to run casinos into the ground – *how the hell is that even possible?* - but somehow continued strutting around like the business genius he obviously wasn't.

For Ted, reality was more than a television game show. His personal draw plummeted to the point he lived payday to payday, like the majority of ordinary working Canadians. Tailored suits and patent leather shoes became things of the past.

By spring 2005 he ruled an empire of three stores. Two of them were in properties he owned, so at least the equity would provide some semblance of padding. *Maybe.*

The closure of his original flagship location was a difficult day. There were no balloons, no ribbon-cutting, no crowd of curious onlookers. And no Alice.

"You think you might want to come down for the last day?"

She looked up from her breakfast. "Why would I want to do that?"

Ted's shoulders were slumped. "I don't know. Just because you were there at the beginning. Thought it might be a little nostalgic."

"I've got meetings with clients, Ted. I can't just bail on them." She got up to pour herself another coffee. "I'm sorry." She looked at him sympathetically. "You should eat something."

Ted poked at his food with a knife. "I don't feel like it."

Alice sat down again. "You given any more thought to what you're going to do?"

"I dunno." He pretended to study the clock on the wall rather than look at her. "Probably go back to selling groceries. Or maybe I'll drive a taxi." He snickered humourlessly.

"No, Ted. Come on. That's a really tough way to make a living." She tapped a hand on the table. "There's got to be something."

"Like what?" He scowled. "I'm nowhere near a good enough bridge player to make a living at it. And I don't know how to do anything else."

"What about a driving school?"

He looked up.

"It's not a completely ridiculous idea. I mean, you are a good driver, and you'd get to keep running your own show." She tried to encourage him with a smile. "There is something to be said for not having to punch a clock."

* * * *

It was a confusing time for his male ego. Ted knew he shouldn't resent it, the afternoon he happened upon evidence that Alice's paycheques were more than twice the size of his. There should have been blood in his mouth from biting his tongue, but he couldn't help it. Jealousy has never been a function of the rational mind.

"I'm not going to apologize for what I make, Ted. I earn that money. I've worked hard for it, and I've made sacrifices."

"I know you have. And I'm proud of you for it." He glanced at the statement again. "It's just..."

"There is no 'just!' There's no but." She snatched the paper from him. "You weren't supposed to see this anyway."

"You shouldn't have left it lying around," he mumbled.

"Well, I'm sorry I did!" Alice shoved the paper into her purse.

Ted poured himself a glass of water and sat down at the kitchen table, hoping the anger would dissipate. Alice pretended to busy herself, shuffling appliances on the counter.

"Why shouldn't I know what you make? It is kind of family business."

Alice wiped a spatula and set it carefully into a drawer. "We're not a family, Ted. We haven't been a family for seventeen years."

I didn't know you were counting too.

He jumped when she slammed the drawer shut. "Do you think I'm happy about it?"

"No."

She turned to look at him. "The fact we're dating doesn't change it."

Ted sighed. "You know, most people don't just keep dating forever."

"As much or as little as you want, Ted. You know that it's never going to be more than that."

He nodded, more in submission than agreement. "There is Rob."

Alice sat across the table from him. "Yes, there is Rob." She sighed. "And I've tried to make sure he doesn't want for anything."

"You've been a great mother. But don't forget I'm still sending support for him too." Ted allowed a hint of bitterness to creep into his voice. "Even though he's twenty-four years old."

"Because he's a student."

"And my mother has paid his tuition!" Ted's voice rose again. "Or has she welched on that when I wasn't looking?"

"No, she hasn't."

Ted wrung his hands nervously before he spoke again. "So that's how a kid can afford a new BMW when his old man drives a beater?"

Alice kept her voice level. "Ted, your car, your life, your company – they're all your business. You're a free man." She looked away for a moment. "I didn't ask for more when you were the one making a fortune."

He stared at her, feeling as though he'd been slapped in the face. "Did you put anything at all away for yourself? Or did you...?"

"Say it! Did I gamble it all away?"

Alice seemed to look in every direction except his. She was quiet when she finally spoke. "We're adults, Ted. We make our choices, and we live with them." She pushed her hair off of her forehead. "I told you then that I couldn't live with yours."

Ted felt like a child, being lectured by a too-strict parent. "I think we did make one good choice together."

Alice looked at him softly, her eyes as beautiful as ever. "More than one." She reached for his hand. "Look, Ted. It obviously hasn't been all bad."

She sighed heavily. "I know things aren't what they were for you. Cancel the support. It was only going to be a few more months anyway. I don't care what the law says about it. I won't complain to anybody."

He muttered something under his breath.

"Pardon me? What was that?"

"I said I think I will!"

"You are going to come when he gets his Masters, right?"

* * * *

Ted had a couple of responsible options for the windfall - funding a new venture, or perhaps doubling the mortgage payments on his condo. He eschewed both. His moral compass was degaussed by the combination of a sense of entitlement and a common rationalization. He suspected, correctly, that the title to Alice's house was free and clear, and only a quick fix could balance the scales. He needed to win his way out of debt, instantly.

The money went to the purchase of lottery tickets. *She did tell me once that lotteries aren't really gambling, right?* And it didn't take time away from his three or four nights a week in her company.

The Bateman prints were sold at auction, the proceeds invested in the lottery. The ultimate return? Thirty dollars. The boy wouldn't notice. He had become strangely distant in recent years, didn't drop in to visit his dad, didn't call to ask advice about a problem with a girlfriend or a professor at the university. Not that Ted would have had any useful advice on either subject. Rob, or RD, as he preferred to be called by then, never got over his disappointment at his father's affair with she-who-shall-remain-nameless, and his post graduate studies were well beyond Ted's expertise.

* * * *

Frank Hamilton took a sabbatical from competition to write a book. It was a slow process, since his heart wasn't in it, but Lily threatened to divorce him if he didn't spend a lot more time at home.

After several months of social bridge games with Frank and Lily, Alice decided she was ready to try on some serious competition.

"Come on, Ted. You've got to take some time off sometime. You're going to work yourself into an early grave."

"You know, a couple of years ago you tried to tell me to go into politics."

"Yeah, well, I was wrong."

They spent a week at his mother's home in Penticton, which – who knew? – hosted one of the biggest annual events on the American Contract Bridge League calendar. No doubt the success of the Penticton Regional had something to do with the plethora of reasonably-priced motel rooms available in the shoulder season.

* * * *

"How long do you plan to keep the house, Mom?"

"I don't know. As long as I can, I suppose. Why?"

"I just worry you might be lonely here. And the upkeep has got to be more than you need."

"It keeps me busy, Ted. That's what keeps you alive. And I've got my friends, the neighbours, and the garden club. Besides, where would I go?"

Ted shrugged. "Just something to start thinking about."

He wasn't sure whether to regret opening his mouth on the subject, on the drive back to Vancouver. Alice stowed her overnight bag between her knees in the front passenger seat. Every cubic inch of available space in the trunk and back seat was filled with heirlooms and assorted junk.

"Gonna take us a month of Sundays to sort all this stuff," Ted laughed. He glanced over at Alice. "You think we should buy an SUV?"

"Ted – Ted – Ted. You do what you want. Remember that technically, there is no 'we.'"

Chapter thirty-six Epilogue

"Ma'am?"

The man spoke tentatively, barely audible over the sound of the beating rain.

"Ma'am! Please."

Alice turned to look at him.

"I can't wait much longer. There aren't many of us on today, and calls are stacking up."

"All right." She handed the poor fellow her umbrella. "Take this. Go back to the car. Just five more minutes?"

She lifted her coat collar as she turned away from him, back to the headstone she'd come to inspect, and back to the memories that should have been more fulfilling.

They'd made love just hours before Ted collapsed. He had rejoiced in her body and she in his, like the first time, as though neither had a care in the world. The doctor was sure his heart failure was unrelated. "A wife can't blame herself for something like that."

"I'm not actually his wife." *What'd I say that for? Doesn't make any difference to her.*

"Then what did bring it on? I thought he was more fit than most men ten years younger."

The woman shrugged, fingering her stethoscope. "Probably genetics. Sometimes you're just dealt a lousy hand." She paused, seeming to give the matter some serious thought. "Is his father still alive?"

"No. He died young too."

The doctor nodded. "I suspect that's your connection." She refused to blame it on Ted's on again-off again smoking habit or his occasional dalliance with alcohol. Alice didn't mention his one vice, the one that couldn't possibly have robbed him of his health. *Could it?*

How many years did we waste? She thought about the lonely nights and the empty mornings, when any number of men were eager to befriend her. Men who couldn't understand why a woman with no ring on her finger would always tell them "Thank you, but not available." The one time she succumbed had been a disaster.

A movement caught the corner of her eye. A gray squirrel, oblivious to the rain, darted across the grass. She reached reflexively into her coat pocket for a handful of peanuts that weren't there. She made a clucking sound with her cheek, and smiled when the animal stopped to look. Trying to laugh was a mistake – it brought on a repeat of the choking tears.

"Ma'am?" The driver was beside her again, holding the umbrella over her head. "I'm sorry, Ma'am." She nodded.

He offered her an arm. "Can you walk, Ma'am? I don't want you to slip in the mud."

"I'll be all right." The headstone had passed muster, shining and new in the weather. She'd known immediately what words would have to appear on it, but it took her days to decide their order.

Why is it up to me anyway? Because nobody else knew him the way I did.

She took one last look back before she stepped into the taxi. Too far away to read, but the message was imprinted on her heart.

Theodore Cronkite
Aug 1958 – Dec 2022
A man of extraordinary
passion and vision

CPSIA information can be obtained
at www.ICGtesting.com
Printed in the USA
BVHW030704220123
656770BV00001B/24